She was only half aware that the candlelight was pinched out. A hand took her elbow as she toppled onto the bed like a statue. Behind her lids the room whirled dangerously. Surely it would stop soon. In a moment it did, and she opened her eyes. She still felt strange, and her hands discovered why. Her clothes! They were gone! "Oh, sweet Mary in heaven!" she groaned.

Then she heard it. That damned low laughter. Mocking her, challenging her!

She tried to sit up, and two hands pressed her shoulders back down onto the bed. She couldn't seem to even think straight. Not with all that brandy running through her blood like liquid fire, searing her; not with the Frenchman kissing her, as if he would lay bare her soul....

"Parris Afton Bonds has outdone herself with this witty, romantic, fast-paced tale."
Heartline

"Parris Afton Bonds is an excellent writer whose work will endure the passage of time. <u>Lavender Blue</u> is truly a keeper."
Linda Hamm Lucas, *The Love Line*

Also by Parris Afton Bonds

DEEP PURPLE

Lavender
Blue

Parris Afton Bonds

Fawcett Columbine • New York

A Fawcett Columbine Book
Published by Ballantine Books
Copyright © 1983 by Parris Afton Bonds

All rights reserved under International and Pan-American Copyright
Conventions. Published in the United States by Ballantine Books, a division
of Random House, Inc., New York, and simultaneously in Canada by
Random House of Canada Limited, Toronto.

Library of Congress Catalog Card Number: 83-90617
ISBN 0-449-90065-7

Manufactured in the United States of America
First Ballantine Books Edition: October 1983
10 9 8 7 6 5 4 3 2 1

For my five sons:
Dean, Kirk, Brandon, Jason, and Ted,
I love you.

Author's Note

Lavender Blue is about the courageous women of every era and area who dare defy convention and flout public opinion for causes they believe worthwhile.

The last battle of the Civil War, fought at Palmito Hill near Brownsville, Texas, occurred more than a month after Lee's surrender to Grant at Appomattox, and the captors ironically became the captured.

I must thank Rita Smith of the Hobbs Public Library and Dan Hamill for their assistance.

—Parris Afton Bonds
New Mexico, 1982

1

"Help! Run! Help!"

"Oh, do shut up, Washington!"

In the bamboo cage suspended from the stand Washington, Aunt Hermione's macaw, preened its scarlet and lime-green feathers at the unwarranted rebuke from its mistress's niece. Scarcely aware of the bird's ruffled feathers, the younger woman paced by her aunt's rocker. Her hoop skirt snagged on the rocker's foot, and she yanked it free.

Help. That was what she needed.

"Jeanette," Aunt Hermione ventured tentatively, her horse face pinched with real anxiety, "won't you consider returning to New Bedford as your father wants? With Armand dead it's not only sensible but quite obvious that you can't continue to keep Columbia going."

Oh, Armand, why? Why us? With you I was content. And now . . .

Now the problem of keeping the plantation stared Jeanette St. John starkly in the face. The latest tax statement proved her inadequacy.

Her father believed a woman's place was running a house—not ruling it. He enforced this dictum of submis-

sion as strictly as he had obedience aboard his ship. A
Yankee sea captain, he had settled in Brownsville, Texas,
after his marriage to invest in some of the steamboats that
plied the Rio Grande River. The following year he sold
the packets to buy the enormous cotton plantation Columbia.

But that turbulent month before South Carolina seceded from the United States her father, burdened by
what he considered his patriotic duty, returned to New
Bedford, Massachusetts. And in turn Jeanette dutifully
submitted to Armand decisions about running her family's
plantation. Yet she knew she understood more than her
husband could ever have hoped to about the South's most
precious resource, cotton. Further, she suspected that her
beloved Armand had no real interest in such a mercantile
venture. Armand should have been a lawyer, a politician,
a minister. Anything but a planter.

Armand's father, who had come to Brownsville as an
agent for one of New Orleans's French houses of commerce, had owned the plantation bordering one side of
Columbia. But through lack of agricultural expertise,
Monsieur St. John was forced to sell his plantation and
return to New Orleans.

Armand had stayed on to marry her. But now he was
gone, too. *Oh, Armand, why?* It was a litany that repeated itself over and over to fill the void in her life.

She circled Aunt Hermione's rocker and went to stand
before the window. In the windows of the jacales lamp-
lights burned against the night. Those thatched-roof huts
of cane sheltered the *campesinos* who worked the plantation's cotton fields. But since the Rebel port of Clarksville
at the mouth of the Rio Grande was blockaded by Federal
sloops-of-war, the harvested cotton sat in Columbia's
sheds and carts. So old Trinidad, Columbia's overseer,
continued to fill the warehouse with cotton that lacked a
market.

Unless . . . unless she could find a way to market the cotton herself. She crumpled the tax statement in her fist. There had to be a way.

Colonel Reuben Jones's Ethiopian Minstrels began their finale with a resounding rendition of "Dixie." Many of the elite in Judge Scharbauer's large ballroom rose to their feet. The song, almost revered as an anthem of the Confederate States of America, brought glistening eyes and patriotic pride to the faces of the old men, the women, and the Confederate soldiers who were stationed at nearby Fort Brown. Even Aunt Hermione, Yankee-born and bred, seemed moved by the moment.

From the chair nearest the French doors Jeanette dispassionately waved a painted sandalwood fan. Its tea-rose color contrasted with the deep-black silk of her ball gown and the black-beaded net that bound her heavy dark hair into a chignon at the nape of her neck. Even her eyes, which were actually an uncommon shade of blue, had a black cast to them that evening.

Jeanette St. John possessed a singular beauty that could not be compared to the more blatant seductiveness of Annabel Goddard. Jeanette's beauty transcended the superficial; it was an essence that as a child had taken the form of an antic sprite. She had been a candle's dancing flame.

Her thoughts ebbed low at that moment. Raffles, buffet dinners, musical soirées, barbecues, and dances! Like the entertainers performing now, the various functions would raise proceeds for the glorious war effort. Accomplishing very little. At least not enough for Jeanette. Nothing would ever be enough for her. Nothing could restore Armand.

Armand. Her fan slowed its swishing flight. Above the pale freckles that bridged her short nose the vivid eyes imperceptibly softened to their normal shade. Gentle, idealistic, handsome Armand. Friend, husband, compan-

ion. A casualty of one of the Civil War's first engage-
ments. How implausible! Seven years of marriage erased
like chalk from a blackboard. At twenty-five she had been
made a widow. And now, almost a year later, the numbness at her loss still had not abated.

Oh, to feel again! To have sensations wash over her
once more like the Gulf at high tide, to be inundated with
the breath of life! Her fan picked up its tempo—half to
alleviate the stifling air in the crowded room, half to alleviate the inactivity that chafed at her.

"Quite boring, is it not?" drawled the rather tall, fop-
pishly dressed man who slid into the vacant seat on her
left. An immaculate hand, rimmed with Mechlin lace at
the wrist, smothered an indelicate yawn. "But then one
feels obligated to attend these fund raisers."

She could almost despise Cristobal Cavazos for his frivolous and flippant attitude toward the war were it not for
the memory of shared childhood games and his droll
humor. He laid the back of one large, swarthy hand
against his lips with a gesture that was almost effeminate
in its grace, and whispered in a pleasant though distinctly
affected voice, "Do look at Annabel's gown, Jen. The décolletage droops low enough to allow the entire Federal
Army to bivouack on maneuvers!"

Unwillingly amused, Jeanette's gaze swept along the
aisles of chairs, moving past the toadlike profile of their
hostess, Pauline Scharbauer, to find Annabel's cameo
head of hennaed ringlets. It was tilted in flirtatious conversation toward the golden one of Major Hampton. The
banker's daughter rapped her fan coquettishly on the
young major's wrist, and Jeanette sighed. Didn't Annabel
ever tire of playing the traditional role of the helpless,
dependent female?

But then had not she played the role to some degree
herself? To recapture Armand's attention, which after his
return from the Virginia Military Institute had strayed to

issues of states' rights and national sovereignity, she had relied on charm rather than use her innate wits. That was what was expected of the female. Certainly not intelligence; God forbid a bluestocking!

She must have sighed aloud, for Cristobal flicked a glance in her direction. His lids drooped lazily in his habitual expression of boredom, but the quirk in his lip portended another sally. "Why Annabel should be interested in Major Hampton is beyond me," he *sotto-voce*d. "*Dios*, the foolish Hampton would charge Hell with a bucket of water!"

"Foolish he might be," Jeanette snapped under her breath, completely out of patience now, "but at least Hampton is serving his country, which is more than I can say for you!"

Cristobal's inane laugh filtered through the last chorus of "Dixie." "*La*, Jen, I have no desire to be a pincushion for either army."

"Ssssh!" Aunt Hermione reprimanded with a nervous glance from behind her osprey fan.

Jeanette sighed. Always the bantering; sometimes light, sometimes fierce. Even as children, it had been that way between her and Cristobal, with the just and fair Armand as arbitrator between his friends. When Cristobal's father, an hidalgo of old Spain's aristocracy and a Knight of the Order of St. James, moved away from the plantation that had shared Columbia's other boundary, the gangling brown boy disappeared from her and Armand's life.

The lanky boy of twelve had come back only the previous month, a massive man of thirty with an undeniably handsome face and a weak will for the pleasures of gambling. And women? Jeanette wondered. She slid a sideways glance at Cristobal's face.

Beneath the slightly waving curtain of rich brown hair were features that could be called firm—a clear-cut jaw, the strong hawklike nose. Only the sleepy brown eyes and the droll grin that disfigured the otherwise well-delineated mouth gave evidence of the spineless character within. At least Cristobal's ready wit and skill at cards seemed to have brought him a modicum of success, for he had returned a fashionable though aimless gentleman.

She told him as much while they watched the guests whirl past in the first dance of the evening, the romantic "Moonlight Sonata." "What, Jen?" he said with good-humored mockery. "You would have me engage in such an unprofitable occupation as commerce?"

She knew what he said was true these days. The once-crowded wharves that dotted the Rio Grande no longer bustled with activity. The warehouses of Brownsville and her twin city of Matamoros, Mexico, on the other side of the Rio Grande stood empty. The long rows of Mexican ox carts and wagons that had lined the riverfront were gone. Rather than plying the Rio Grande's snaggy sandbars with cargo, the steamboats of Kennedy, King, and Stillman were now armored with cotton bales to serve as the core of the Confederate Navy. Shipping was drastically curtailed due to the restrictions of the web of Federal vessels patrolling the vital trade arteries of the Gulf of Mexico.

"Of course, Jen, you must give me credit for some ambitious enterprise. I am contributing to the war effort in my own way."

Her eyes narrowed in disgust. She was incensed more than usual that evening with Cristobal, with his passive, toilless existence—so different from Armand, who had cared so deeply about everything and who had given the ultimate: his life. "I can just imagine! Your bar bills, I'm sure, help support the Confederacy—as no doubt do your tailor's bills."

Cristobal fingered his waistcoat of claret silk with a sheepish grin. "These duds I picked up in Madrid—or was it Rome?"

"So that's where you've been all these years—Europe."

"And that, my dear, is how I am helping the Cause."

"What—gallivanting about Europe?" Jeanette asked, impatiently tapping her foot and only half listening. She was tired and dreaded the nine-mile trip back to Columbia.

"*Dios,* no! I have been engaged by several European publications to write articles on the Confederacy's progress in the war."

Startled, she looked up into the handsome face that should have graced some valiant soldier rather than the dandy before her. "You—sinking to begrime your hands with labor?" she quipped, but with some of his infectious good humor. "Surely you will cover nothing that will take you too close to the battle lines."

Cristobal yawned again. "Naturally not. I seek to rid myself of *ennui*—not my life. I am preparing my first article on the blockade runners." His deep voice took on a theatrical urgency. "Those brave men who defy the might of Federal vessels imprisoning the Confederacy's coast."

Like a worrisome mosquito Cristobal's words hounded Jeanette after he took his leave of her. Unheedful of the amorous glances various partners cast at her, she danced through two waltzes and a quadrille pondering what Cristobal had said.

The guests assembled at the Scharbauers' town house were the most prominent, the wealthiest, the handsomest. Beneath the hundreds of brilliant candles the women's silks and satins glittered and shimmered. The soldiers paraded flashy gray uniforms decorated with the yellow stripe of the cavalry or golden epaulettes and braids on their crimson shell jackets.

So far the remoteness of Texas shielded the state from the brunt of the conflict. Because Columbia's citrus fruit crops could still be sold in Texas, Jeanette's problems in maintaining Columbia were minimal compared to those of landowners in the rest of the Confederate States. No doubt this irked her father, who thought a woman should not be capable of running a plantation; that was a man's occupation. But how long could she continue before finances forced her to accede to her father's desire that she come North to live with him?

She had to find a market for her cotton.

And then she knew what it was Cristobal had said that stirred some far recess of her brain. Why not a blockade runner?

Why not indeed a blockade runner!

When an admiring sergeant went to get a cup of peach brandy punch for her, her gaze rapidly scanned the crowded dance floor for Cristobal's taller frame. Why couldn't she and Armand be one of the couples? But that part of her life was past and done with.

At last she spotted Cristobal. At the refreshment table, of course. Impatiently she tapped her foot, cursing society's taboo against a woman seeking out a man. Fortunately, a few minutes later he passed close enough for her to speak. "I do declare you haven't paid me a whit of attention tonight, Cristobal." With a quick snap of her wrist she spread her fan open in her best imitation of Annabel Goddard and flirtatiously smiled up into Cristobal's umber-brown eyes.

He turned, casting her a quizzical look, and she wondered if she were carrying her coquetie act a little too far; but no, Cristobal had been gone a long time. Almost eighteen years. Time could have changed the headstrong hoyden he had known, if he remembered her that clearly.

"My dear Jen, I am quite honored that you should desire my attention when you have already turned down five of Fort Brown's finest soldiers requesting the honor of a dance. And, frankly, quite puzzled, since you know how dancing bores me."

It was she who had forgotten Cristobal, the boy, whose sharp mind challenged hers. Her lips formed a plaintive pout. "My feet feel like Terry's Rangers just rode across them, Cristobal. I'm tired of dancing."

"Oh, surely, you jest."

She ignored the derisive grin but made the decision to temper her flirtation. Cristobal seemed impervious to women's wiles and affected more by the latest words of fashion and style that filtered over from the Continent.

When the next dance began and a mountain of a soldier who had crushed her feet earlier in the pigeon wing and hornpipe started toward her, she turned to Cristobal, saying, "I'm hot! Let's escape into the courtyard for a breath of fresh air. I want to hear more about the exciting blockade article you're preparing."

Cristobal obligingly took her elbow and steered her toward the veranda's open doors. "And I thought women were weary of war stories."

"Oh, but I find them so dashing and romantic!"

The exotic scent of the orange and lime trees wafted through the evening air, and a tropical moon rocked just above the high adobe walls of the courtyard. The Scharbauer town house was one of Brownsville's most fashionable and, like those of the few other prominent families, it was surrounded by squalid Mexican mud hovels that lined the back alleys and dusty streets.

Jeanette leaned against the post of the flagstoned well and languidly sipped at the brandy punch. Cristobal stood before her, one hand above her head on the post, bracing his large frame. "However on earth does one go about running a blockade, Cristobal? And where do the contacts come from—I mean, how does one sell off the cargo?"

"That, my dear," he drawled lazily, "is precisely what I should like to know. Some deuced Frenchman seems to have the best success at avoiding the Federal fleet—at least so go the reports I've gleaned out of General Bee. But our illustrious general is so obtuse about blockade runners that I daresay he would not know the difference between a double-barreled shotgun and his nostrils."

"Frenchman?" she asked, seizing on the lone piece of information. "What's his name?"

Cristobal picked an imaginary piece of lint off his mulberry-colored short frock coat. "Kitt—something or the other. No one seems to know much about our self-proclaimed Rebel."

"But where does he put into?" she pressed. "Clarksville?"

"*La*, Jen, if I knew that, I'd have my story. I'd interview the buccaneer firsthand." He fixed a singular drooping eye on her. "Why all the interest?"

The flush that colored the broad sweep of her cheekbones and washed out her freckles was not feigned. She would have to watch herself. She took a quick swallow of the now flat punch. "Oh, but a real buccaneer, Cristobal. This Kitt sounds so—so mysterious and daring."

"And a mercenary out for his own profit. No doubt most uncouth. I imagine your buccaneer must go for weeks without the amenities of a bath or razor. And the ilk of people he would consort with—well, my dear . . ." Cristobal flitted a handkerchief before his aristocratic nose as if scenting something unpleasant.

Jeanette gasped as Cristobal's swishing handkerchief landed in her crystal cup. "*Dios!*" he swore and dipped his fingers into the cup to retrieve the soggy portion of material. Without warning the cup tilted precariously, and the sticky punch sloshed over the rise of her breasts revealed by the sapphire-blue tulle bodice.

"Hell and damna—" Quickly she bit her lip. But her eyes rolled with exasperation as Cristobal plunged the brandy-soaked handkerchief into her cleavage in a fruitless attempt to absorb the liquor that dribbled down between her breasts.

"What—whatever is going on?" demanded an imperious feminine voice.

With little hope that the question could possibly be directed elsewhere, Jeanette cautiously poked her head around Cristobal's broad shoulder. From behind her lorgnette, Elizabeth Crabbe, the matriarch of Brownsville society and the possessor of a voluble tongue, glared with shocked outrage. Next to her stood Claudia Greer, the hostess's married daughter, and Jeanette caught the sympathy in Claudia's plain face. However, on Elizabeth's other side Aunt Hermione looked as if shock would topple her into the cistern behind her.

His hand still lodged between Jeanette's breasts, Cristobal said drily, "I fear this is going to be difficult to explain."

2

"However will I explain what happened tonight to everyone?" Aunt Hermione whinnied. "And what, God forbid, will my dear brother say when word reaches him of your outrageous behavior?"

Jeanette barely heeded Aunt Hermione's agitated prattle during the hour-long drive along the dusty River Road that had been built as a military highway during the Mexican War of 1846. Absently she looped the black silk Lyons shawl over her shoulders, though the summer breeze that mercifully rustled in from the coast some twenty miles distant hardly warranted the wrap.

"Dear me, a widow scarcely a year and already those young soldiers were ogling you tonight, Jeanette. Crude, unchivalrous men. That is what war does to men. Turns them into animals. And Cristobal—I would never have thought it of him. He seemed to have such impeccably good taste. Men in my day . . ."

Why not run the blockade?

Preoccupied with the plan taking root in her mind, Jeanette scarcely noticed as the brougham rumbled down Columbia's long drive guarded by tall, stately palms. The trees seemed to march against the night's star-studded sky like platoons of well-drilled infantry, never out of line, never out of step.

Aunt Hermione droned on while the carriage clattered over the short wooden bridge that spanned the *resaca*, a water-filled channel cut by the overflow of the Rio Grande, and rolled to a halt amid retamas, mimosas, and pepper trees. The trees fronted a two-story house, a strange mixture of Southern colonial architecture with its white columns and New England slate shingles and dormer windows.

Aunt Hermione's gnarled hand plucked at Jeanette's pagoda sleeve. "Jeanette? You haven't heard a word I've said."

Absorbed in thought, Jeanette descended from the carriage to climb the pillared veranda's wide brick steps. Aunt Hermione, her face drawn now with real concern, hurried after her. The gaunt old woman's black cape flapped about her like crow's wings. For years now she had hovered nervously over her charge. Jeanette could even remember the occasion that triggered Aunt Hermione's arrival and the end of her childhood's carefree days: the afternoon her father caught her riding astride in boy's britches with Armand and Cristobal. Up until that time his lack of a son and the death of his wife in the throes of yellow fever had fostered a neglect of his daughter.

Not so that afternoon. Her father's ruddy face had paled; his jowls had quivered. "I won't have it! Sure, you can read and ride. But can you knit? Can you cook? You're a girl, Jenny, not a boy. God, but I wish your mother were alive!" And that was the summer Aunt Hermione had come to stay, had come to train Jeanette in a woman's role in life.

"Talk about the soirée tonight will be all over town by tomorrow, Jeanette. I just knew we should have delayed your first outing. Whatever shall we do?"

"What?" Jeanette turned in the parlor to focus her distracted gaze on her father's sister. "Why, nothing, Aunt Hermione."

The old woman's mouth dropped open, but Jeanette turned to climb the worn-carpeted stairs to her bedroom. She walked around the four-poster bed where she and Armand had lain entwined and went to stand absently at the window, her mind sorting out what would be needed to put her plan into action.

All those years marriage with Armand had occupied her mind and heart. If only . . . if only there had been a child to link her with Armand, to bridge the gap gouged by death. As it was, of Armand she had only her wedding ring and the letter from General Beauregard advising her of her husband's death. Armand's wounded body slowly putrefying in the filthy Yankee Fitch Prison, General William "Monster" Morgan's refusal to render medical attention to the prisoners . . . These were things she did not often let herself think about.

Instead she had concentrated on keeping Columbia running in the face of what seemed insurmountable odds. But now—now the blockade runner, the mysterious Kitt, offered hope.

Hope that Aunt Hermione seemed intent on dashing. For early the next morning the old woman cornered Jeanette in the parlor. "We must do something, Jeanette, to allay the gossip that will surely circulate."

"What gossip?"

"Why, about last night," Aunt Hermione stuttered. "About you and Cristobal. And what he was—was doing out in . . ." she trailed off, unable to finish describing the mortifying scene.

Jeanette thought Aunt Hermione seemed about to swoon. She paced the parlor, trying to think of a way to placate the old woman. Her aunt sat in the Boston rocker and clasped and unclasped her liver-spotted hands in agitation. From the cage hanging in the stand next to the rocker, Washington jutted its hooked beak at Jeanette and cawed, "Help! Run!"

She wanted to run. Instead she said with a stoicism born of what seemed long suffering, "I have explained what happened. A simple accident. It could have happened to—" She halted at the thud of the door knocker.

"That must be Cristobal!" Aunt Hermione said.

"What could he possibly be doing here at this time—"

"I sent Trinidad to Cristobal's quarters in Brownsville," the aunt explained.

Tia Juana, Jeanette's old black nurse, waddled past the parlor door to answer the knock. She had been with the Van Ryan family since Trinidad married her and brought his young bride to the Texas border to escape the persecution that followed the mixed marriage between the Mexican and the Negress.

Weighing in excess of two hundred pounds, Tia Juana had run the house to suit Jeanette's father and ruled Jeanette and Trinidad to suit herself. They both loved her. No hand could soothe a child's fevered head as hers did, or lovingly stroke a man as she did the pint-sized Trinidad.

"Well, knock me over," the strapping black woman exclaimed, "if'n it ain't Cristobal Cavazos!"

The tall, elegantly dressed man replied something in Spanish and kissed the black woman's piano-key-sized fingertips. When Cristobal released her hand, she snorted her contempt for the boy who had grown into the man before her. "Hmmph. Clothes don't make no man!"

"Cristobal!" Jeanette impatiently called out. "Do come in and unscramble this awful mess to Aunt Hermione's satisfaction."

Cristobal entered the parlor and swept both women a

bow that would have been the envy of St. James's Court. "I am at your service, Miss Van Ryan," he told the flustered old aunt.

Jeanette maneuvered her hooped skirts around the chaise longue to come before Cristobal. She was short, barely five feet, and he was well over six feet; yet she glared at him with all the defiance of David facing Goliath. "Please clarify to Aunt Hermione what happened last night."

He raked a well-defined brow. "What happened?"

Jeanette stamped a kid slipper. "Cristobal!"

"Ahhh, yes. I see." He turned from the furious blue eyes to meet Aunt Hermione's anxious ones. "I spilled some wine on your niece's—uh, bosom—"

With a moan Aunt Hermione's hand fluttered to her flat chest.

"Aawwk! Help!" Washington squelched.

Cristobal cast an uncomfortable glance at Jeanette. It was the first time she had ever seen him ill at ease. He cleared his throat and finished with one of his silly laughs that was meant to be reassuring, "I was merely making reparations, Miss Van Ryan, when you and your companions happened to chance on your niece and myself in the courtyard."

Aunt Hermione began rocking the chair in discombobulated motion. "Jeanette's reputation will be ruined," she moaned half to herself. "Your father will think me the poorest of guardians if he hears of this. There is nothing left but for you to offer marriage, Cristobal."

"What?" the other two cried in unison.

"Aunt Hermione," Jeanette said when she regained her faculty of speech, "you've lost your senses! You're getting senile! Utterly mad! I could never remarry."

"Pshaw!" the old lady said, more firmly now that she had arrived at a solution. "People who are not in love

marry all the time. I should have married that old under-
taker instead of waiting for some Lancelot to ride along
and whisk me off to Camelot. Now it's too late," she
mused. "Old Orville lies in one of his own coffins."

Jeanette could see that this conversation was going to
be a new low in an already hellish day. "I'm not waiting
for Lancelot or any man to—"

"You could come to care for another man—yes, even
Cristobal here—just as much as you did for Armand," her
aunt continued, unperturbed at the volcanic tremor that
seemed to be threatening her niece.

"I will never care for anyone as I did for Armand,"
Jeanette said, underscoring each word with clenched jaw
muscles.

"Ahhmmm." Both women turned to look at Cristobal.

"Ladies," he interrupted, "your discussion does me
great honor, but I must beg off."

"What?" Aunt Hermione demanded, shocked far beyond her previous dismay.

"Oh, do listen to him," Jeanette pleaded. It wasn't just
the thought of marrying another man that upset her. It
was the knowledge that with Cristobal underfoot, all her
hopes of running the blockade would be demolished.
Slow-witted Aunt Hermione would be unlikely to guess
the furtive operations she had in mind. But Cristobal . . .
Very likely he would suspect something.

"To put it indelicately," Cristobal said, "my interests lie
elsewhere."

"Another woman?" Aunt Hermione demanded, incredulous that any woman could take precedence over her
niece. Had not Jeanette been the toast of the Rio Grande
Valley for one brief summer after her return from Phila-
delphia? And then Armand St. John had secured her as
his own.

"No . . . not another woman," Cristobal said hesitantly.

Jeanette's breath sucked in. Did she correctly interpret his innuendo? She found it difficult to believe that her childhood friend, the handsome man who stood flushing before the two women, could be one of those strange types said to prance about New Orleans' Latin Quarter.

Now Aunt Hermione blushed to the very roots of her pewter-gray hair. She grabbed up the fan from the cherry drop-leaf table and began to fan herself rapidly. "I see . . . I see." Then: "But, yes! That solves everything!"

The two turned incredulous eyes on the old woman. "Well, my dear, since you don't—don't want another man—oh, this is so difficult to explain."

"Do not tax yourself, Miss Van Ryan," Cristobal said drily.

"—to love you as Armand did," Aunt Hermione continued, and Jeanette knew stopping the old lady now would be like halting a runaway locomotive, "and Cristobal has no wish to proceed in that direction with you, dear . . . why then there is no conflict in interest. You can marry one another and both go about your own ways," she finished up with a grand flourish of her fan.

Cristobal rolled his eyes and shrugged his broad shoulders. "I fear your aunt has a bee in her bonnet."

"Never!" Jeanette cried. "Elizabeth Crabbe will have to throw tomatoes at me in front of the opera house first! General Bee's troops will have to lock me in the stockade. The nuns at the Immaculate Conception Convent will have to burn me at the stake."

"Be reasonable, dear."

"I'm afraid she's beyond reason," Cristobal wryly counseled the old woman.

"I would rather live out my days as a widow of questionable virtue than marry again!" With that pronouncement Jeanette picked up her skirts and headed for the stairs.

Her lips curved into an elfin smile, her first genuine smile in a long time. Her blue eyes twinkled, revealing the essence that shimmered just beneath the young woman's surface and lent her an aura of exquisite beauty.

A giddy widow involved in amorous dalliances would hardly be thought capable of running supplies against the mighty Federal blockade.

3

Trinidad Cervantes knew everyone and everything that happened in the Rio Grande Valley, but Jeanette wondered if Columbia's old foreman could help her track down the elusive Frenchman, Kitt.

Trinidad was a dried-up, wizened little man with a monkey face and agile bowed legs; he always insisted that his growth had been stunted when he was a jockey by the horse trainers putting him on too light a diet and burying him up to his neck in the manure box for too long a time. After that, her father's offer to oversee Columbia had seemed to the little man like a miracle from St. Jude.

It was true that Trinidad could neither read nor write, nor did he know a note of music, but many a so-called educated white man envied him his accomplishments. He spoke both Spanish and English fluently and played the violin like a virtuoso. He made beautiful rings and bangles out of tortoiseshell with only his pocket knife, a round stick, and a pot of hot water for his tools. He also made fancy ropes for bridle reins and girths out of horsehair. But it was his gentle love and concern, which her stern father had been unable to demonstrate, that endeared Trinidad to Jeanette.

Trinidad had cousins and nieces and nephews in all the villas strung along the Rio Grande line like glass beads on a necklace. If anyone could elicit a piece of information, he could. Yet she had been riding with the leathery brown old man since sunup and had uncovered nothing about the Frenchman.

She had reasoned that perhaps the Frenchman was running contraband in one of the small ships of light draft that could operate in the shallow coastal waters where ships of the line could not venture. Perhaps, as a few other blockade runners did, he sailed into one of the inland waterways or even slipped in over the bar at the mouth of the Rio Grande, and transferred his contraband to lighters, large, open barges.

Working their way down the river toward the coast, she and Trinidad stopped before every adobe jacale to question the inhabitants about the Frenchman. The sun, an orange-hot coal, now rode high in the blue-white sky, and she was tired and her thighs were sweaty in the boy's dungarees. Yet she said nothing to Trinidad of her parched throat or muscle-sore derrière, for he had wholly disapproved of what she had in mind.

"Eet ees bad enough that you must dress and ride like *un muchacho*," he reproved her in that avuncular way he had used on her since she was three and old enough to sit astride a horse. But she had not ridden horseback since she went off to the finishing school at twelve, and she was dearly paying for it now. That she straddled a scurvy burro, a jenny, did not help.

Trinidad continued his diatribe, unaware that she had reined up her burro and was no longer following him. "But thees mission you are on—*híjole, sobrina*," he said, using the Spanish equivalent for niece, "eet could land you en the calaboose. And whachaya think, if the *Yanquis* catch you, they hang you for a traitor." He snapped his horny fingers. "*Muy pronto*, no?"

Jeanette drew off her floppy hat and let the long braid
she had tucked into the crown fall between her shoulder
blades. She turned her face to the treeless shoreline, hoping to catch some of the breeze that was nudging the
tide's waves toward the beach. But the wind playfully
hovered just off the sultry coast. Overhead a flock of
curlews wheeled. With the back of her arm she shielded
her eyes against the sunlight that glared off the white sand
and watched the curlews' arrowhead formation with distracted interest. "Trini," she mused, "maybe this Kitt—
maybe he doesn't operate off the coast at all. Maybe he
operates from right there out of Fort Brown."

Trinidad heeled his burro about and loped up alongside
the young woman he loved as much as his own eleven
children. "One of the *soldados,* eh?"

Jeanette began to fan the soiled hat before her face.
"No," she said slowly, "I'm sure I would have recognized
him among the soldiers I danced with. His face would
have betrayed his strength of leadership, his cunning, his
bravery in serving a noble cause."

Trinidad guffawed and slapped his bony knee. "You,
sobrina, ees *una romantica*—and a leetle bit loco, no?"

She sighed and smiled wistfully. "Yes, I daresay I am.
This Kitt is probably all Cristobal says he is. A crude ras-
cal out for his own profit."

In the village of Bagdad on the Mexican side of the
border Jeanette's search was finally rewarded with a clue.
She should have guessed that since Bagdad was a neutral
port it would be simple to bring cotton across the river
from Texas and load it on one of the vessels anchored in
Bagdad's harbor. The Federal blockaders could not inter-
vene until the ships cruised outside the territorial limits.

Situated between a stretch of sand dunes, Bagdad's flat
beach fronted the Gulf of Mexico. The village of fisher-
men's board shanties offered tolerable anchorage and harbor facilities for the growing number of vessels—now a

dozen or more—that were participating in the dangerous occupation of shipping Confederate cotton.

Beneath her hat's floppy brim Jeanette's eyes swept uneasily from one side of the dirt street to the other. Saloons and bars jostled for elbow space with homes whose pastel paint was peeled off mud-brick walls by the sun and wind and salt. Apparently she was not the only one with the idea of transporting cotton to the Mexican port. The dusty streets were rife with men—Mexican teamsters, cotton buyers, cotton sellers, speculators, peddlers, foreigners. Their clothing, hair, and beards were saturated with so much dust that they looked like millers, and the horses and mules shook their heads to throw the dust out of their ears.

Although the sun was still high, balancing atop the spire of the unfinished cathedral, people were spilling out the swinging doors of a crowded cantina when Trinidad roped in his burro. The painted placard over the cantina's door announced: LA FONDA DEL OLVIDO, the Inn of Forgetfulness.

"Enchanting," Jeanette said.

"You weel wait here."

"No." She slid a leg over the burro's scraggy back and hopped down. "Now is as good a time as any to put my masquerade to the test."

"*Dios mio,*" the old foreman groaned, shaking his sombreroed head. He should have told the girl's father every time she snuck out her bedroom window, using the trellis as a ladder, to scour the countryside at night with Cristobal and Armand. Perhaps a few well-placed whacks—no, it would not have changed the girl. Only made her more rebellious and obstinate than she already was.

Sawdust sprinkled the hardwood floor of the smokefilled cantina. A brass rail was flanked by ornate cuspidors and the mahogany bar was banked with customers—businessmen, soldiers from Fort Brown, drifters, and gaily painted girls whose attributes spilled over their low-cut, black-laced necklines. Jeanette hunched her shoulders so that the buckskin shirt hung loosely, concealing the small breasts. She jammed her pale, delicate hands in her pants pockets, assuming a masculine stance.

"Hey, *paisano*," a mustachioed monte dealer called to Trinidad. "No *muchachos* in the place."

Jeanette shifted to the other foot and braced her mouth in a sinister mug. She was careful to keep her hat's brim shadowing her blue eyes, though many a Spanish conquistador had left blue-eyed, fair-haired descendants. "I'm not a boy," she gruffly told the dealer in her best Spanish.

Trinidad winked broadly. "I have brought my nephew for—some experience."

Nearby the men who girded a green-baized table mounded with silver dollars and gold pieces chuckled and elbowed one another. "Ahhh, yes," the dealer grinned. "Perhaps Maria or Hermosita?"

"No, no," Trinidad said. "She must be young. Rubia—is she still here?"

The dealer jerked his head toward the stairs. "She has a select clientele, *paisano*. But you can try your luck."

The stairs creaked beneath Jeanette's boots. A threadbare runner showed the way down a dimly lit, seedy-looking hallway. From below drifted the American hoedown, "Little Brown Jug," banged out on a tinny piano. Trinidad stopped before the third door on the left and knocked. "Rubia, it is Tio Trinidad."

Jeanette sighed. Another niece.

"One of my sons knows Rubia," Trinidad explained baldly before the door parted to admit them.

Jeanette took one look about her at the gilded mirrors, the velvet draperies, and the painting of the nude woman partially shielded by a boa fan, and decided that in com-

parison similar places in New Orleans must look like
Methodist revival meeting halls. Such ornate trappings in
such a claptrap establishment!

And such a woman who turned from the oval mirror to
face her! Jeanette judged the woman, dressed in a demure
gown of dove-gray muslin with a high white collar, to be
twenty-one or -two. Her golden-skinned face was devoid
of makeup, her lips soft, her pale hazel eyes vibrant
against the honey-blond hair that clouded her shoulders.

Rubia, Spanish for blond. And to think this regal crea-
ture of undoubted Spanish heritage was a lady of the
night!

The young woman set down the ivory-backed brush and
smiled. *"Tío, cómo está? Y qué pasa por sus hijos?"*

Raised among the *campesinos* and, of course, with
Cristobal as a friend, Jeanette easily followed the conversation in Spanish. She had to repress a smile when the
young woman reproved Trinidad for bringing the slim,
callow youth to her. But Trinidad, removing the sombrero
from his grizzled head, replied, "It is not for that we
come, Rubia. We come for information. We look for a
man—*un francés, se llama Kitt."*

The face, like a beautiful flower at sunset, closed over.
Jeanette's heart leapt. The young woman knew something!

Rubia took up the brush and began toying with her
curls. *"Por qué?"*

"You have heard of him?" Jeanette asked, unable to
constrain her excitement. "You know him?"

Rubia's pale-eyed gaze moved up and down Jeanette's
disreputable-looking person. Her lids narrowed. "Who is
the boy?"

"Another of my brother's *sobrinos*. He will say nothing."

"And I can tell you nothing—until you tell me why, *tío*,
you wish to find this *hombre*, this Frenchman, Kitt."

Trinidad turned the sombrero in his hands and re-creased the high crown. He flashed Jeanette a furtive look. "We are in need of someone to transport certain cargo."

Rubia nodded her head. For a moment she tapped the brush lightly on the dressing table's tiled top. Jeanette held her breath. To come so close to finding the mysterious and elusive Kitt . . .

Then, "A water boy, Alejandro, may take you to Kitt— under certain conditions. You will most likely find Alejandro pushing his cart along the oceanfront, *tío*."

Thirty minutes later Jeanette sighted a little Mexican *aguatero* trudging along the hard-packed sand behind an ox cart loaded with water barrels. With Trinidad close at her heels, she threaded her way between the kegs, boxes, and bales of tobacco, cotton, and hides waiting to board the few ships, mostly English merchants that sat three miles out in the Mexican harbor.

Alejandro, who could have been no more than eleven or twelve, possessed angelic, bird-bright eyes. From his dirt-smeared, cherubic mouth drooped a cigarette butt. Trinidad explained what they wanted, and the urchin flipped the butt out on the sand. "*Sí*," the boy replied indifferently, as if it were of little consequence to take them to the famous or infamous blockade runner, depending on which side one was for. "Come back after sunset. We go then."

For more than an hour Trinidad and Jeanette, trying to look as churlish as the Mexican water boy, sat in a sleazy cantina that fronted a sea-rotted wharf while they waited for night to pull its blanket over Bagdad. By the time they left she was more than a little dizzy from the smoke and the noxious fumes of the pulque and mescal that lay like a fog over the cantina.

She found she was to grow even more dizzy a short time later, for Alejandro informed the two of them that once they boarded a lighter, he would have to blindfold

them. She was slightly taller than Alejandro, but when he
started to knot the smelly bandanna about her eyes, she
could see his disgust at dealing with such a sissy-looking
boy. Beneath the floppy brim of her hat she glared back at
him. What would a boy have done in similar circumstances? *"Caramba, mono!"* she cursed gruffly, calling
him a monkey. "I could tie the thing better and faster
myself!"

She caught Trinidad's approving grin and the boy's expression that lost some of its contempt, before the world
was blackened by the bandanna. It was a curious feeling,
the lack of sight—the shifting motion of the lighter's
planks beneath her feet, the skipping of the cool wind
across her cheeks. She could have sought the refuge of the
lighter's cabin, which was little larger than a pup tent. But
she preferred to taste the sea's salt tingling her lips and
hear the surf's rhythmic pounding against the sandy shore
as the lighter moved out into the harbor. Time ceased al-
together.

There came the booming of the lapping waves against
something broad—a ship's hull? Then the thud of the
lighter bumping on wood and the sudden jouncing. After
that she detected the swish of what must be a rope ladder,
followed by unintelligible conversation far above her. Alejandro put a ladder between her hands. "Climb," he instructed.

The rope was rough against her palms, and as the ladder swayed with her weight she was glad she could not
look down. The scent of smoke—a pipe, perhaps—
reached her, signaling she was nearing the top. And a
keen sense of joy filled her. Soon she would be able to
participate once more in something that had meaning.

It wasn't just her hope of bringing revenue to Columbia
again. Nor was it just the idea of avenging Armand's death
that was responsible for giving her life substance once
more. Steadily there grew in her a vision of aiding the

Confederacy—a vision born of one brief visit to Columbia back in 1859 by Robert E. Lee.

At that time Mexico was undergoing constant political strife, and Brownsville received, with almost equal frequency, the bullets and the refugees of battles between rival Mexican factions in Matamoros. Deserters from the various factions looted both sides of the river impartially, and so great was the disorder that Lieutenant Colonel Robert E. Lee was sent out from San Antonio to investigate the situation. One evening after dinner he had remained at the table with her father and Armand.

From the parlor she and Aunt Hermione could hear the men talking, could hear Lee's low voice speak of his love of the South and his concern for its future. Though he had freed his slaves years before, he still held a passionate devotion to the South.

After he left, when they were in bed, Jeanette wrapped in his arms, Armand said quietly in the dark, "I felt I was in the presence of a man who was cast in a grander mold and of finer metal than other men."

She had felt the same. She had been impressed with the fairness and kindness that surrounded Lee like an aura. Much later she often wondered if Armand realized he was himself cast in that same mold of fairness and kindness.

But just now the vision of actually aiding the Confederacy paled in her excitement at meeting the recklessly daring and resourceful Kitt!

Hands grappled under her arms and hauled her over the ship's bulwarks. Vertigo attacked her and she lurched unsteadily on her feet until hands at her shoulders steadied her. A few voices could be heard, mostly Spanish; then—yes, she picked up a rich male baritone speaking in French. Oh, why hadn't she tried to learn more of the language from Armand?

Another voice, at her shoulder, replied, *"Oui."* Her arm was gripped, and she was led off. The shutting of a door combined with the resinous scent of cedar. The same voice that had answered at her shoulder, sounding like that of a younger man, said in Spanish now, "Our captain wishes to know what is it you want of him?"

"Can we have our blindfolds removed?" she asked, forgetting that Trinidad was to have taken the part of the negotiator.

The melodious baritone voice she had known was Kitt's snapped an order in French, and she felt her elbow released. Taking it as a signal that permission was granted, her hand slipped up to the bandanna only to be checked by a banded grip at her wrist. At once she could sense another presence standing immediately before her—the heat of a body, much larger than hers; the warm, rum-scented breath.

Him.

4

The squeaking of the door's hinges told her that one or more people had left the room. "Trinidad?" she whispered anxiously.

No answer. Where had they taken him? The man who stood before her, so close, spoke now, and his breath rustled the stray tendrils that had escaped the braid concealed beneath her hat. *Mon jeune homme, à quoi . . .*"

It was useless; she got no farther than, "My young man, to what . . ." and then she was unable to make any sense of the low, melodious words he spoke.

She began to shake her head to indicate her ignorance of the language when she was surprised by another voice in the room—the younger one that had spoken before, translating the Frenchman's commands to Spanish for her. "Our captain requests that you do not remove the blindfold, as he desires to keep his identity a secret—and he wishes to know to what he owes the honor of your presence?"

She sensed that the Frenchman studied her closely during the exchange of words. The hand that encircled her wrist like a manacle released hers. She dropped her hand to her pockets in a boy's swaggering stance and pitched her throaty voice at an even deeper level. "Tell him I have heard of his reputation for evading the Federal blockaders—that he has yet to lose a ship. Tell him I have warehouses of cotton that I wish to sell."

Another exchange in the fluid French, and the young voice said in Spanish, "There are other ships in the harbor willing to take on your cargo."

Such an uncomfortable feeling not to be able to see to whom one is talking! It had to be something like that of a *penitente* at the confession box. No wonder she had never embraced Armand's Catholic convictions. "Yes, but those ships offer only money or mercantile goods in exchange— liqueurs, dress material, ladies' hats. I also want guns and ammunition—and quinine for the Confederacy."

The translation was made. A low chuckle escaped the man who stood immediately before her. She turned her face back up in the direction of his. "You are not in it for the 'Cause'?" she asked, disillusion slowing worming its way into her brain. Then quickly she remembered to spit on the floor in an imitation of the *aguatero*.

The younger man, whom she suspected by the accent to be a Mexican, made the translation to his captain. The man before her—he had to be very tall, judging by the source of his voice—laughed again and uttered something in French.

The Mexican said, "The captain says to tell you that he is in it for himself."

"I will give your captain more than a fair share of the proceeds from the sale of the cotton, more than the standard five thousand dollars a blockade-runner captain gets for a round trip."

It was an easy promise. In the textile mills of England four million workers were dependent on Southern cotton. And in France six hundred thousand people were likewise employed. Europe was willing to pay for the cotton.

The words flowed between the two men, then the Mexican replied, "The captain says that since he owns his own vessel, he is making money quicker than he can invest it, that—" he broke off as the Frenchman interrupted.

She felt what seemed to be the back of the Frenchman's fingers lightly stroking her cheek. The Mexican made a choked sound and continued. "My captain says that—he sometimes prefers—beardless young boys in his bed."

This was indeed no gallant Armand she was dealing with. Her mental image of a brave and dashing gentleman rapidly evaporated. Sweat broke out under the band of her hat. Where in tarnation was Trinidad? She gathered her wits about her. "Tell him—tell him I prefer girls."

Another low laugh followed the translation. Suddenly her hat was jerked off, and her wrist-thick braid swung down to flop against her shoulder blades. The Mexican swore. The masquerade was over! A hand pulled the braid over her shoulder to lay upon her rapidly rising and falling chest. His fingers continued holding the braid, playing with it. Her breast tingled at the sensation of those fingers resting so brazenly against it.

He murmured something, and the Mexican actually snorted. "My captain also enjoys girls. He is still willing to consider a trade other than money for transporting your cotton aboard his ship."

Her mouth dropped open at the blatant suggestion. Her interest in the French blockade runner dropped well below freezing. "Tell the *gentleman* his ship can rot in Davy Jones's locker first!"

At that the Frenchman erupted in laughter. The weasel! He was enjoying toying with her. Watching her squirm. "I wish to leave now," she said stiffly.

In her anger she missed the exchange between the Frenchman and his man, but the Mexican said, "He tells you to go back home—where a woman belongs."

Where a woman belongs! It was too much! Her hand swept out to make sharp contact with the Frenchman's jaw. She heard his grunt with a grim feeling of satisfaction—until he jerked her braid, yanking her head forward. She stumbled against him, and his hands grabbed her by her shoulders to steady her. He held her close against his chest. One arm—its muscles seemed as large and thick as an anchor's cable—slid about her waist. His free hand grasped her braid and tugged, forcing her chin up.

"Let me—"

But his mouth silenced her. His lips ground against hers with a hunger that stupefied her. Armand's passion had been sweet, tender . . . nothing like this savagery she was experiencing. Her head was bent so far back she thought her neck would snap. Frightened for the first time in all the harrowing day, she shoved her hands against the massive chest until he released her.

"Tell your civilized captain"—she gasped for breath—"that I shall seek out the ships anchored at Bagdad until the day comes I find a captain who isn't so mercenary!"

The Frenchman did not let the Mexican finish the translation but caught her to him once again. His lips softly moved over hers, as if he were memorizing the shape of her mouth. Then he released her before she could recover from the shock of the second kiss and vent her anger. *"Bon soir, ma chérie,"* he said and, turning her around by the shoulders, placed a well-aimed whack on her bottom.

Tia Juana laid a finger as large and black as a shotgun barrel to her lips. "Ssssh, missy."

Jeanette tiptoed through the kitchen. But her head brushed one of the many copper plates and kettles suspended from the ceiling. Like dominoes the pots and pans clanged one against the next. The old black woman's pupils rolled heavenward to display their whites.

"Tia Juana, what the thunder is—" Aunt Hermione

charged through the door and hauled up short. Jeanette thought the old woman looked as if she would have an apoplectic fit. Not even the news of Armand's death had seemed to shock the woman as much.

"I can't believe my eyes!" The old woman practically whinnied. "All those years trying to train you to be a proper lady—and this." Her accusing finger trembled as she pointed at the offending getup. "This!"

Jeanette almost expected a snorted neigh from the horse-faced woman. "I told you I was going out riding for the day with Trinidad."

"But not—not dressed so scandalously. And not riding all day—and night! I've been beside myself, Jeanette. Thinking that you'd been carried off by a band of Kicka-poos—or worse, those awful Mexican desperadoes."

Tia Juana, who stood before the stove, flashed Aunt Hermione a withering look and with a haughty expression on her pitch-black face returned to dicing scarlet chilis.

Jeanette crossed to the sink. "But you can see I am per-fectly safe. We were delayed by a rain shower." Which was true, since showers occurred almost daily that time of year, cleansing the air of dust and sand. She pumped some water over her hands, splashed her dirt-streaked face, and mumbled, "And I plan on riding more often. The year of mourning has made me forget how pleasur-able riding can be."

The following day the muscles of her bottom protested just the opposite. Pleasurable riding was not to be had, at least on one of Trinidad's burros. She would openly ride one of Columbia's fine bays before she would submit her posterior to that torture again.

With each movement of the bay Jeanette ached abom-inably, but her need to find a willing blockade runner was greater than her suffering. Remembering the whack, the insulting kiss, the cavalier treatment she had endured at the hands of the French blockade runner, Jeanette grew hot with indignation. From now on she would carry a knife or a derringer when she sallied forth on her mission, though she little knew how to use such weapons.

The British and French merchant vessels she and Trinidad called on that afternoon openly admitted that, rather than returning with bulky firearms, they preferred liqueurs and silks and other items that occuped a small amount of space in relation to their value. Then, too, they were unwilling to risk the ire of the United States prize courts if they were caught. Penalties were a lot stiffer for smuggling arms and ammunition.

If there was a bold and recklessly brave man among the blockade runners who was interested in her proposal, she didn't find him that day. She returned early enough to change and bathe for the opera she had promised to attend with Aunt Hermione. Sitting through the tedious *Faust* that night was even more agonizing than riding had been. Every so often she would shift uncomfortably, and her rustling taffeta skirts would bring a baleful eye from Aunt Hermione. Intermission could not come quickly enough.

Lady Olivia Mountbatten was in the midst of her grand aria, the glorious finale to the first act, when Jeanette spotted Cristobal in the box of no less a personage than General Bee and his wife. The plump little woman looked perfectly delighted at something Cristobal whispered behind the back of his beringed hand, one of his witty *bon mots*, no doubt.

Perhaps Cristobal had better success than she had in locating a blockade runner with bravado! When the intermission came and the soldiers crowded the curtained entrance to her box, she expressed her desire for fresh air with the hopes she could corner Cristobal in the opera house's lobby below.

Aunt Hermione practically beamed with pleasure that her headstrong niece had regained her senses and was behaving like a lady instead of some hoyden. It had never occurred to her that after the year of mourning Jeanette would turn wild again. Aunt Hermione had thought that marriage with Armand had once and for all settled the chit down. To see the young woman married off once more under the thumb of some strong-willed man would mean her duty to her niece and brother had been carried out!

Escorted by her entourage of military admirers, Jeanette found Cristobal surrounded by a coterie of Brownsville's younger people, who appeared to hang on every utterance of the effete fop. But Cristobal did cut a fine figure. The new tight black trousers, which had replaced the wide peg-top fashion, displayed his splendid physique. A droll smile lit his heavily lidded eyes at her approach with the three soldiers trailing.

"A lovely peacock among turkeys," he quipped.

In the general laughter that followed the man on her left, a lieutenant who stood some seven inches shorter than Cristobal, said, "I take umbrage at that, sir, and wish to call you out!"

With a bemused expression Cristobal looked down from his height at the little man. "Whatever for?"

"For the insult, of course!" said the lieutenant, whose face was quickly taking on a choleric color.

"Fie!" Jeanette intervened with a disarming smile for the young people gathered about. "The two of you look like a cock and a bantam." She held out a dainty hand. "Cristobal, do escort me back to my box and tell me of your latest travels."

"*La*, Jen," he said when he had taken her arm and they had moved away from the others, who were still chuckling over the incident, "your rescue came in time. That little poppinjay would have been snapping at my heels all evening."

"I was afraid your bravery would cost the life of one of you," she snapped.

"*Dios!* I'm not so foolish as that," he said with his imperturbable bonhomie. "About my travels, did I ever tell you that there is a most fragrant, flowering shrub along the Mediterranean called the lavender? The exact same shade as your eyes—lavender blue."

Her fan never stopped its swaying motion. "You do say the most flattering things, Cristobal. But tell me, how is your article going? Have you located our mysterious Kitt?"

"Not a scent of a trail!"

"But where all have you looked?"

He fixed her with an amused glint in his eye. "My dear, I have looked in establishments that a proper young lady like yourself would never dream of entering."

She held back a grin of triumph. She had succeeded where a man had not. She had found the elusive Frenchman—to no success. "But surely you have heard the whereabouts of other blockade runners who are willing to . . . run risks out of the ordinary?" If she could just worm one name out of him.

"Bah! They are here today, gone tomorrow. I heard through a good source at the Pelican Pub that the *U.S.S. Albatross* captured the blockade runner *Two Sisters* off Brazos Santiago yesterday."

He turned a humorous countenance on her. "But surely, Jen, you still aren't attracted to such rogues as the French blockade runner?"

"Hardly," she snapped heedlessly. Yesterday had cured her of any idealistic notions she had entertained about the Frenchman. There were other ways to market her cotton before she would have to resort to his contemptible terms!

5

The trellis swayed precariously. Jeanette held her breath. No longer was she the elfish tomboy who had scaled the trellis like a buccaneer the mast. She often lamented over the way her once slender frame had filled out. The budding breasts whose existence had sorely annoyed her at twelve had bloomed into a lushness that often threatened to spill out of her low-cut dresses. Yet the armoire's mirrored doors reflected the slim hips of a woman who has yet to bear a child. Would that she had.

When no noise of cracking latticework followed, she relaxed and drew a deep breath. The scent of the fragrant roses that laced the trellis mingled with that of luscious oranges and bananas from the Columbia's fruit groves beyond. Quickly she skimmed the rest of her way down the network of slats.

"Hell and damnation!" she hissed when she reached the bottom. She thrust her forefinger in her mouth to suck where a thorn had pricked it.

Spitting out the blood that salted her tongue, she laughed aloud. It had been even longer than the period of mourning since she had enjoyed herself. Perhaps since that day when Aunt Hermione had made her put up her hair and let down her skirts and society had cast her into the role of a young woman.

From behind her a voice cautioned, "Ssssh!" In the moonlight she made out Trinidad's weather-beaten sombrero. "You laugh loud enough to wake the cemetery. You want your aunt she should hear us?"

But she knew old Trini was in good humor also. Riding was in Trinidad's blood. The little man's rounded shoulders squared, his back straightened as for the first time in more than a year, he sat astride a superb horse. With the effects of the war, the bays had been reserved for drawing the brougham only. In Richmond and Wilmington and Charleston Thoroughbreds now pulled caissons instead of carriages.

Jeanette tried to repress her own capricious good mood. But as the bays clip-clopped their way along the River Road toward Brownsville and Matamoros she laughed gaily. The delicious solitude of the dark, when no proper lady would be about, the feel of the invigorating night air on her face, and the freedom of her body unrestrained by stays and hoops only heightened her spirits.

The old Mexican overseer cocked his head, and she said, "Trini, sometimes I think that when God cut me out of His bolt of cloth, somehow He slipped on the pattern and I wound up a female when I should have been a male!"

Trinidad chuckled. "*El Señor,* He never slips up. One day, *sobrina,* you weel find thees pattern from which He made you."

She doubted it. There was no pattern for a twenty-six-year-old woman who behaved like a sixteen-year-old boy . . . except for the mentally incompetent. That was it, she really must be deranged. Only an imbecile would set out on such a futile expedition.

She laughed again, and her exultant laughter echoed up and down Brownsville's sleeping streets. Even the saloons

and mescal joints snoozed in drunken slumber. Not so
Matamoros. The cantinas that wedged every corner were
more active than a Baptist riverside revival. Drunks staggered out swinging doors as ready replacements shoved
their way in. A brassy trumpet mourned the loss of fortunes on the monte tables. Sloe-eyed women with painted
faces struck seductive poses as they displayed their wares
outside cantina doors and in the rooms above.

But Jeanette had had enough of cantinas three days before. She let the bay pick its way through the refuse-
ridden Plaza de Mercado toward the Camino a Los
Cemeterios while she formulated the rest of her plan. The
bay danced to a halt in front of a stucco building that had
openings for rifle barrels in the second-story walls and a
large dome used as a lookout post rising above the flat
roof. The walls were pitted and scarred with bullet holes
from the numerous revolutions. This was the regional
headquarters for the Mexican Guardia Nacional. Two soldiers came sleepily to their feet at the approach of the
peach-fuzzed youth and the stooped old man.

Fearlessly Jeanette looked over the soldiers' bell-
mouthed *escopeta*. The shotgun was almost an antique. "I
wish to see your *capitán*."

"He sleeps."

"It is important," she pressed.

The soldier, whose jacket was stained and sloppily but-
toned, shrugged at the other, and replied, "Come with
me."

They followed him into a room where light peeked
through chinks in the mud-brick walls and, at the soldier's
bidding, waited while he disappeared down a hallway.
The room contained a battered desk and only one chair,
but Trinidad found a nail keg for Jeanette to sit on. Soon
the soldier reappeared, followed by a stocky man struggling into the jacket of his uniform. This was the officer
whom Trinidad told her was known for negotiating deals

above and beyond the call of duty—and his office.

He eyed them suspiciously over the bristle of his handlebar mustache. "*¿Pues?*" he grumped. "Well? Well? What is it that brings you bats out at this ungodly hour of the night?"

"Cotton," Jeanette said in a young man's low-pitched voice.

"Cotton?" the captain roared.

"Cotton," Jeanette answered, unperturbed at the way the captain's mustache flapped with the jowls that worked in muted outrage. "More cotton than you ever dreamed." She hurried to explain the plan she had formulated over the last two days—the idea to establish an overland route from the railhead between Galveston and San Antonio for shuttling cotton to Matamoros by teamsters.

"Why Matamoros—why not Bagdad?" the captain asked when she had finished.

"Because I want guns and ammunition, and the European blockade runners don't like to risk running firearms through the Federal blockade on the Gulf. But with you as a middleman—and taking a handsome profit—cotton could be freighted to Guaymas on the Pacific in exchange for guns and ammunition from the merchants who risk no blockade."

"Ask for wagon loads of whores! Ask for barrels of *aguardiente!* But do not ask for guns and ammunition!"

The captain flung a hand at the *escopeta* the soldier cradled. "Do you think my men would shoulder a weapon as outdated as a bow and arrow if we had the means to obtain modern firearms? We need them to fight the French. Even at this minute *los franceses* wait like sea wolves outside Veracruz's harbor to set up their Austrian Maximilian as Emperor of Mexico. Bah!"

Political machinations in that decade were rife. The French, through past-due debts owed by Mexico, hoped to gain control of that country's unstable government, which was already torn asunder by its continuous internal revolutions. Of course, France's intervention violated the Monroe Doctrine and forced the United States to align with Mexico's fugitive President Juárez. Thus the Confederacy and France found themselves strange bed partners, both allied against the United States.

"Then why not buy the firearms?" she ventured. "Mexico has cattle—that means beef and hides. Food and shoes for the European countries."

The captain grunted, and his great mustache flapped. "Because of Juárez's order to defer payments on our national debt, other countries refuse to deal with us. I am sorry, *joven,*" he told the young man, "but I cannot help you—nor myself, *ay de mí!*"

On the trip back to Columbia Jeanette slumped low on the bay's back. Anything she hoped to do for the Confederacy, anything she hoped to do for Armand's memory, even for Columbia, would have to be done in a woman's limited capacity. Knitting socks and underwear and making bandages and canteen covers. Her contemptuous snort nearly equaled that of the weary horse.

She crawled into her four-poster just as dawn shafted the eastern sky. But sleep eluded her as the memory of the blockade runner's kiss plagued her thoughts. The kiss had not been that repulsive. Surely some terms short of total capitulation could be agreed on.

While the last blistering rays of July sun gilded the cathedral spire, the brougham rumbled through Matamoros, an old fortified city that once offered Easter-egg painted homes, semitropical fruits, exotic flowers, and salt marshes converted to tree-shaded lagoons.

"Not like it used to be when we would come over for all manner of fiestas and fandangos," Aunt Hermione declared and pulled her black lace shawl more tightly about her. "A romantic place, Matamoros was then, with gallant caballeros and handsome soldiers everywhere. But now, now—it's not safe for a woman to be about."

Now cotton was beginning to flow out of the South through Texas to Matamoros and from there to the neutral port of Bagdad, which the Federal Government could not blockade. The formerly sleepy little border town of Matamoros was overflowing with twenty thousand speculators from all over the world. The influx of foreigners was catered to by the accoutrements of most boom towns—brothels, gambling houses, and innumerable saloons.

Yet, like the much-smaller Bagdad, Matamoros had scarcely any sidewalks, no gas works; the streets were not graded and ordinarily had an average depth of eighteen inches of mud. There were likewise no waterworks and peons hauled silty water from the river for two dollars per forty-gallon barrel.

Aunt Hermione's fan indicated the peons who lounged about the Plaza de Hidalgo in bare feet and dirty sombreros, the drunken soldier who lurched from a hitching post to the plaza's iron picket fence, the three beady-eyed pistoleros whose hands rode their gun belts. "Rape— mark my word, Jeanette. The Yturrias' ball is not so important to take a chance on—"

"Rape," Jeanette finished with a sigh. "Aunt Hermione, rape is particularly unnecessary in a town with such a supply of hospitable prostitutes. You have little to fear"—or hope, she added mentally—"of rape."

On the other hand, Jeanette knew *she* would have to worry about rape that night—unless she played her cards right, which was just what she had in mind.

Behind the Yturria's high, pink adobe walls the ancient and patrician names of Mexican history were represented—with the exception of Cavazos. But then Cristobal was off researching his article—no doubt in a saloon. For once she was glad he was not along to relieve the tedium with his foolish yet funny repartee. He would make an excellent red herring that evening.

Many women would readily believe she could leave the ball to have an assignation with such a handsome and distinguished man. The women would be quite willing to overlook the inane laugh and the affected mannerisms for a heavy diamond ring on their finger, bought with a lucky or skillful hand at cards, and their name coupled in marriage with the Cavazos name, which still retained the grandeur of its aristocratic past. More than once that evening Jeanette mentioned Cristobal with lowered lashes and a giddy smile at the other young women.

Only with Claudia Greer did she lower her guard. But then Claudia, like Armand, had always been sensitive to others and would have seen through her sham. Even now the plain-faced woman perceived how forced was the bright smile that Jeanette wore. As a properly married woman with a husband away at war, Claudia joined the dowagers and duennas. These women sat against the adobe walls of the large lantern-filled courtyard, away from the fun and festivities.

Claudia put her hand gently on Jeanette's and lowered her voice so the other women would not hear. "I know it must be very difficult for you, Jeanette. I know how much you loved Armand . . . and how very much he loved you."

Jeanette blinked back the tears of shame at her deception and answered honestly, "Sometimes I forget, Claudia. Sometimes it seems that I never was loved; that Armand was a trick of my imagination."

"I think it's time's way of lessening the hurt of losing a loved one. But I don't think the Lord ever meant to limit our love to just one person." Her stubby-lashed eyes searched Jeanette's. The young woman's mouth, much too large for her narrow face, smiled tenderly. "Don't wait for the perfect person, Jeanette. There are no perfect people, only perfect moments."

But Claudia had not known Armand as she had.

Jeanette stayed just long enough in the Yturrias' courtyard to mingle with the citizens of Brownsville and Matamoros and dance a few waltzes with the officers who had come over from Fort Brown. When the mariachis launched into a melancholy rendition of "La Golondrina," she drew her aunt away from the rotund and pompous Señora Morales to murmur, "I have decided to leave early, Aunt Hermione, but our carriage will be at your disposal whenever you desire to leave."

Her aunt, annoyed at being drawn away from the gossiping ring of matrons, nodded distractedly. Then her ears almost perked up like those of a horse that had just scented danger. "What? What? However are you getting home?"

Jeanette's lips curved in a mischievous smile. "I'm not going directly home, Aunt Hermione. A gentleman of our acquaintance awaits me."

Aunt Hermione's eyes rounded like horse blinders. "My smelling salts," she wheezed.

Jeanette took the fan from her aunt's trembling fingers and waved it before the old woman's face, whispering, "I shall be very discreet, I promise you."

When she had installed her pallid aunt in a comfortable chair in the Yturria *sala*, a drawing room of opulent furnishings, she made her way to the large, hand-carved double doors at the front entrance where Trinidad waited on the brougham's box. She was grateful for the dark as she awkwardly levered herself up and settled her massive hoop skirts over the sides.

"*Loca!*" Trinidad said, shaking his head and flipping his whip over the bays' backs. "You are crazy in the head, *sobrina*. Too much sun as a child!"

"Not enough sun as a woman, Trini." She lifted her face to the stars. "It's a glorious night."

"Eet's a dangerous night. I heard the owl, *tecolote*, he hooted twice just at sundown."

"Bah! You and Tia Juana are too superstitious. Did you leave the message with Rubia?"

"*Sí*. But she made no promise that the Frenchman would come."

"I'm taking a room tonight at the Fonda del Olvido—" Jeanette held up a forestalling hand. "I'll be perfectly all right with your niece Rubia. Just be waiting for me tomorrow morning on the first stage back to Matamoros."

Grumbling all the way, Trinidad drove her back to the plaza where the stagecoach stopped on its ten daily runs over the twenty-odd miles between Matamoros and Bagdad. Jeanette wrapped her shawl about the lower portion of her face to conceal her identity, but fortunately she was the only passenger on the stage's last run of the day.

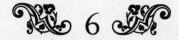 6

As she climbed the rickety stairs of the Bagdad cantina, excitement bubbled in her like champagne. For too long life had held little challenge. Rubia, beautifully gowned in rose jaconet with a white chimesette filling in the V neck, answered Jeanette's knock.

Ruefully Jeanette thought that of the two of them she herself looked more a lady of the night, dressed as she was in the sapphire satin and only a touch of ivory lace to camouflage her low neckline.

Rubia's face was expressionless, but Jeanette could see the curiosity and—was it resentment?—that lurked in the pale hazel eyes. "Kitt, the Frenchman, has agreed to see you," Rubia said. "Why I do not know." She nodded her head toward the other end of the murky hall that was lit by a single candle sputtering in its socket. "He waits for you in the last room on the left."

When Jeanette knocked, a rich baritone voice said, "*Entrez.*"

The room was as black as Hades, and she wondered if maybe that wasn't where she might be. Facing Satan. Her eyes peered among the shadowy forms of the room's furniture, and a voice said in muffled Spanish, "Come here—

to the corner, *por favor*." She recognized it as belonging to the Mexican on board the blockade runner's ship.

Now, as her eyes focused, she could see two figures sitting at what appeared to be a small, round table, their backs half to her. She groped her way past the foot of the bed and located a chair across from the two.

"*Sientese, señorita,*" said the one to her left, the Mexican, instructing her to sit.

The leather chair, which was wedged into a corner, squeaked as she seated herself and settled her skirts. She wished she could make out the faces of the two opposite her more clearly, but each wore a sombrero pulled low. Even their clothing was dark—leather vests of black or brown, she couldn't tell for sure, and dark shirts. She could make out a pistol lodged in the Mexican's wide belt. She shivered. Below the table the Frenchman no doubt sported a brace of pistols strapped to his hips. She must not let herself forget that this was not like the games she had played as a child with Armand and Cristobal. These men had no consideration for a lady. But then wasn't that what she wanted? To be accepted on the merits of what she could accomplish for the Confederacy—and not on the merits of sex?

She fixed her gaze on the Frenchman, for it was he who decided her fate; yet she could no more make out his features than she could see the back of her head. "I have reconsidered," she began in Spanish. "I feel that we still might come to terms."

She waited while the usual translation was made. "His terms, my captain asks?"

This was going to be touchy. "A compromise."

She heard the humor in the Mexican's voice as he gave the Frenchman her reply. Annoyed, she did not wait to hear his captain's comments, but interjected, "Tell him that for the arms and ammunition I will play him a game of chess. If I win, he receives his share of the sale of the cotton—in gold. Nothing more. If he wins—then, his

terms. I spend a night in his bed for every delivery of
arms his ship makes."

She expelled her last breath. It had been difficult to say
what she had, but the worst was over now, for she had no
doubt but that she could win at chess. She had played the
game too often with Armand and Cristobal to lose.

The tallow candle on the far wall fluttered to life. In the
flickering dim light Jeanette could make out now why the
two men's voices were muffled. Bandannas shielded the
lower half of their faces, so that only the shadowed portion
between the sombrero's brim and the bandanna was visi-
ble—mere slits that watched her. She thought they
looked more like desperadoes than privateers.

Waiting for one of them to say something, she was half
afraid the Frenchman would turn down her proposition—
and half afraid he wouldn't. She wished there were more
light. Her bravery was wavering like the candle flame. At
last the Frenchman murmured something, and the other's
chair scraped the floor as he rose to leave. Beneath the
Frenchman's unwavering surveillance, she shifted uneasily. It wasn't fair that he could study her, while she
could barely see him. He had even had the foresight to
position her so that the candlelight was behind him.

It wasn't too late to change her mind. There were easier
ways to help the Confederacy, to avenge her beloved.
Plaiting palmetto hats and making canvas knapsacks. Did
not Southern homes hum with the spinning wheel and
clack with the loom? She could still sell her cotton in
return for the necessities required to keep Columbia operating.

She rose to go, and a swarthy hand shot out to capture
her forearm. With gentle pressure the Frenchman levered her back down into the chair. *"Asseyez-vous."*

Sit down. He had made that plain enough.

"You really are despicable," she said with a charming
smile, careful to keep to English.

No response.

"You two-headed jackass," she said sweetly, enjoying the moment. "Men like you are no better than worms."

The door opened and the Mexican entered, this time without the bandanna about his face. The candlelight behind him accented his wiry, reed-thin figure. He carried an onyx chess set, and when he set it on the small round table between her and his captain, even with his sombrero shadowing his face, she could identify the Mexican as a mestizo by the obvious Indian features.

"*Buena suerte*," he murmured before he left the room. Jeanette wondered if the wish of good luck was meant for her or the Frenchman. The closing of the door seemed to be the sealing of her fate. Her glance quickly swept the room—not as well furnished as Rubia's. Small, musty. A white iron bed with, incongruously, a tin *retablo* of the Virgin Mary over it. A bureau of dark wood that sloped to one side. The chipped pitcher and washbasin sat precariously on it. No window. No escape.

Back to the Frenchman. His eyes, dark and luminous, watched her intensely. His large, brown fingers began to set the black and white pieces in their positions. She took a deep breath and removed the shawl from her head. There was no backing out now. She started pulling the eyelet-lace gloves from her fingers.

"*Vous avez le blanc,*" he told her.

He was giving her white, the advantage of the first move. "How chivalrous of you," she cooed, still in English. Immediately she moved out her bishop's pawn. With luck she could get the match over quickly—with the fool's checkmate that utilized only three moves.

Apparently the Frenchman was no tyro at the more intricate plays, for he responded by moving his black knight, which demolished her original plan of early attack, easy conquest. She sighed inwardly. It was going to be a long and difficult game. At one point the Mexican entered and set two glasses—hers was cracked—of harmless-looking amber liquid before them. "Mescal," he said before closing the door behind him. She left the glass untouched. She was not so foolish that she would let the Frenchman inebriate her.

The game continued. Black and white pieces began to vanish from the board. She drummed her fingers. He rubbed the bridge of his nose. She sacrificed two pawns for his knight; he yielded three pawns for her bishop. She wished the bandanna didn't conceal his face so well. If she could only see his expression; perhaps the droop of his mouth to give her some clue as to his intentions. As it was, the relentless gaze of his brown eyes told her nothing.

Piece after piece was vanquished in the fierce mental combat. Her nerves were as taut as one of Trinidad's violin strings; her palms were damp with perspiration. Her opponent was as good as or better than Armand and Cristobal!

Nervously her fingers played with her remaining fortresslike rook. With it, and her queen, she might just possibly corner his king in checkmate. But if she did not succeed with the next move, it was the beginning of the end.

Then, before she realized the position he had maneuvered her into, he swiftly moved his bishop diagonally across the board. His gaze sought hers across the table. *"Echec,"* he said evenly.

She closed her eyes and opened them again, hoping the board would look different. It didn't. Her king was forced to move and sacrifice her queen to his bishop. She watched with a shuddering breath as his strong fingers plucked her queen, her strongest piece, from the field of battle. Bitterly her lips curled at the crippling blow. Her lungs expelled air heavily, and her hand lifted the glass. In one breath she swallowed nearly a quarter of its contents. Her esophagus went into paralysis. Every taste bud screamed in agony. Her pupils dilated like kaleidoscopes.

Immediately he was at her side, his huge hand pounding her back. His husky chuckle was muted by the bandanna. *"Avez-vous abandonné?"*

"No!" she gritted, when air had returned to her seared throat. She understood the question only too well. "I don't wish to concede!"

He reseated himself, sprawling in the chair, and refilled her glass. Wildly her gaze swept over the board, searching for an escape for her king—and for herself. The damned Frenchman had to be a chessmaster! She knew now how the paltry number of defenders must have felt at the Alamo with Santa Ana's legions moving in for the slaughter—except with her queen captured she held no musket for her defense. And the Frenchman's ravishment of her would be, in a way, much worse than the final death before the firing squad. It would be a betrayal of her memory of Armand and their love. For her it would be tantamount to adultery.

She positioned her rook, her fortress, between her king and his dangerous queen, only to realize immediately his knight now had her cornered. The rook slipped from her grasp to clatter on the board. She shrugged her shoulders dispassionately. "I yield," she said in Spanish and reached for the glass. Avoiding the triumphant glint in the dark eyes across from her, she swallowed the entire contents this time.

The effect was devastating. The sausage curls before her ears seemed to spring out and roll back like sprung window shades. Her deflated lungs gasped like bellows. She struggled to her feet. Her chair overturned behind her, shattering her eardrums with the noise.

She was only half aware that the candlelight was pinched out. A hand took her elbow as she toppled onto the bed like a statue. Behind her lids the room whirled dangerously. Surely it would stop soon. In a moment it

did, and she opened her eyes. She still felt strange, and
her hands discovered why. Her clothes! They were gone!
"Oh, sweet Mary in Heaven!" she groaned.

That damned low laughter! Mocking her, challenging
her!

She tried to sit up, and two hands pressed her shoulders back down into the comfort of the mattress. *"Ma
chérie, j'attends pour toujours pour ceci."*

Whatever was he saying?

She gave herself over to the large capable hands that
stroked her shoulders, her neck. Warm lips moved over
hers, lightly—as the wings of Death? Surely she could not
be held accountable for what she found no pleasure in.

Armand . . . oh, Armand, her soul cried out.

A hand took the fingers of her left hand, holding them
gently. Lulling her . . . deceiving her. For in the next
moment she felt her marriage ring slipped from her finger. The thief! Yet to raise her head in protest did not
seem worth the effort of enduring the torpedo that rock-
eted through her brain.

Then her outrage at the theft was diverted by the lips
that nuzzled at one breast. She lay rigid. Paralyzed by
what he was doing. It had been so long. His teeth gently
nipped one flaccid nipple, and her body arched at the unexpected sensation. And then he was kissing her again—
softly, sweetly, it would almost seem, so that when she
felt his tongue teasing her lips and teeth, it was no intrusion, no violation. It was as if he were not demanding but
asking for her participation.

She opened her mouth, surprised at the pleasure she
had forgotten. Had she and Armand settled into such a
dull routine of lovemaking? She couldn't remember, but
then she couldn't seem to even think straight. Not with all
that mescal running through her blood like liquid fire,
searing her; not with the Frenchman kissing her, as if he
would lay bare her soul.

Then, a slow stirring of excitement. After a moment her natural reticence was diluted by the pleasurable feelings given by the Frenchman's bold tongue, and her tongue dared to touch the tip of his.

The hand that tenderly cupped her breast encouraged her even more, and her tongue engaged in an erotic dance with his. At times she had thought that Armand was a little shocked by her active response in their lovemaking. Maybe ladies were not supposed to enjoy the act, but it had always been difficult for her to remain passive.

When the Frenchman's fingers massaged her nipple to a tumescent peak, she moaned low in her throat.

"*Oui*," he whispered against the hollow at the base of her neck. "*C'est ça. C'est meilleur.*"

Oh, what was he saying? What was she doing! What was *he* doing?!

She tried desperately to close her legs against the hand at her knee. "*Non, non,*" he said in a low voice that tickled her ear. His tongue traced the delicate convolutions of her ear, and goose bumps prickled her flesh. Forgetful of her intentions to resist, she parted her thighs for the hand warming her skin in deliciously stroking motions that moved ever upward. The goose bumps were chased away now by the heat radiating from that area his hand softly rubbed. "Ohhhh," she cried low, half in pleasure, half in shame at the soft, squishing noise emanating from between her legs.

He laid a gentle finger against her lips. "*Que cela ne vous embarrasse pas.*"

He had perceived her embarrassment and sought to reassure her. But it did not help. Never had she experienced such a lack of control over herself. He repeated his words, softly still but with an unmistakable relentlessness, as if what and how she felt mattered. It dawned on her then that perhaps it did matter to him—that to see her lose herself to his lovemaking was the ultimate domination for the man. She twisted her head from one side of the pillow to the other to escape his questing kiss, but he anchored a hand in her hair, holding her head immobile in a gentle grasp. *"S'il vous plaît, mon amour."*

Please, my love?

Even as she acquiesced, the muscles in her legs relaxing, he moved upon her. His body entered hers in slow, gentle increments. Her body buckled with the unexpected bulk that filled her—until there was nothing but him. A year. Had it really been more than a year since she had known the warmth of Armand's body covering hers? Again, she had forgotten. That warm, pleasurable feeling brought on by Armand's lovemaking.

The Frenchman weighed a ton! Then his weight was forgotten as the magnificent body began moving in and out with breathtaking strokes. She tried to recall Armand's handsome face . . . with the austere features of an ascetic. That sensitive mouth . . . those warm, intelligent eyes. Strange that the only two men ever to possess her were Frenchmen. And there it was—the Frenchman again. There was no escaping the thought of him. Or escaping him.

Involuntarily her arms slipped about his narrow waist. Her hands slid up the broad back, her fingers feeling with surprise the muscles that ridged it. She clutched him to her, unconsciously urging him with little moans. Suddenly she tensed. As if from someplace far away, something beckoned—strongly. There was an inexplicable urge to move toward it. Her body took command, carrying her toward that calling force. She lifted her hips, arching to meet the Frenchman's thrust, slamming forward against him with her need.

At last he answered her body's demand. For one electrifying moment she was suspended. Then little orgasmic shudders quaked her body. With a cry she went slack in his arms. From afar it seemed she heard him whisper, *"La petite morte."*

The little death. Never had it happened to her.

She slept the sleep of death. But sometime during the night she was awakened by the clink of a glass or bottle. She gasped. Cool liquid trickled down her stomach, pooling in her navel. A strong scent of sweetness cloyed her nostrils. She tried to focus her eyes on the shadowy figure who straddled her hips, but what with the dark and her splitting headache—with a groan her head fell back on the pillow. She abandoned the idea of identifying the Frenchman—her lover. She gave over to the tongue that dipped into her navel's recess and penciled a trail over her belly.

"Brandy," he told her, and she nodded mindlessly, letting her body float on the tidal wave of his lovemaking. Oh, sweet Mary! Was that really his tongue licking the sticky brandy from between her fingers . . . tickling the arches of her feet . . . stroking the backs of her knees? Abruptly the warmth of his body departed, and she heard a woman's voice sigh with keen disappointment and longing.

"*Le baiser français,*" he said with soft laughter now.

She nodded again, not caring what it was he whispered—until her legs were ignominiously hoisted over his shoulders. Without warning she felt his head dip between her thighs. Violently her hands shot out to shove his head away, but his tongue persisted in its pursuit of the delicate folds. At last she stopped tugging at his thick head of hair and surrendered to the exquisite sensations that winged through her. Clutching his head to her now, she went limp with the unbearable pleasure.

Le baiser français. The Frenchman's kiss!

7

Le baiser français!

The Frenchman's kiss.

Jeanette's broad-brimmed straw hat swished furiously from her head. A heated flush stole over her face.

"Your complexion is positively beet-red, Jen. The sun too much for you?"

"What?" She looked up from her picnic plate into the dark-brown eyes of the dandy who stood before her with Annabel on the lush grass of the public square. In the square's center stood a Liberty Pole around which a space had been enclosed for the graves of officers of the Ring-gold Battery who were killed during the war with Mexico. Where was Armand's grave?

"I'm sorry, Cristobal. What did you say?"

"I think I like your complexion much better this way," he said with that inane little laugh peculiar to him. "A little color to it. Almost golden tan like it was when you were a child."

"Fie! A lady's complexion should be magnolia-white." Sighing, she replaced the hat and tied its lilac streamers that matched her dimity day dress beneath her chin. As if she really cared what the sun could do to her complexion.

57

"A lady can never be too careful with her skin," red-headed Annabel reproved.

Her perfectly oval face was renowned in the Valley for having the creamiest skin. And, to Jeanette's chagrin, she never failed to mention Jeanette's freckles whenever the subject of complexion arose. She did not fail this time either, though she was more circumspect than usual. Her Dresden blue eyes gazed demurely at Cristobal, who leaned insouciantly against the courthouse's shading oak, before looking with simulated pity at Jeanette. "If you're not more careful of the sun, Jeanette, you'll look just like one of your plantation darkies."

"Does Columbia own darkies, Jen?" Cristobal drawled. "I would think Armand would have been against slavery."

"Of course he was against it. No one owns slaves in Lower Texas. Except on a limited basis. It's easier and less expensive to pay wages to the Mexicans."

Cristobal arched a black brow. "Are you sure the reason darkies aren't owned in the Valley isn't simply because their masters know it'd be too easy for them to escape across the Rio Grande?"

Her mouth full of fried chicken, she could only wrinkle her nose at him. It was always that way between the two of them—Cristobal countering her statement with another. Whatever the subject, she could depend on the two of them to disagree. Only now Armand was not there to mediate their heated debates.

"I don't want to get into an argument over theoretics," she said flatly when she had swallowed.

The question of a Civil War over slavery was simply one she could not understand. In fact, she had her doubts whether that was the real issue. Armand had said several times that it was more a struggle between the North and the South for political and economic power. He had believed in stronger states' rights and a less powerful Federal Government. She only believed in the worth of a human.

And that human was gone.

"Major Hampton says that the Yankees have darkie regiments," Annabel said.

"Ladies," Cristobal said in a bored voice, "the politicians are talking enough about the war today without us dwelling on it." He straightened and said, "Anyone for some lemonade?"

Annabel rose to her feet to clasp Cristobal's proffered arm, but Jeanette declined. Annabel Goddard obviously had her sights set on Cristobal, as she had on Armand just after he returned from the university. She was a clever, scheming, man-hunting coquette, and for a while Jeanette had wished ardently that she could be just like her. And then miraculously Armand was ignoring Annabel and asking Jeanette to marry him.

She felt out of place there in the sunshine, with Armand gone, his body somewhere beneath mounds of damp dirt and darkness. She would much rather have been with Trinidad and two of Columbia's trusted *campesinos*. They were delivering three wagon loads of Columbia's cotton to Bagdad's wharves. There the little Mexican *aguatero* would see that the bales reached their consignment—the abominable Frenchman!

Perhaps it was just as well she attended Brownsville's Fourth of July barbecue, even though it meant listening to the eloquent but boring speeches delivered by the city's politicians and Fort Brown's military leaders. She did not want to chance meeting that Frenchman again until . . . until the arms were delivered and it was time for another shipment of cotton—and another payment to him. She shuddered with shame, horrified at the memory of the previous night. The chicken in her mouth tasted like ashes, and she dropped the drumstick back on her plate.

She had betrayed Armand's memory. She had reveled in the Frenchman's arms like—like some whore! Oh, dear God!

A little boy in knee britches scampered by yelling after a hoop, and she cringed. Her head! The damnable mescal. Her lids closed against the brilliant sun that threatened to bring her liquor-soaked eyeballs to a boil.

"Some lemonade to cool you, Jen?"

She looked up again at Cristobal, who held out a porcelain cup to her, and had to laugh at his devilish expression. They both were recalling the last time they were together with a cup between them. It had almost cost them their freedom. "No, thank you, Cristobal. I don't dare chance you dropping a handkerchief in my cup again."

She rose from the grass. "Where is Annabel?"

"Elizabeth Crabbe cornered her."

"That I don't have to worry about." She straightened her full skirts over her hoop. "In Elizabeth's eyes I have become a pariah since she caught you with your hand—"

She colored and caught the silly grin that played about his lips. "I think I shall leave early with Aunt Hermione. It's a long way home, and I'm a little tired."

Actually, she would need the siesta that almost everyone observed in that semitropical climate when, come two o'clock, awnings were pulled down and shutters closed for the afternoon. Rarely did she feel the need for a siesta, so restless was her nature these days. But she knew there would be no sleep for her that night. Nor the next two nights after that.

She and Trinidad would be following the stagecoach route north to the railhead of Alleyton. The two of them would be stopping off along the way to talk to the owners of remote ranches that she hoped to enlist as way stations. With luck, when she was finished, an overland route would be set up for Confederate cotton unloaded at Alleyton to reach the neutral port of Bagdad and eventually European markets.

Her *campesinos* would work as teamsters to shuttle the

cotton. In return she would receive forty percent of the profit—half of which she wanted in arms and ammunition. But still it would cost her. For each shipment of firearms that arrived in Bagdad—a night with the Frenchman!

The reins held loosely in her hand, Jeanette slouched in the saddle and tried to get what sleep she could as the bay picked its way over soil too poor to sustain even prickly pear. There were only a few greasewood with devil's pincushions embedded in the sand drifts around their roots. A rustling in nearby chaparral snapped Jeanette's chin up. With a small cry, she hauled in on the reins, almost rearing the bay. But the moonlight disclosed that it was only an armadillo and not one of the savage Kickapoos or marauding Mexican bandidos that gave Aunt Hermione palpitations of the heart.

At her side Trinidad scowled. "Thees ees no job for a woman," he muttered.

She sighed. "Not you, too, Trini." How ironical that only the Frenchman—only Kitt, as Rubia had called him—was indifferent to the absurd idea that a woman could be a gun runner. And a good one, it would appear. For the few loyal rancheros with whom she had spoken along the road to Alleyton were willing to act as way stations for her for the cotton wagons moving south to Mexico and the ammunition wagons that would be rolling north to the Alleyton railhead.

As it was, Trinidad was incensed that she had had to bargain with the rebel Frenchman for his aid. According to Trini, it should have been given freely. She knew if she had told Trinidad what her bargain would be costing her, her overseer would readily murder the Frenchman. And that puzzled her—the price the Frenchman demanded. His blockade running surely earned him enough money to buy the charms of any number of women. Indeed, something about the young woman Rubia indicated that she was quite willing to share the Frenchman's arms without payment if she weren't already doing so.

So why me? Jeanette asked herself. Oh, she knew she was attractive, if she listened to the soldiers who were openly courting her now that her period of mourning was officially over. But there were women more attractive. And, as she pondered it further, it occurred to her that the day the Frenchman stated the terms of the bargain she looked very disreputable—a dusty-faced young woman dressed in a boy's dirt-stiffened clothing. *So why me?* she asked herself again.

Again and again throughout the long ride she would curse the despicable French mercenary—and then she would curse herself for the way her spine tingled in memory of his seductive voice. What did he look like? He was probably as homely as Abe Lincoln himself. At the vision of the President of the Union making passionate love to her, an uncontrollable chuckle erupted, and Trinidad cast a dubious look at her and shook his head gloomily. With another grunt of hopeless resignation, he parted from her beneath Columbia's fruit groves, taking Jeanette's bay to the stables with him.

The trellis sagged beneath her weight as she levered herself up to her bedroom window. By the gray light of dawn she unbuckled the gun belt, stripped off the dust-caked pants and shirt, and packed them, along with the Mexican-cobbled boots, in her father's large iron sea chest that she kept below the window.

She whirled at the light knock at the door, but let out a weary sigh of relief when Tia Juana's deep, scratchy voice called low, "Miss Jeanette?" Then: "You feeling better?"

Jeanette swept the carnation-pink cotton wrapper from the foot of the bed and tied it about her before opening the door to admit old Tia Juana. The rotund Mexican woman winked broadly, saying, "Brought you some Mexican chocolate. Told your aunt dat Yankee tea she sends up no good for dem sick headaches."

Repressing a smile, Jeanette took the cup of hot chocolate. She sat down on the velvet-padded wicker chaise longue, snuggling against its broad back and tucking her stockinged feet up under her. "Tell Aunt Hermione that my headaches are just about gone and that I'll be down later."

Tia Juana nodded with another conspiratorial wink and trod out of the room. For years Aunt Hermione's "sick headaches" had kept the poor old woman to her room for days at a time, and now the malady proved beneficial to Jeanette's purposes. And, truth to tell, she did have the beginnings of a headache brought on by two sleepless nights of riding. She grimaced, wondering if it were possible to have a hangover linger for three days.

She finished off the cup of chocolate while she made a rapid calculation. Six bales to a four-mule team at five hundred pounds a bale . . . and if she took five loads a trip, $6 \times 5 \times 500$, or 15,000 pounds at—what was cotton going for a pound now?

King Cotton's price fluctuated erratically, but it was becoming a popular medium of exchange for the struggling Confederacy. A multimillion-dollar business, if she figured it correctly. A lot of money was to be made by those willing to run the risk of the blockade, because once the war ended cotton would be a glut on the market. But now—now there was cottonmania. The European textile houses cried for the precious commodity.

She untangled her legs and crossed to the secretary. Setting down the cup, she picked up the *Houston Tri-Weekly Telegraph*. She scanned the index: bacon 55 cents a pound, butter $1.75, coffee $2.75, cotton . . . "Sweet Heaven above!" she breathed. "Seventy cents per pound of lint." Her fingers went for a pen and scribbled out her computations. Why, that was $10,500! And the European market paid five times that amount in gold specie. Even split in half with the planters who raised the cotton, her share would keep Columbia operating and buy a lot of arms and ammunition as well!

Her mouth stretched grimly. She did not even have to split her share with a blockade runner—not as long as she was selling her body. Oh, God, that her beloved should see her now; Armand, who expected only the most worthy actions from the damned human race.

The long penholder slid from her fingers, and for a moment her head drooped. Wearily she rose from the desk and went to lower herself on the four-poster. Sleep. That was what she needed. Later, when she awakened, she would know that what she was doing for the South was right.

Cristobal flipped the coins on the table and led Jeanette out of the coffeehouse. No doubt a lot of tongues would waggle the next day about her outing with Cristobal. Which was just what she hoped for. A frivolous, flirtatious young woman would scarcely be suspected of running cotton.

They stopped by Portilla Pena's Book Shop to pick up a volume of Poe's poetry for Aunt Hermione. But when they were ready to leave, she impulsively said, "Let's ride out to Boca Chica. They say oysters can be had by wading knee deep in the ocean and picking them up."

"What?" he quipped. "You'd bare your feet like a child?"

The idea sounded wonderful. "No. But you could."

"But, Jen," he drawled, "why go to the effort of searching for the cursed clams—"

"Oysters."

"—when you can purchase them at Market Hall for little or nothing?"

She flashed him a withering look and mounted her bay without waiting for his assistance. She rode sidesaddle this time, properly dressed in her sable-brown riding habit— veil, gloves, and all. Cristobal was no less costumed in a camel-colored riding jacket with britches of Bedford cord and Napoleon boots.

The two of them cantered out of the city along the River Road. It was a mistake. As they came to the out- skirts, soldiers could be seen bathing in the river. Every so often, caught in the unsuspected undercurrents, some- one drowned. She hurried her bay on past the patches of brush and palmetto and did not slow the mount down un- til the Palo Alto Prairie, a vast, level grass-covered plain, came into view. Here and there they passed small ranchos with fences made of brush, for there was no timber.

The muted slap of water against sand warned of the ocean's proximity. Then the wide sweep of the ocean sud- denly lay before the two riders. Cristobal helped Jeanette dismount. "Let's walk," he said.

She fell into step beside him. They walked in comfort- able silence, the only sound the swashing of the surf and the crunching of their boots on the hard-packed sand. She wondered what went on behind Cristobal's mild eyes. What did a vacuous person such as he think about? Ar- mand would have told—

As if picking up on her thoughts, Cristobal said, "You've never talked about Armand, Jen. Are you over his death?"

How callous. "No." The sun was hot, and she longed to remove her jacket and hat, her gloves and shoes. To let the salty wind tangle her hair and to dig her toes in the warm sand. But etiquette forbade it.

Cristobal bent and picked up a smoothly worn seashell. "You don't like to think about it, then?"

"There is nothing to think about." Except her bitter

sense of wrong. How did one tell a person that he was occupying space, breathing air better meant for someone else?

"Will you remove that deuced top hat, Jen? The veil keeps flapping in my face like a swarm of angry mosquitoes."

She laughed then and gladly accommodated his request. At least Cristobal never conformed to convention.

The sand was washed smooth by the tide, which occasionally cast upon the beach pieces of boxes, barrels, and bones of ships. Near the white rim of the surf a Portuguese man-of-war lay like a shriveled, phosphorescent bladder, and Jeanette knelt to marvel over it. Which was the second mistake of the day. For when she removed her sand-coated gloves, Cristobal said, "Your wedding ring, Jen . . . it's the first time I've noticed you without it."

She looked up guiltily to meet his inquisitive gaze. "I— I misplaced it."

He eyed her narrowly. "A wedding ring is hard to misplace. Columbia isn't hard up for money, is it, Jen?"

"No. I'm not having to pawn my jewelry like some of the South's women."

If only the ring were pawned. Then she could find a way to retrieve it. But it was stolen. The Frenchman had stolen not only her wedding ring but the innocence that had belonged to Armand. And she grieved more for the latter than the former.

She rose to her feet and gave Cristobal a sadly whimsical little smile. "You were right. Hunting for oysters wasn't that good an idea."

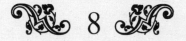 8

Jeanette rubbed the bay's foam-flecked barrel and tossed the blanket over the stall's wall. The musty scent of hay and manure filled her nostrils as she led the horse out to walk around and cool off. The night was still star-studded; dawn was some hours away. And she was still exhilarated with the feeling of having accomplished something really worthwhile—all on her own.

She had made that first trip running cotton. True, it was Columbia's cotton, the last of it. And she had been gone only overnight—long enough to haul the cotton downstream, ferry it across to the Mexican side, and from there transport it to the Bagdad warehouse the Frenchman had specified was to be used in his absence.

Trinidad had grumbled about her making the run with only his son Felix and a few other *campesinos* to accompany her. But she had to feel she was doing something for the Confederate Cause. And she told herself she would feel even better when she had munitions and medical supplies to deliver to the Confederacy purchasing agents in Alleyton.

How she would later arrange the two-week round trip by wagon to Alleyton without her aunt guessing what she

was about was something that plagued her. As it was, until the Frenchman's sloop returned to take on another cotton shipment, she would have to store the cotton she
brought back from Alleyton in Columbia's old Santa Maria
Chapel. It was nothing like the Convent of the Immaculate Conception with its three stories and cloistered arch-
ways and lichen-covered surrounding wall. But the Santa
Maria Chapel, founded by the Oblate Fathers, had a
charm of its own.

The abandoned adobe building with its ochre-brown
walls fronted a bluff overlooking the sluggish El Rio
Grande del Norte and the old Military Road. The chapel
was perfect for hiding the cotton until it could be ferried
over to the Mexican side of the river. But suppose the
Frenchman did not return for another cotton shipment?
Suppose he kept the proceeds from its sale?

She knew that a steamer with an average capacity of 800
bales earned as much as $420,000 on a round trip. A
shipowner could shrug off the loss of a vessel after two
safe round trips through the blockade of gunboats that
cruised restlessly in search of prey. It was something she
had fretted about over the past week, for his sloop should
have put into Bagdad by now. Of course, there was bad
weather to consider, the lack of coal at a harbor, or the
moon—for no steamer wanted to make the run in bright
moonlight through the cordon of Federal revenue cutters
that prowled the seas.

After Jeanette led the bay to the water trough and
penned him up, she made her way to the cluster of jacales. An oil lamp burned in Tia Juana and Trinidad's. She
knocked on the rickety corncrib door and at Trinidad's
"*Pásale,*" entered. The old man sat alone on the cornhusk
mattress. Apparently Tia Juana had already gone up to the
house to start the kitchen fires.

A rank *cigarro* perched on Trinidad's seamed lips as his
pocketknife whittled away at a child's whistle. "*Cómo se*

va?" he asked, squinting up at her through the haze of smoke.

"*Excelente.*" She took the dusty hat from her head and began to unplait the heavy braid that hung down the center of her back. "I passed two other wagon trains of cotton on the Mexican side of the river. It seems all of a sudden everyone is anxious to cash in on the white gold. Do you know, Trinidad, they're saying now you can almost follow a trail of lint all the way from Alleyton?"

Her hand paused at its task of unraveling the braid. She tilted her head to one side. "You're quiet. Has something happened?" She came alert. "Did Aunt—"

The old man shook his head. "No." His hands stopped their whittling, and he fixed a rheumy eye on her. "I saw the *aguatero* yesterday. He had a message. The Frenchman's sloop ees een. Your supplies—they are ready. Alejandro says you are to come by for the invoice."

Her nimble fingers returned to unplaiting her hair. She bit her lower lip. Wasn't this what she was working for, ammunition and firearms for freighting to the Confederacy's battle zones? And, of course, she could keep Columbia operating. Was it really such a high price to pay?

"You do not want to see the Frenchman, eh? That one, he gives you trouble, *sobrina?*"

She looked sharply at Trinidad. She could not afford for his avuncular protectiveness to interfere with her mission. She smiled wanly. "Sometimes I wish he would. I told you I am a romantic at heart. But the Frenchman—he has only a profit in mind. He thinks of me as nothing more than a dirty urchin like our *aguatero*, Alejandro."

"I do not like eet that you go alone to him. What if he should discover you are not a boy?"

She managed to laugh lightly. "You saw Rubia, Trinidad. Dressed as I am, I would not hold the attraction for him she does."

"Then you have not seen yourself, *sobrina*."

She slept late that morning, until past noon, then went down to the parlor to tell her aunt that her sick headache seemed to be passing.

"Those headaches are bothering you more and more often, dear," Aunt Hermione said. Her knitting needles never stopped clicking as she continued: "It's a wonder mine aren't any worse with the way things are—the French armies swarming against the Juaristas on the other side of the Rio Grande, that Mexican bandit Carbajal ravaging the Valley, and Union gunboats patrolling the Rio Grande's mouth."

"War!" Washington squawked. "Help! Run!"

Jeanette ignored the macaw. Over the cup of Mexican chocolate Tia Juana had brought her, she said, "You sound as if you're a dyed-in-the-wool Rebel, Aunt Hermione."

Aunt Hermione's lashless eyes blinked wide. "For land's sake, no. But soldiers are soldiers, dear, whether they're French, Confederate, or Federal. And it's not safe for a woman in times like this. We should thank our lucky stars we're so far from the battlefront."

Jeanette swallowed the words on the tip of her tongue along with the hot chocolate. No need to alarm her aunt by telling her that with the increase in contraband trade out of Bagdad Federal troops might at any moment decide to close off the Mexican trade by invading Brownsville. Fort Brown's four hundred soldiers would be defenseless against any concerted Federal effort.

Fortunately the Union Admiral Farragut felt that such an invasion was not worth the heavy losses of soldiers he would suffer due to yellow fever. Every summer the peal of the funeral toll signaled yellow fever's presence.

When her aunt informed her she would be attending a quilting bee that afternoon, a sigh of relief flooded over Jeanette. There would be no need to fabricate a lie for her absence. Surely she could make the . . . payment on the war stores within an hour. She simply had to abstain from drinking anything potent. Besides, meeting with the Frenchman during the day appealed to her for other reasons. There was something about doing what she would have to do in the dark, at night; something that seemed to compound her guilt, though she could not put her finger on it. Perhaps meeting the Frenchman in the daylight hours seemed more a business arrangement and less like a—a clandestine affair.

And, of course, it was less dangerous to traverse Bagdad's streets in the daylight, even though she did not plan to bring Trinidad with her. He must never suspect the price she was paying. Her shame was great enough without guilt she would feel over involving the loyal overseer in a defense of her virtue.

She wore the boy's disguise again, hoping that her miserable appearance might dampen the Frenchman's ardent appetite. The foul-smelling, dirt-stained garments certainly put off the people with whom she shared the Matamoros–Bagdad stage. It was the first time in six weeks she had returned to Bagdad, and she was amazed at the forest of masts in the waters. Where before she had counted maybe twenty ships, there now had to be sixty or seventy vessels; from schooners and sloops weighing twenty tons to brigs weighing two hundred. They were from every nation, eager to capitalize on the cotton trade which was so vast that control of even a part of it could mean millions.

The narrow, winding streets swarmed with Confederate deserters and Union sympathizers; with German, Danish, Dutch, Spanish, and French seamen; and with peddlers, gamblers, swindlers, and smugglers. She almost despaired of ever locating Alejandro among that backwash of the world. She swaggered up and down the length of the harbor, afraid of being approached by some drunken jack-tar.

The September afternoon was hot and muggy with not a breath of wind to evaporate the perspiration that beaded around her hatband and beneath the heavy buckskin shirt. Alas, she could not discard either the hat or the shirt, as some of the sailors coiling ropes or mending nets had done.

It was Alejandro who found her. "I have been waiting for you," he told her in Spanish without removing the cigarette butt from between his lips.

So, the French blockade runner was not about to let her take the war stores and leave; not without his commission. She shrugged off her misplaced optimism and followed Alejandro to the lighter used for ferrying freight from the shore to the ships at anchor. This time he did not blindfold her. She would finally see the scurvy scoundrel.

She and Alejandro rode the long steady roll of white-capped waves, neither of them speaking. Without the blindfold, she found the sloshing of the small vessel on the immense body of blue-green water much more frightening. No doubt her complexion was the same shade of green.

Mal de mer. Seasickness. She knew her father had suffered great disappointment that she had been a girl, the only child. There were no sons to follow him to the sea. Perhaps that was why she always tried to do whatever sons did. Climb trees, read, ride bareback. And yet her efforts had gained her nothing. Only her father's wrath that she could not fit into the disciplined life he knew as a sea captain. But at that moment she wasn't just seasick. She was scared witless.

In the occasional glance Alejandro shot in her direction she detected contempt for the puny boy she presented. Yet she suspected he also resented that another "boy" could so easily obtain the time and attention of the privateer whom Alejandro obviously held in such high esteem. Oh, if she could change places with Alejandro. If she were only a boy; no, a man who could move so easily within his world, unhampered by the restrictions of society.

She repressed the urge to reach out and run her fingers through the urchin's windblown hair. Instead, she steeled herself for the approaching meeting with the Frenchman. She sorely missed Trinidad's comforting presence. Alejandro pulled the lighter alongside a long, low, lead-colored steamer. The extreme rake of her masts and three funnels gave her a fast look. With crisp and graceful lines, she was obviously built for speed. Her short mast flew the French flag and bore the name *Revenge*.

With a bravado she did not feel Jeanette climbed the swaying rope ladder on the steamer's starboard side and swung up over the railing onto the white deck. Scored by brass tracks for gun carriages and dotted with piles of solid shot standing handily in racks near each piece, it glittered in the hot sun.

Four or five seamen were scrubbing the planks with vinegar and holystone and hosing down the decks. One of them, a weather-beaten sailor, bare-chested and in white trousers rolled to his calves, ambled toward her on bandy sea legs. Before she could ask directions to the captain's cabin, he produced a red handkerchief from his hip pocket and proceeded to blindfold her. "Sorry, son—captain's orders," he explained.

If that was not indignity enough, he caught both her wrists and bound them behind her with hemp. Once again she faced a world of darkness as the sailor propelled her forward, saying once, "Watch your step." For what, she did not know. Apparently she navigated the deck safely, for a few seconds later he halted her and she heard his rap against the solid door. And then that marvelous, deep voice: *"Entrez."*

The door closed behind her. She knew she was alone with the Frenchman. His soft laughter infuriated her, and through gritted teeth she said, "Are you so brave a privateer that before you face a female you need to have her trussed up like a Thanksgiving turkey?"

She heard the creak of chair leather and then his footsteps coming toward her. Her lungs ceased to function. *"Non,"* he replied in that same laughing tone and added something—she wasn't quite sure what—about a woman and a man. Most likely about a woman pretending to be a man. For the umpteenth time, she wished she remembered more of Armand's language.

"Where is my ring?"

The Frenchman spoke, softly. So close was he, his breath fanned her face.

Exasperated, she stomped her foot. "I can't understand you. Where's your friend, your translator?"

A silence followed. He made no move to touch her, and the dreaded waiting was much worse than if he had gone ahead and raped her. Then at least the waiting—six weeks of waiting—would be over with. Suddenly her hat was removed and her braid swung free. Then she felt herself scooped up against his chest. She remembered now—he was tall with broad shoulders and a solid build. That one night she had spent with him had revealed that much to her . . . and that he had an abundant head of hair. Oh, sweet Mary! She blushed with the memory of his parting words—taunting words. *"Le baiser français!"*

Abruptly her body was released to sink into a mattress. Her heart began to chug erratically. She waited for the mattress to groan with his weight beside her, but his footsteps took him away. Her ears strained to hear—and picked up the sound of splashing water. Then . . . shock as a cool, wet cloth rubbed over her face. And more shock as she realized he was unbuttoning the shirt to throw it open. She tried to move away, but her arms and bound hands were immobile, jammed beneath her by her own weight. Worse was to follow as her buckskin pants were slipped down along her legs to plop on the plank floor. The wet cloth returned again to bathe her shoulders, the valley of her breasts, under her arms. Down past her navel. Gently parting her thighs. The humiliation was too much! Oh, if only she could will herself into a dead faint for the next hour!

Hour? The Frenchman's lovemaking took that much time and more. How long she could not remember later. The effect of the blindfold was to produce a curious sense of timelessness, of drifting. She was only aware of the hands that ceaselessly caressed her skin; stroking her shoulders, her calves, the indentations and curves of her body—yet never touching the places that she had been taught were forbidden. Places that she was to learn were extremely sensitive. He whispered words that she suspected were sexual in nature. Desperately she tried to make herself unresponsive to what he was doing to her. But it was impossible. Her body betrayed her, reacting with quivering anticipation of the next step in his slow seduction of her.

At last his fingers touched her breasts, and her nipples sprang erect. A small sigh escaped her parted lips. He whispered something at her ear, and the strangeness of the French language did not conceal the triumph in his voice. "Oh, get it over with, you cursed jackal!"

Still, he made no move to enter her, but continued the erotic play on her body. "Please," she whispered hoarsely. "*S'il vous plaît*," she begged with the little French she knew.

When he continued to drop careless kisses in the hollows of her neck and elbow, the indentation of her navel, and along the slope of her hip bone, her body arched toward him in a language of its own. Mercifully, he recognized the language. His torso moved up over hers, and she welcomed the warmth and the weight. He stroked her slowly, deeply. It was not enough. Her body moved in tempo with his, seeking the fulfillment she sensed was so near.

Then it was approaching, that glorious explosion of all the senses that was almost painful in its intensity. She ascended, she soared, and finally she floated in that sweet neverland of release. At that moment she was so full of him that she knew she would recognize him even if she found herself next to him in a crowd—he had a subtle musky odor that she found tantalizingly masculine.

The back of his hand caressed her cheekbone, bringing her back to reality. He still lay half on her, his heavy calf draped over her knees, and she turned her head in his direction. "I hate you," she whispered. "I hate you for what you are. I hate you for what you do to me. For what you've made of me." Her voice dropped to an almost inaudible, agonized rasp. "And I hate myself."

She knew he did not understand her and so did not worry about his reaction to her words. Yet there was something in his silence—as if the sadness in her words prevailed in the room. He moved away from her, and the bed creaked, relieved of his weight. His silence was unnerving. After a moment the mattress gave again beneath the pressure of one of his knees, and her body jerked as he unexpectedly ran the wet cloth between her thighs, cleansing her of their lovemaking. "Damn you to hell," she croaked, then resorted to Spanish when the English was not sufficient for her loathing of his impersonal treatment.

That he understood. He laughed, and she liked even his sardonic laughter better than his silence. With the ease of a man in excellent physical condition he rolled her onto her stomach. At once her arms stung with the pain of the blood rushing back through the vessels. Unwillingly, she whimpered, and his hands began to massage hers. "*Je te prie pardon.*"

Surely she had not understood correctly. The Frenchman's actions were confusing. She wanted to put him in a pigeonhole, but his inconsistent behavior, his elusive personality, would not permit her to do so.

"What?" she derided. "You're actually asking me to forgive you?"

"Yes, I am," he said gravely.

Then, before she could ponder his reply, he was dressing her and turning her over to someone whom he called Solis.

Outside, the handkerchief was removed and the sunlight blinded her. Trying to focus, she blinked, at first seeing only a smooth olive-brown chest. As she rightly guessed, the man was the wiry mestizo she had glimpsed at La Fonda del Olvido. Like the other sailors, he was dressed only in trousers. She dreaded meeting his derisive gaze, but above the flat cheekbones his eyes were compassionate. Which only made it worse.

"The lighter is waiting," Solis said gently.

Making no reply, for in truth she didn't trust her voice, she turned and let him lead her back to the rope ladder. She was as taciturn as Alejandro, who steered the lighter back to the wharf. Her mind cringed as she recalled what had transpired that afternoon.

And in the next horrifying moment she realized that the Frenchman's last words to her had been in English!

She whirled back to face the sloop and raised her fist against the sky. "You French bastard!" she shouted.

P. 73
A SLOOP IS A SMALL SINGLE
MAST SAILING SHIP
IT MIGHT BE A "SLOOP OF WAR" BUT
DOUBTFUL

9

"Young man, the Cause is deeply indebted to your bravery and your generosity," Colonel Ford said, gravely shaking Jeanette's hand. "I only regret that your Mexican citizenship prevents you from officially serving the Confederacy. With your ingenuity, you could no doubt win a battle single-handed."

Praise was rare from John "Rip" Ford, who was no less than a former Texas Ranger, doctor, lawyer, and was now Commander of the Sub-Department of the Rio Grande. Jeanette left his tent that night feeling that his warm words of gratitude were worth all the planning, the hard riding, the sleepless nights of the last five days. Even worth the prostitution of her body. For that was what it really was. She tried not to let herself think about those two debasing times she had given herself to the Frenchman.

She wondered if a man could ever understand the humiliation of being sexually used—of having one's own body turned into an instrument of betrayal. Perhaps that was why she felt such a sense of achievement in delivering the war materiel to the Alleyton railhead. She had surmounted odds that many a man would have found difficult—the most difficult being the obstacle of subterfuge that she, as a female, had to undergo.

She watched as soldiers, dressed in yellowish gray tunic coats and pantaloons, began to unload from the four burro-drawn wagons the supplies bought with the contraband cotton. Item by item was checked off by a pimply-faced sergeant and then stacked on the Alleyton railroad loading platform.

She knew the exact count of every item. Had she not earned each one? Two thousand British Enfield muskets, fifteen new French artillery pieces with ammunition, forty thousand rounds of small-arms ammunition, whole bushels of gun caps, along with Sharps' breech-loading carbines and even some unwieldy blunderbusses from God knew where. She calculated that those Enfield rifles that cost twenty-one dollars apiece in England were costing the Confederacy fifty and sixty in Bagdad.

And what had been her price? Costly. The Frenchman had forfeited a goodly sum for an afternoon with her in his bed.

With Felix, who was as large as his father Trinidad was small, and four of Columbia's faithful *campesinos*, she began the drive back to Brownsville with the cotton-filled wagons. The ancient Camino Real north from Matamoros was rapidly becoming the Cotton Road. In the moonlight a trail of cotton lint brilliantly marked the deeply grooved wagon route. Though it was the fifth of December, the first frost of the year had yet to come.

Even wearing sturdy leather gloves, Jeanette's hands were chafed from handling the lines and working the whip. Her back ached from jouncing in the springless wagon, and her voice hurt from shouting vituperations at the burros. And she loved it. She reveled in riding along through the starry night—carrying out a forbidden and dangerous mission. It was exciting and stimulating.

Much more so than remaining home. The inactivity at Columbia was unbearable. Even Cristobal, her one source of amusement, was off again, pursuing another story. She had tried to involve herself in the running of the household, but between Aunt Hermione and Tia Juana the great house was kept in impeccable condition. And lately there had been little need for bookkeeping with the market for Columbia's citrus fruits and cotton severely limited by the war.

And then, too, there was José Carbajal. Because this latest of the revolutionaries to besiege Matamoros roamed about the Rio Grande, she had insisted Trinidad remain at Columbia. The little old man had offered little resistance. Perhaps after twenty-six years of serving as a surrogate uncle he knew her well enough to know she would do what she wanted anyway. Still, caring for her as he did, the old man felt, like all males, that a woman had her place—her role—in life.

With a bitter taste on her tongue she recalled some of the men in Brownsville who through bribery had either wrangled medical certificates stating they were unfit for military service or who suddenly elected to serve with "home guards" that were far from the battlefront.

Men! The lazy, cowardly Cristobal. The unscrupulous, exploitive Frenchman!

So engrossed was she in her mental damning of the male sex she did not at first notice the two men. Dressed in matted bobtail coats and dirty coonskin caps and sporting long grizzly beards, they moved stealthily out of the shadows of one of the isolated elm motts that dotted the flat landscape. "Hold at it!" ordered the one cradling a rifle with its bayonet pointed directly at her.

In the wagon behind her she heard Juan petitioning the Virgin Mary and all the saints for protection. More and more often bandits were plying their trade along the newly created cotton route, whose traffic was growing daily. Robbery and murder marked the route as well as the cotton lint. She should have brought a rifle or revolver. Hindsight did not help her now.

"Well, well. Will yew lookee at this, Clem," said the other man, whose walleye seemed to rove in all directions at once so that she did not know to which he was referring—the cotton bales or her. He spit a clump of tobacco. "Wagons full of cotton bales." He grinned then, showing brown-stained teeth. "I bet yer pockets are loaded, too. Contraband fetches a good price these days, don't it, Clem?"

"Shut up," the one with the bayonet commanded. He moved his nag alongside her wagon. "Strip, kid. All yew greasers—strip down."

Sweat broke out on her palms. The fringed leather jacket she wore against the cool December night suddenly seemed as hot and heavy as a coat of armor. If only it were as protective. She swallowed. "Do as Clem sez," the wall-eyed man said and prodded her shoulder with the tip of his bayonet.

Her blacksnake whip snapped up and left the plaited imprint of its thongs across the man's face. She had missed! She had aimed for the rifle! He yelped and dropped the rifle, but Clem's jerked to his shoulder to fire. Oh, God, she did not want to die yet! The blast shattered her eardrums. She blinked and saw Clem slide off his horse like a sack of potatoes.

She whirled to face the other man, but he was already hightailing it for the sunrise as if a posse were on his heels. The riderless horse pounded close behind the bandit.

"*Dios, perdóneme,*" Felix rasped, begging God's pardon, and lowered his Mexican pistol.

Spanish expletives and words of gratitude directed to patron saints filled the night, but Jeanette's ears droned

with a faint buzzing. She closed her eyes against the grue-
some sight of the blood-spattered man stretched out in
the dust beside the wagon. Still, she was unable to pre-
vent the churning of her stomach. She leaned over the
wagon and threw up in the dust.

"Señora, you are all right?" asked Pedro, who had lost
an arm in a cotton press.

She nodded weakly. When the threatened fainting spell
passed, she feebly cracked the whip over the burros.

"*Hija! Ándale! Vaya!*" came the shouts from the Mexican teamsters behind her, anxious to get safely back to
Columbia.

But all that Jeanette could think of was the man who
had died before her eyes. If Felix had not killed him, she
would have tried. It frightened her . . . the violence
which she had just realized she was capable.

By the time they reached Columbia's boundaries, a
blinding rainstorm obscured everything but the hundreds
of water toads that suddenly appeared. Shivering with
cold, Jeanette collapsed into bed for an entire day, secure
in the knowledge that even at that moment Trinidad was
having the *campesinos* stack the cotton bales in the already packed church.

Aunt Hermione was beside herself with worry. When
Jeanette made her way downstairs that evening, her aunt
plied her with hot camomile tea. "It's bad enough that
you disappear to spend days at a time with your—your—"

"Lover," Jeanette supplied, holding a handkerchief to
her nose to forestall another ghastly sneeze.

"But to walk along the beach with him—in the rain—
for all to see."

"It was raining," Jeanette mumbled against the handkerchief. "There was no one out walking to see us."

"Exactly. No one foolish enough to go out in this
weather. And no one foolish enough to flaunt their affair. I

don't know what's come over you, dear. Why, in my day, if a woman wished to have an—an affair, she did it discreetly."

Jeanette slid a glance at her aunt, who moved her knitting needles fast and furiously. "Have I been indiscreet?" she asked cautiously. "Has anyone mentioned seeing me about—with a man?"

"Why, no. No, dear. But that's just the point. Why can't you just marry this man—make it all proper?"

Jeanette stifled a smile. "What if he's married, Aunt Hermione?"

The old woman gasped. "Oh, no! After all the Sundays I have dragged you to church. You wouldn't dare commit adultery, Jeanette! Would you?"

She smiled sadly. "No, Aunt Hermione. I daresay this man has not the slightest intention of ever facing an altar."

"Then why don't you invite him to the city's New Year's Eve ball? Perhaps if he saw what kind of people you come from, your background—perhaps it might put some ideas in his head. Do I know him or his family?"

"No, I don't think you do. Besides, he wouldn't come to the ball. He—he doesn't like to be around a crowd."

The old woman sniffed disdainfully. "No doubt some Union deserter seeking the safety of the border. I hope you aren't thinking of marrying someone like that."

Exasperated, Jeanette set down the cup, sloshing the tea in its saucer. "Can't you understand that I am not now, nor will I ever be, interested in marrying anyone? And, if I recall correctly, several months ago you were very interested in marrying me off to a man who never even had the courage to fight in the war!"

"But Cristobal has good breeding and background," Aunt Hermione continued, unperturbed by her niece's outburst. "And I do hope he will be back in town for the ball. His presence adds the perfect touch to a party.

Promise me you'll go to the New Year's Eve party. Dancing with Cristobal would at least lend some respectability to the evening."

Jeanette rolled her eyes to the ceiling, giving up on ever communicating with the well-meaning old woman, but agreed to attend the ball. She would have that long to calm down Aunt Hermione's shocked pride—and talk her out of the idea that marriage with Cristobal would be such a perfect solution.

In the meantime, while she waited for word from the Frenchman, she recruited Trinidad as a shooting instructor. She knew she had been lucky with the bandits. She did not intend to depend on the whim of the gods the next time. Foregoing stays and hoops, much to Aunt Hermione's displeasure, and wearing only a slatted sunbonnet, she rode down to the abandoned church with Trinidad. Twenty-five years earlier, the monkeylike man had fought at San Jacinto alongside Sam Houston and Deaf Smith for Texas independence, and that afternoon brought his old Navy Colt six-shooters with him.

"*Híjole!*" he swore as he tossed the empty tequila bottles in the air and she missed each shot. "Did I not tell you thees was no job for a woman?"

"*Cállate!*" she said impatiently. But her impatience was with herself, her lack of skill. "Men weren't born knowing how to hit a bull's-eye. Toss another bottle. I'll hit one yet." She did, but by that time she had run out of ammunition and daylight and bottles.

Never had the soldiers looked so dashing and so handsome, the women so lovely. The upper story of the market, which was used as an assembly room for public receptions, had been cleared of chairs. Its chandelier blazed with a hundred sparkling candles over the multitude of guests gathered to welcome in the New Year of

1863, which suddenly looked so bright for the Confederacy.

Since there were no telegraphic signals south of New Orleans, the people of Brownsville had only just learned of General Lee's victory at Fredericksburg, Virginia, nearly three weeks earlier on December 13. As a result of the terrible defeat, General Grant removed General Ambrose Burnside from the command of the Army of the Potomac.

Yet even here in Brownsville, the Confederacy's southernmost city, not every citizen was loyal to the Cause. Indeed, over a third of Texas was pro-Union. Many, like Jeanette's father, had emigrated to Brownsville from the North. Others had lived all their lives in the Deep South but were loyal to the Union and had moved to be closer to the border of Mexico, whose President, Juárez, was sympathetic to the Federal Government.

If any of them discovered Jeanette's furtive activities, her hope of aiding the Confederacy would be endangered. Thus she flirted outrageously and whirled through the waltzes and quadrilles with one soldier after another, praying that no one would ever associate the shallow, slightly promiscuous widow with anything that required substantial thought. Her aunt was right. For all purposes she and the feckless Cristobal appeared to be a perfect match.

As it was, Cristobal did not return in time to illuminate the New Year's Eve ball with his presence. And neither had the Frenchman returned to Bagdad.

This upset Jeanette far more than Cristobal's absence upset Aunt Hermione. Almost every day that first month of 1863, Jeanette either sent Trinidad or rode herself to the Bagdad wharves to search among the forests of masts for the *Revenge*. Although she dreaded seeing the steamer, knowing what its captain would require of her later, she dreaded even more its absence, which meant a costly delay in her gunrunning.

It had been more than three months since his steamer had put out to sea. He should have returned by now. Had the *Revenge* been captured? Or had he merely decided it was not worth his while to run the Brazos Santiago's Federal blockade? After all, there were other Confederate ports that would pay dearly for his services.

And Confederate women.

Damn the blackguard to Hell!

10

With seeming nonchalance Jeanette leaned against the peeling stucco siding of the wretched cantina that fronted the busy Bagdad harbor. As she huddled in a thick, grimy navy coat, her boy's disguise protected her from the flotsam and jetsam of humanity that crowded the streets. For more than a week her anxious gaze had constantly scanned the Gulf of Mexico's horizon for the *Revenge*. At last, the sloop had put in with the high tide that chilly gray February morning.

Jammed into the coat's pockets, her hands clenched and unclenched furiously. Impossible! But too obviously true. Lighters moved to and from the *Revenge*, depositing their cargoes on the shore. As she watched through anger-filmed eyes, the loads of contraband were deposited in two separate areas for the customs officials. At one end of the wharf Solis supervised the loading of war materiel that presumably would go to the same warehouse from which she made her last collection.

But at the other end—God rot the Frenchman in Hell! The contraband being stacked there under the supervision of one of Juárez's soldiers was not the niceties desired by people deprived by the war—fine silks, foreign coffee, el-

egant dinnerware. No, the contraband was also war materiel. Arms and ammunition that the Frenchman had
declared he would dare risk at only one price—her body!
As surely as burros brayed, the Frenchman was not col-
lecting a night in Juárez's bed as the price for his services.

She had sold herself for naught! She could just have
easily paid for the arms and ammunition, the quinine and
medical equipment, from the proceeds from the sale of
the cotton. She had debased herself—no! The Frenchman
had debased her. Her sacrifice for the Cause was reduced
to a farce. She was little more than a whore! Oh, how the
Frenchman must be laughing at her noble sacrifice! How
amusing she must be to him!

Damn him!

Tears of helpless rage blinded her eyes during the
stagecoach trip back to Matamoros and the journey from
there to the Santa Maria Chapel where she changed back
into her camisole and day dress. All that afternoon she
paced her bedroom like a restless spirit would wander
through a haunted house, knowing there would be no
peace for the soul until she was avenged.

Several times the back of her hand came up to wipe
away the tears that flooded her eyes. The beauty of the
marriage she had shared with Armand was sullied beyond
reclamation. No modern-day instrument, no thermometer
or scale, could gauge the depth or intensity of her hatred.
She abhorred herself only a little less than she did the
Frenchman.

And she would tell him so in the most scathing terms
and have done with the scoundrel, that scum of the sea,
once and for all. She waited impatiently through the rest
of the day for him to send word via Alejandro that the
supplies—and his invoice—were ready. Word did not
come that day, and she had to suffer through one of Aunt
Hermione's poetry-reading parties. Browning, Carlyle,
Poe—the literary giants of the day all had their works

read. Washington thought the reading tedious, for after each lady had read and taken her seat the bird responded with a "Help!"

"Quoth the Raven, Nevermore," Jeanette hoped fervently.

She sat in the parlor with a vacuous smile pasted on her face, delivered pretentious praise for writers whose works held little interest for her, and trilled laughter reminiscent of Cristobal's chortle. But she passed when her time came for a reading, and Aunt Hermione directed a worried frown at her.

Tia Juana was unlacing Jeanette's stays that night when Aunt Hermione came into the bedroom. Her lantern-jawed face puckered in an uneasy expression as she moved nervously about the bedroom, touching Jeanette's brushes on the dressing table, fingering the ivory voile curtains at the window. "Is it that man you've been seeing, Jeanette?" she asked at last. "Have you two had a lovers' quarrel?"

Jeanette sliced a glance at Tia Juana. The old Mexican woman wore a guarded expression. Shrugging the dress off her shoulders, she passed it to Tia Juana, commenting airily, "Of course not, Aunt Hermione. I guess I'm just a little tired tonight."

"You've been riding too much, that's what." Her aunt peered at her closely. "And look at your complexion. Tanned! Dear Lord, Jeanette, there won't be a man who'll look at you if you don't start protecting your skin. And look at your hands, will you!"

Jeanette pulled her hand from her aunt's grasp. "I'll put some rosewater and glycerin on them before I go to bed."

Having extracted the promise that Jeanette would also wear her cotton gloves to bed, her aunt departed, leaving Jeanette to wait through a long, sleepless night for the Frenchman's summons. It came early the next morning with Trinidad's appearance at the kitchen door, talking in low tones with Tia Juana. The black giantess patted the little man's leathery face consolingly. Jeanette wondered if the two had guessed what her mission had cost her or knew of the Frenchman's deceit.

At the old chapel she changed into the boy's clothing. But this time she tucked Trinidad's navy revolver into her pocket. With Trinidad at her side she rode the bay through Matamoros and on to Bagdad, rather than wait for the stage. As usual, Alejandro could be found pushing his water cart along the wharves. And, as usual, the boy contemptuously spit a wad of tobacco on the splintery planks on which they stood. At another time and place Jeanette would have had to smile at the dirty-faced splay-footed boy. If only she and Armand had had a child . . . Her hand ached to ruffle Alejandro's shaggy brown hair.

As it was, the tension, as strong as the cable that held the ships at anchor, permitted her only the merest physical motion. Trinidad put a hand on her arm. "I go weeth you, *sobrina.*"

She shook her head. She could not afford to involve him in what could well be a violent confrontation. "Wait for me here, Trini. I'll need your help."

"Sometheeng ees wrong. I sense eet."

She forced a smile. "Something is wrong—your imagination." She turned her gaze back to the Gulf. It looked black under a sky boiling with gray, bilious clouds. An appropriate day, she thought grimly, for the task at hand.

A lighter bobbed the waves toward them. A woman clutched its railing with one hand and her hat with the other. Even with the porkpie hat hiding the blond hair, as the lighter drew closer Jeanette recognized the woman by her regal bearing. Rubia. The swine of a pirate had the insolence to make love to another woman before he coerced her to crawl into his bed. Oh, God, the meeting she always dreaded could not come quickly enough this time!

She was half-tempted to shoot the snake with the derringer she carried for protection, but she had not sunk so far that killing came that easy. Not yet.

Rubia's gaze passed over the two dirty boys who took her place on the lighter with only the barest flicker of interest. But Jeanette's eyes, blue-black as the ocean beneath her soil-stained hat, burned in wrath. The cold wind clawed at her clothing as she rode the lighter out to the *Revenge,* but she scarcely noticed how icy her face had become as she kept it relentlessly turned toward the Frenchman's steamer.

Through the endless night she had thought this moment would never come. Now her breath was ragged; her heart thudded out its impatient fury. Her feet carried her swiftly up the rope ladder to the deck. Solis met her with that same deferential smile that changed to an apologetic one as he held the blindfold to her eyes and knotted it behind her head. After binding her hands behind her, he led her toward his captain's quarters. Her heart galloped like a racehorse's. The door shut behind her. And though there was only silence in the cabin, she knew the Frenchman was there. She could scent him—as the lioness scents danger. Her enemy!

Waiting, she shifted her weight with the roll of the ship. Why didn't he say something? Then at last she heard his booted tread, bringing him nearer to her. When his hand, warm, firm, was laid on the side of her neck, she flinched. *"Mon âme, m'as-tu manqué?"* he asked in a husky voice.

She shrugged her shoulders. "You know I don't understand French." It was said carelessly, in an attempt to disguise her rage.

His lips brushed hers, lingering at the corners of her mouth, but she sensed the hunger contained in the light kiss. For what seemed a long moment he stood before her, so much taller. Silent. His hand gently rubbed along her neck, his thumb playing with the hollow at the base of her throat. As if he had come to some decision, he scooped his arm behind her knees and back to hold her against his chest. Her hat slipped from her head to plop on the plank floor. Then the bed rose up to meet her. She expected the attack now. The removal of her trousers and then being taken. She would let him believe he would have his way with her as usual—and at the last minute she would put an end to this damnable farce.

With some surprise she felt him stretch out on his side next to her. She thought she heard a sigh. She tensed, waiting for his hands at her clothing. But instead a callused finger traced the bowlike curvature of her upper lip. He said something she could not understand. "Speak in English!" she snapped. "I know you understand it."

His lips covered hers now, and his tongue pried her teeth for admittance. Her body would not heed the warning screamed by her brain. Traitorously her teeth parted, her tongue met his, answered the question posed: her want of him. Her torso shifted to strain against his long, hard, well-aroused frame. When his lips at last released hers and his fingers went to her coat, her head moved frenziedly from one side to another. She could not give in to the lure of this man's sensuality. She could not let the man who had defiled all that had been good and honorable seduce her so easily.

"My—my hands," she gasped. "Free them." His fingers halted at her buttons. She was glad he could not see her eyes. "Please. I want to . . . I want to feel you . . . as you feel me." Still he paused, and she blurted out, "I want to touch you . . . everywhere."

She heard his sharp intake of breath. The waves slapped against the ship's hull while she waited for his answer. "Non."

She gasped, thwarted. "You tricked me," she cried out in a tear-rasped voice. "You—you opportunist, you scurvy swine. You have been selling firearms to the Mexicans!" She hiccoughed on her tears but hurried on, "And I bet you didn't take a soldier to bed as your price!"

"*Non,*" he said again, gently but firmly. "*Tu te trompes.*"

She cared not what his reply was. There was only her hurt, her anger. "You rutting beast!" It came out a hoarse whisper. "Do you think I would ever let you touch me again?"

Her hands itched to scratch his eyes out, to mark his flesh as he had marked her soul. With an enormous effort, spurred by her outrage, she twisted her arms, struggling to free her hands. "*Doucement,*" he said in a calm voice that only infuriated her more so that she was kicking and screaming expletives she was scarcely aware she knew.

He wrestled with her, trying to pin her motionless. And that was when the derringer went off. The explosion ripped through the room. The acrid odor of gunpowder filled her nostrils—as the Frenchman's surprised groan filled her ears. The sound of pounding feet on the deck echoed outside the cabin, and the door's hinges creaked as it was shoved open.

"*Madre de Dios!*" she heard Solis swear.

Hands were jerking her roughly from beneath the dead weight of the Frenchman and thrusting her outside the cabin. Another voice said in the King's English, "You blimey little slut! There will be hell to pay for this!"

The English sailor left her then, and she huddled against a damp, briny coil of thick hemp rope. It seemed forever that she sat there, growing cold as the sun hid behind the clouds and the wind off the Gulf blew angrily about her. She shivered, more with terror than cold. What had she done? How could she take another life so carelessly. So this was what war did to people. Hardened them. Made them hold life so cheaply. And now she had destroyed the only lifeline she could establish to run the cotton. Her noble plan to aid the Confederacy was shattered just because her pride had been trampled.

Men were right. Women could not make good soldiers. They allowed their emotions to get in the way. And her tears soaked her blindfold as she waited for judgment to be passed on her.

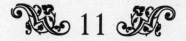

11

The tall figure, so dark it almost blended with the night's velvety backdrop, stood on a narrow wrought-iron balcony that was identical to a score of other balconies that decorated the homes in the French section of Brownsville. Settling one hip on the balustrade, the man leaned back against the iron-laced column and, lifting his flushed face to the frost-scored February wind, exhaled a wreath of smoke.

"Monsieur, you are still much too ill to be out," a little man, a dwarf, reproved in French.

With an amused twitch to his lips the man looked down at his valet. "Fresh air is beneficial to a fever, *n'est-ce pas,* Henri?"

"*Non!*" reprimanded the dwarf, a Frenchman of the Gascon type with glittering black eyes and thick, coarse, jet-black hair. "Not when you've been severely wounded and you persist in standing bare-chested on a winter night!"

He padded over to the man and passed up to him a Turkish silk brocade dressing gown of an elegant cerulean blue. "At least drape this over your shoulders, monsieur."

Hampered by bandaged ribs, the man allowed Henri to

wrap the dressing gown about him. When the dwarf left, muttering dire predictions of consumption, the man returned to his cigar—a long-nine brought out on the Havana run. Still, he was destined to be interrupted once again, this time by a slender, wiry Mexican.

"*Caramba*, Cristobal!" The gaunt young man crossed the balcony's threshold. "You should be abed!"

Cristobal emitted a grunt of smoke. It was hopeless. His two friends were worse than the doddering old sister at the convent who had bandaged the gun wound. "How about sharing a glass of brandy, Solis?"

"Bah! A keg would be more like it. It's the only way you'll get the young woman out of your mind." He punched a finger at Cristobal's chest, and his friend winced. "She has claws, eh?"

"At last," Cristobal said drily, "we've found something we can agree on."

"I warned you that you were playing with fire." Solis ambled off to the sideboard in the adjoining room. "A little spitfire."

"A spitfire no taller than an Enfield rifle and weighing less than a keg of whiskey."

"Why did you ever agree to run guns for her, *amigo?*" he threw over his shoulder.

Cristobal inhaled one last time and tossed the cigar over the railing. "I've asked myself that a hundred times if I've asked it once." And he knew the answer. When someone wants something badly enough, it doesn't matter the terms or conditions.

And he had wanted her since—since he was a boy. The lissome girl had been a bright flame dancing with warmth, enchanting two little boys, keeping pace with them, daring them, taunting them, laughing with them. And even after the *gringos* had taken his father's ancient land holdings, after the *Yanqui* courts of law had confiscated what should have been his inheritance—one hundred *sitios* of land granted by the King of Spain in 1757—he still wanted the *Yanqui* sea captain's daughter. Through all those years of his family living in poverty, living off the bounty of French relatives who made his family grovel, he had not forgotten Jen.

One day he would return to Texas, a land almost as large as the Republic of France, as a man in his own right. He struggled for an education, working the docks of Nantes to pay for a tutor. Had he also in mind returning one day to win the *Yanqui* girl who possessed all the pluck of a worldly adventurer?

He didn't know. He never assessed the feeling for her that was so much a part of him. But during the years he was trying to establish a line of packet ships between New York and Nantes, he had not lost that want of her. There was not a night in all the hellholes he had slept in that the mere memory of those lively, lavender-blue eyes did not invade his heart's light.

He had told himself the feeling was only one of nostalgia. Even when he learned she had married his best friend and his guts ached with the thought of her belonging to anyone but him, he told himself that were he ever to meet her again, she would be a plump little wife approaching middle age.

Sacré tonnerre! When he returned to Brownsville, he found Jeanette St. John was even more attractive as a woman. Character now molded her face. Had Armand been responsible for that growth of her spirit, that vitality? He thought not. Armand had been a dreamer, not a catalyst.

But Jen had wanted a man who sighed longingly in fourteen-line iambic-pentameter poetry. And so he had been willing to play the effete fop in order to enjoy the flame of her presence—although the pretense had served him on innumerable occasions when dealing with the Federal Army and Navy, neither of which would normally divulge confidential information to a blockade runner.

As the hapless, lazy hidalgo, he had been able to learn much more—for instance that Brownsville, Galveston, and Indianola each had three Federal blockaders, sloops-of-war on station with two actually on duty at all times. They lay off these towns' long white sandy beaches, along which continually strolled Texans to watch these men-of-war. And the men-of-war waited, knowing that when a favorable moment arose—a fog bank, a stormy, dark night—the blockade runners would make a dash for it.

Yes, knowing that a Federal sloop's engine had blown, or in one instance that an iron-clad had every man down with yellow fever, helped him immeasurably.

Solis returned with two glasses and passed one to him. The mestizo's dark eyes glowed in their sockets like coals. "You know that it was wrong, Cristobal—taking the young woman as you did, bargaining with her for . . ."

"For her love," Cristobal murmured harshly, not bothering to hide the pain in his face.

"To Juárez's victory over the French pigs," Solis said, raising his glass and tossing down the contents. "Bah!" He wiped the back of his sleeve across his mouth. "You really have become a hidalgo. *Aguardiente* goes down much better."

Cristobal cut an amused smile at the friend who as a child had faithfully served his father; faithfully enough to follow him willingly into the exile of poverty in France. Keeping with that tradition, Solis now faithfully served him. He raised his glass to Solis. "To Juárez—to Mexico."

"Tell me, *amigo,* why did you ever agree to run the guns for the little boy-woman?"

Cristobal shrugged. "I told you—that it was to help fight the *Yanquis.* Did they not take my inheritance?"

"*Sí,* but the *Yanquis* support our own cause—Juárez's government. And you were already running guns against the French, when she came to you. Why take more

chances with the *Yanquis*—when your services are much
more needed by Juárez? And don't tell me it was for a
woman—the boy-woman. You already have enough
women—*Dios*, Rubia is enough woman to last you until
the mescal's worm rots."

Cristobal tossed down the brandy—and was reminded
of Jen, of the way her face had blanched then washed back
in crimson when she so boldly swallowed the entire glass
of brandy. The corners of his mouth twitched. It did seem
pretty damned silly to tell someone you would risk your
life for a single night in the arms of one special woman.
He had known it would be the only chance he would ever
have to love her as he had always dreamed of doing.

And, then too, there was the knowledge that if he did
not agree to run the guns for her, with her will and determination she would eventually find a way—and at what
price? Her midnight visit to the captain of Matamoros's
National Guard proved that. Did the little fool not realize
the danger she was placing herself? And then where
would her grand idea of serving the Confederacy be?

He sighed, relieved at least that he had had the foresight to keep a tail on her at all times, for all the good it
had done in that last little encounter she had with the two
highwaymen. The tail had not counted on Jen making
such good time. But then the tail did not know Jen the
way he did. No one did.

Not her father. No, not even Armand. God rot his noble memory.

"Another brandy, Solis."

"The Lord have mercy on us!"

The shriek only whispered through Jeanette's dream,
and her legs and arms stirred in lazy protest. Sleepily her
hand groped for the mosquito netting that had been
draped across the bar against the annual swarm of insects
that took wing with spring's warm weather—as if the net-

ting could shut out the repeated shrieks for heavenly intervention.

The cries only became louder, and then the netting was jerked open. Groggily Jeanette slit one lid. Wide-eyed and snorting, her aunt looked like a horse just confronted with a rattling sidewinder. "They're here! Listen! The guns. They'll rape us all! Get your clothes, Jeanette. We're going to the convent."

Jeanette sat up and pushed her braid over her shoulder. She tried to focus her eyes—and her thoughts. Aunt Hermione stood before her in a high-necked muslin nightgown with a spoon bonnet perched on the bird's-nest hair. Jeanette gave up and, shutting her eyes, languorously stretched her arms.

"Whatever are you talking about, Aunt Hermione?" she yawned.

She had spent a long night supervising the moving of cotton bales from the church to the warehouse at Bagdad. She gingerly rubbed the small of her back. In the haste to beat the dawn, she had even assisted the *campesinos* in hefting the heavy bales.

With the sleepy smile of a satisfied cat she stretched again. Things could not be working out better. Fortunately for the Cause, the cursed Frenchman had survived. And apparently his close brush with death had deterred him from further pressing his charms on her. Miracle of miracles, Alejandro had passed the message to Trinidad that the Frenchman required only the standard five thousand dollars for each round trip. It still left her enough profit to cover Columbia's operating expenses, though her reduced share from the sale of the cotton decreased the amount of war supplies she bought off the *Revenge*. But as long as she did not have to see the Frenchman again, it was enough.

So why had she awakened with the name Kitt on her lips?

"What am I talking about?" her aunt echoed. "Land's sake, girl! Can't you hear the explosions? Trinidad says Federal landing boats are shelling Brazos Santiago beach with field guns. Hurry!"

"Hell and damnation!"

"Jeanette!" Aunt Hermione gasped.

Jeanette sprang from the bed. Mechanically she began yanking clothing from the wardrobe and tossing the articles on the bed. Her camisole, the day dress of magenta faille, her corset. The steel hoops of the cage crinoline got twisted in the bedsheets. Drat! She had known to expect an invasion by the Federal armies. Her Morocco gaiters— no, the heavy brogans would be better. She began lacing the high tops. The Yankees couldn't permit the Confederacy's contraband trade out of Bagdad to continue its phenomenal growth and still hope to win the war. Where was her polonaise? But she had counted on the invasion coming when Fort Brown was better garrisoned—and better supplied.

She jerked on the hoops, and they became even further entangled with each other and the bedding. "Get Tia Juana up here to lace me, Aunt Hermione," she muttered in distraction, fighting with the crinoline that seemed to have taken on perverse animated capabilities.

The great house locked up at last, Aunt Hermione was ready to evacuate. Accompanied by a grim Jeanette and Tia Juana, who muttered darkly about Yankee scum, the old woman ordered Trinidad to drive them to the convent. The shelling, which had sounded only like a distant drum, increased in volume to resemble crashing thunder. From the fan-leaved palm trees along the River Road an ashy pall could be seen hanging like a curtain just beyond Brownsville. The city's streets were empty of morning traffic when Trinidad reined the carriage to a halt before the gray-stoned convent.

Jeanette made no move to get out of the carriage, and

Aunt Hermione said impatiently, "Dear, do hurry. The beastly soldiers could enter the city at any moment."

"I'm not going to the convent right now," Jeanette answered, just as impatiently. She had to find out exactly what was happening. "Tia Juana, guard Aunt Hermione for me."

"Have you lost your mind, child!" Aunt Hermione shrieked. "There's going to be rape and murder and—and, get down from that seat this instant, Jeanette St. John!"

Jeanette laughed gaily. "Fie, Aunt Hermione. How often does one get to see the real fireworks? It's been deadly dull, and I mean to enjoy the excitement!"

Tia Juana smacked a good-bye kiss on Trinidad's forehead, but Aunt Hermione's mouth fell open. Her bird cage dropped to the ground, powdering the old woman's skirts with a thick white film of dust. For once she disregarded Washington's shrieked imprecations. "I know you're a flighty girl, but this is sheer madness!"

Jeanette waved merrily and instructed Trinidad to drive on to Brazos Santiago. "I'm writing your father!" Aunt Hermione yelled after the departing carriage. "Do you hear me, Jeanette St. John?"

The carriage rocked on down the road that in the dry season lay ankle deep in dust and in the rainy season was a sea of mud. Jeanette felt a twinge of guilt at the worry she was causing her aunt. But she had no other choice than to carry on the charade of a giddy young widow. At least until the South won the war and Armand's memory was vindicated. Besides, she was a grown woman now, and there was nothing her father could do to stop her.

❧ 12 ❧

Shaded by the lime-green eyelet parasol, Jeanette reposed in the canoe's bow. She felt almost guilty at the pleasurable respite she was taking from her underground activities.

As the boat drifted on the popular salt lake outside Brownsville, her long fingers indolently swished through the cool aquamarine waters. A warm May breeze whispered through verdant branches of weeping willow, salt cedar, and fanned palms. It played with the tendrils that twisted free of the elaborately crimped curls at her temples and before her ears. Refracted light off the water dappled her upturned face. If only the peaceful afternoon did not have to end so soon.

That Saturday was the first break from work she had known since the attempted Federal landing at Brazos Santiago. Fortunately, the sandbar at the mouth of the Rio Grande had prevented any large men-of-war from sailing on down to Brownsville, and the few landing boats were swamped in the surf off the island.

After that scare, her aunt had declared she was returning to New Bedford where it was safe for women and had immediately written her brother of her intentions. Though

103

Jeanette knew she would miss the dear, muddled old woman, she felt that her aunt's decision to leave was a blessing in disguise—at least her own disguise could be discarded around Columbia, and she would have more freedom of movement without worrying about being observed.

Realizing that the United States did not intend to let the contraband trade continue, she had worked feverishly since the Federal Navy's aborted attempt at landing. Soon—maybe in months, maybe weeks—the Federal Navy would try again, this time to take Brownsville, which was the true heart of the contraband trade. Therefore, she instructed her *campesino* teamsters to make as many runs as possible while they could. Already the Santa Maria Chapel was packed with cotton. Even the choir loft overflowed, and not another inch of space could be found to accommodate the bales. Now she had no choice but to await the return of the *Revenge,* which was due at any hour now.

In the meantime she only wanted to relax and escape the demands made by the double life she was leading. How fortunate that Cristobal had returned to Brownsville just the night before; for despite his silly laugh and his pretentious manner, his *bons mots* were making the afternoon pass most agreeably.

Lazily Jeanette opened her eyes to regard her friend. He had draped his fawn-colored redingote over the bench seat in front of him and rolled his cambric shirt sleeves to the elbows. As he idly dipped and lifted the oars, the tendons and muscles rippled along his forearms.

Her gaze moved to the shirt's open collar and the corded neck. Then she perused the chest that stretched the cambric tightly with its movement. After lingering there a bit longer than necessary, her gaze dropped down past the long legs to the Wellington boots, of the best leather, of course. Slowly her heavy-lidded eyes returned to the thighs. They were sheathed in close-fitting nankeens that revealed their solidity. She continued her desultory inspection, focusing now on the buttons below the waist.

Involuntarily she blushed, her eyes riveted to the hard rise displayed there. A magnificent specimen of manhood! Too bad it was wasted on—other men.

She knew she should condemn Cristobal's preference for the male sex, but she could not. She truly liked him, for all his feckless ways. And besides, who was she to pass judgment on him, when she—when she had done things she could not be proud of, either. When she had done things since last summer of which she was terribly ashamed. Why, just the act of boldly sizing up Cristobal's masculine attributes! It was an urge that had never crossed her consciousness in all her married life. She grimaced. That just illustrated once again how degenerated the Frenchman had caused her to become. He had opened up to her, like Pandora's box, a sordid world that even at this moment continued to pique her curiosity. Never, if she lived to be a very old lady, would she ever forget *le baiser français!*

Seeking to shake the discomforting memory from her mind, she returned her thoughts to her companion. She peered at his handsome face through a thicket of ebony lashes—only to find his gaze steadily fixed on her with what she suspected was amusement at her covert assessment of him. She colored hotly and hid once more behind the façade of the coquette.

"You don't think me terribly unladylike for asking you to take me canoeing, do you, Cristobal?" she teased and flashed flirtatious dimples.

The rich brown eyes with tiny creases at the corners seemed to mock her. Or was it her imagination? For at the next moment he chortled. She repressed a shudder, for his laugh was like a fingernail scraping down a chalkboard.

"Jen, I've only been in Brownsville a day, and already the tedium was wearing away at me. Couldn't have been more grateful for the message Trinidad brought. I'm afraid, dear girl, that the gaiety of New Orleans night life spoiled me."

"You were there doing another war story?"

He had the good grace to flush. "Supposed to," he corrected. "For the *London Times* on the New Orleans-to-Matamoros contraband trade. Alas, not all my time was spent on research. But, gad, you've heard how gloriously debauched New Orleans is."

She studied him openly now, noting the lines of fatigue that grooved either side of his mouth. "You look like you spent the entire time you were in New Orleans being properly debauched."

Cristobal laughed and pulled in the oars. Water droplets off the oars splashed musically back into the lake. He raked a brown hand through his curling mass of mahogany hair. It persisted in escaping the center part he affected, which, along with the side whiskers, had been made popular by the Crimean War. "I confess to the debauchment, but as to how proper it was, you'd have to ask the ladies of the night."

Her parasol dipped dangerously toward the water and her eyes widened in dismay at the implication behind his words. Cristobal apparently participated in—and enjoyed—the most intimate of relationships with women! The idea depressed her somehow, for with him she had always presumed herself safe from the unwanted flirtations made by other men. With him she could relax and be herself—almost.

She saw that he was watching her reaction, and she sat upright, saying boldly, "I was under the impression, Cristobal, that you—uh, had no interest in the female sex."

"*La*, Jen, that was to stave off your aunt. Surely marriage taught you that men like a certain type of woman sometimes."

Her eyes blazed back at the light that danced in his. "No, it did not, Cristobal Cavazos! There are some men who are above such wickedness . . . who are noble and good . . . who believe in fidelity and—and go through life loving one woman."

He picked up the oars again. "And women—are there any such women? Besides yourself, of course. I can imagine how devoted you were to Armand. And know how you've martyred yourself to his memory."

"What do you mean?" she asked sharply.

"Why, simply, dear girl, that you would never think of taking another man—er, into your bed again. In marriage, of course."

Her composure shaken, she twirled the parasol in agitated jerks. "Of course." Why must she continue to let the guilt of the nights spent in the Frenchman's arms disconcert her? She must realize she had simply made a mistake. But, oh, what it had cost her!

She forced a coy pout to her lips and said reprovingly, "But really, Cristobal, this is a subject that no proper lady should discuss."

His lips twitched with that foolish grin of his. "How positively ill bred of me to lapse into such an indelicate conversation. As you said, no proper lady would think of discussing such a subject."

Which is why I have always found you so delightfully entertaining, my love.

"I don't care what he wants. I'm simply not going."

"There! Look for yourself, Jeanette." Aunt Hermione tossed on the parlor's drop table the letter that had been forwarded from New Bedford by the United States Consul in Matamoros. "My brother says you have no choice."

Disbelievingly Jeanette picked up the folded sheets of

foolscap that bore her father's near-indecipherable scrawl. Her aunt said apologetically, "When I wrote your father, telling him I wanted to go back to New Bedford and you preferred to remain here—well, I really did not know, dear, that your father would do this."

But the order was before her—in the strict, commanding language of a sea captain. Always he had tried to regiment her into the unquestioning, disciplined behavior he demanded of his seamen. He had tried to control his daughter in the same unbending, authoritarian manner in which he had run his ship.

So far she had managed to resist that iron will that made no allowances for the fact she was not a seaman but his daughter. Sometimes she resisted through outright defiance, sometimes by subtle evasion. But this time it looked as if she did indeed have no choice.

Her father's letter made it undeniably clear that he considered it unsafe for a woman without the protection of a man to remain in a city facing seige and that he expected her to leave immediately for New Bedford with her aunt.

Because Jeanette was far past her majority, legally she did not have to submit to her father's dictums. She could rebel and remain in Texas. But the last sentence in the letter, stating that since Armand was dead he was planning to put the plantation up for sale, staggered her.

It wasn't just that she loved Columbia and its wild, strong terrain—and loyal, fun-loving people so much. It was also the realization that with the sale of Columbia her scheme for aiding the Confederacy—and eventually establishing her own independence—would die, for there would be no base for her clandestine operations. Where would she store the cotton and firearms that crisscrossed each other at Columbia on their way to their respective destinations? How could she work out of quarters in Brownsville without her movements being observed?

For long, frustrating moments she stood as if paralyzed, holding the letter before her unseeing eyes, oblivious to her aunt's rambling apology. Instead, Jeanette's mind busily searched through the maze of possible alternatives to obeying her father's ultimatum. One by one she rejected each alternative as being unsatisfactory either to her father or to her own plans.

And then she knew. She whirled from her aunt and, lifting her hoops, ran upstairs to her bedroom. Without bothering to seat herself, she leaned over the cherry-wood secretary and dashed off a letter to her father. With luck and a fast horse she could get the letter to the United States Consulate in Matamoros and see it off on the next sloop bound for either Boston or New York.

But it would take more than luck to carry out the rest of her plan. It would take some glib talking, and for once she was not certain if she was equal to that task. Cristobal might be a lazy, jaded fop, but he was sharp. Would he go along with her suggestion?

13

Jeanette took Tia Juana with her. The old Mexican woman sat in the carriage next to her and grumbled the entire nine-mile trip into Brownsville. Trinidad merely hunched his bony shoulders to show his disapproval and kept his attention on the team of horses. "The old horned devil has possessed you, missy," Tia Juana said, not letting up in her diatribe. "Better one of my *remedios* than to do this."

Jeanette wasn't so sure herself. Facing Cristobal with her preposterous suggestion seemed almost but not quite as bad as undergoing one of Tia Juana's folk cures that went back to the dark magic of Africa. The old woman was a *curandera*, a healer, or what some of the Anglos referred to as a witch doctor. The last time Tia Juana had tried to practice a *remedio* on Jeanette was the year she was nine. She broke a wrist falling from her horse as she attempted a jump previously cleared by Armand and Cristobal. The old woman's cure had been horse manure packed over the break, a method that had sent Aunt Hermione into a frenzy. The two women had battled for almost an hour over the proper treatment. In that time

Jeanette was off again, riding, and eventually the wrist healed of its own.

Privately Jeanette wondered if her head had ever healed. Tia Juana seconded the thought, saying, "You must be bewitched. Why ever would you want to marry dhis—" her ham hock of a hand waved contemptuously and the fat beneath her arm shook, "dhis popinjay? He struts like a Mexican cock."

"That you don't have to tell me."

"Den I will tell you that I also have an incantation for bewitchment, *niña*."

"It will take more than an incantation," Jeanette pronounced grimly.

For a while the three sat in silence as the team of bays clipclopped down the River Road with its arch of palms of great height and age. Then Trinidad spoke up, saying just loud enough for them to hear, "You are still in love weeth Armand, and still very angry weeth that blockade runner, no? But I don't think you know what you are doing, *sobrina*."

"I know exactly what I am doing," Jeanette bristled. "And that blockade runner is nothing more than—than a speculator, a mercenary, a pirate! Furthermore this is— it's a marriage of convenience. *If* I can persuade Cristobal to marry me," she muttered under her breath.

"There!" Tia Juana pounced on the statement. "Dat's yor problem. Any young man wit' dah sense God gave a goose would hop into marriage wit' you quicker than a cat on a june bug. So why Cristobal? Even if he is a man of my husband's people, he is still a lazy good-fo'-nuttin'!"

"If I must be protected by a husband in order to remain at Columbia, I don't want that husband to be a soldier. They have a penchant for dying. And that leaves Cristobal."

She did not add that since Cristobal seemed to prefer

the loose ladies of the night, the prospects of marriage
with him were just that much more appealing. He would
not bother her with his desires. She would not be further
sullied by anyone else's lovemaking; for in her heart of
hearts she was still and always would be Armand's wife.

The solution seemed simple. If only Cristobal would
find it so simple.

For this confrontation she had dressed, appropriately,
in a Zouave military jacket over a scarlet Garibaldi blouse
braided in black. The black silk skirt had a scarlet band at
the bottom that matched her blouse and scarlet hairnet.
Her Glengarry Scotch cap was tilted at a belligerent angle, though more from her high chignon than from her
attitude, which, if anything, bordered on apprehension.

If ever she needed courage it was now. Everything de-
pended on her ability to persuade Cristobal—something
she'd never been able to accomplish in their childhood.
And something told her that the dandy Don Cavazos was
no more biddable now than he was twenty years before.

Trinidad halted the brougham before a two-story brick
establishment similar to all the others in that area of town,
largely due to the iron grillework at the windows and narrow balconies that betrayed a French influence. The little
old Mexican waited, petting his beloved horses, while the
two women entered the building and climbed the stairs to
Cristobal's set of apartments. Jeanette paused before the
door to draw a deep breath of courage, but Tia Juana
reached past her and banged on the wood with her fist.
"Better to git dhis over wit', missy."

A dwarf bid them enter while he went for "Don
Cristobal." Tia Juana plopped her bulk at the end of a
Louis XIV chaise longue, but Jeanette paced about the
room in agitation. Peripherally her mind noted that the
room lacked the usual clutter of knickknacks. In fact it was
sparsely decorated, but the appointments were in good
taste. A few paintings caught her eye and imagination as

did a bronze sculpture of a charging bull and a pewter humidor of unusual shape.

She turned as Cristobal halted in the doorway. He quirked a brow, his normal sleepy gaze moving from her to Tia Juana and back to her again. He was dressed in buff-colored riding britches with Hessian boots and a white muslin shirt that bloused at the wrists. Apparently he had already been riding, for his thick hair was rumpled. With whom? Annabel?

"Gad, Jen, your expression is positively dolorous," he said with his imperturbable but dry good humor. "Has someone died?"

Yes. My heart. Oh, Armand. Why did you have to ride off to battle? I want you in my arms, my gallant husband, not in some nameless grave.

"I have come with a business proposition," she said briskly.

A droll smile tugged at his lips. "Business? Since when, dear girl, have I ever bothered my head with business?" He folded his arms over his chest and crossed one booted foot to lean against the doorjamb. "But do continue. This promises to be a most diverting day after all."

She clasped and unclasped her hands. His sangfroid was unnerving. She cut a glance at Tia Juana. The old black woman understood. She hefted her massive frame from the chaise longue, saying, "I'll wait below with Honeypie."

Jeanette wandered to the French doors that were thrown open to let in the sunshine. Below her the *dulce* woman hawked her sweet confections in competition with the tamale woman who fried her tempting dish over a portable grill across the street. But Jeanette neither heard the *dulce* woman nor smelled the pungent hot tamales.

"You mentioned a business proposition," Cristobal prompted in his pleasant but distinct voice.

She turned and forced her gaze to meet his inquiring

one across the breadth of the room. To ask a man to marry her! It galled her beyond anything she could recall. "I need a husband," she said baldly. Her eyes flashed an unholy blue, daring him to laugh just once.

Nothing. Neither surprise nor laughter. The usual affable face wore a mask that gave her no clue to his feelings or intentions.

Cristobal pushed off the door and indolently walked toward her. Reluctantly she let him take her elbow and steer her toward the recently vacated chaise longue. "Apparently this will not be one of our brief little chitchats."

He took the wing chair opposite her, leaned forward, propped his forearms on his knees, and clasped his large brown hands. His handsome face wore none of its usual superciliousness. She breathed a little easier. Thank God! For once it would seem he was inclined to talk about something in a serious manner.

"If I remember correctly, Jen, you swore before your aunt and me you would never marry. Why the change of heart?"

Or is it a change of body? Are you carrying my child, which you think is the Frenchman's child? His heart suddenly started thudding like the piston rods in the *Revenge's* engine room.

She reached into her reticule for her fan, anything to play with. "Fie on you, Cristobal," she said and splayed the fan. "How unchivalrous of you!" Demurely she lowered her lashes. "Does a lady have to confess her reasons?"

He straightened and settled back in the chair. So she was once again assuming the role of the frivolous flirt. He much preferred the boy-woman. With an inner sigh he donned his own mask for the role he was expected to play. "You brought up that loathsome word, business," he reminded her and crossed one boot over the other knee, waiting.

"Then let me substitute the word assets." Where to begin? "If—if we were to marry, can you not imagine the monetary comforts you would enjoy?"

"And the problems of running a large estate," he said drily.

Well, at least he had not burst out in that obnoxious laughter. "Wrong." Her fan snapped closed, and for a second her pretense dropped. "A contract would specify that the St. John–Van Ryan interest would retain control of Columbia."

"But with the marriage to me, the St. John name would come to an end," he pointed out, his drooping lids concealing the intensity of his gaze.

"True," she admitted. The fan began to swish again as if to dispel the depression that had seized the young woman. Was she once more betraying Armand? With the marriage to Cristobal not even Armand's name would remain to remind the world he had once existed. "But my father, through our overseer Trinidad, would continue to govern the estate. On your part you would receive a handsome monthly allowance that would permit you the freedom to pursue your . . . pleasures to an even greater degree."

His lips twitched in wry amusement. "You mean subsidize my gambling expenses—among other things?"

"Exactly."

"You are buying my name, then," he said bluntly. "Why?"

She had not expected that. "What?"

"Did I stutter?"

How much to tell? Cristobal was no fool. Better to tell as much of the truth as possible. "My father wants me to return to New Bedford, where he feels it is safer for women. And I—I don't wish to be under his thumb." She hurried on. "He would have me settle down, a staid and proper widow. I'm too young to be put away in a rocking chair. I want to enjoy myself. Surely you, of all people, can understand, Cristobal."

"I understand, I think. You are suggesting that you wish to carry on your social affairs after marriage the same as you do now."

"Exactly. I knew an enlightened man such as yourself would understand." She prided herself that the conversation was going along so easily. "Oftentimes I may choose to absent myself from Columbia to pursue the small little pleasures denied a widow."

So, it was not a child she was carrying, but the Confederacy and Armand's memory she was protecting. "Why me, Jen?"

Her mind worked furiously. "Another husband might expect me to—er, remain in my own bed, and"—she could feel the heat of the blood flushing through her face—"and I knew that you preferred"—this was not going so well, after all—"that you preferred—uh, gray doves."

"Prostitutes?" he substituted.

The fan was oscillating like a windmill in a storm. "Yes!" she groaned.

He slumped farther into the chair. His supple fingers formed a pyramid beneath a jaw that, curiously enough for a man of his fastidiousness, was still unshaven at that hour of the morning. At last he said, "I'm to understand you do wish to forego with me the intimacies of marriage?"

"Yes! Yes." Oh, if she could only get this horrendous ordeal over with!

"*La*, Jen, your proposal is not very flattering to my ego."

"Since when have you ever worried about someone else's opinion," she laughed, reverting for a moment to her old self. "Your ego is large enough to sustain my womanly blow." Then, anxiously, "Well? Will you agree?"

He could think of a dozen reasons why it would be utterly imbecilic to marry her, the most important being the knowledge that she would hate him forever when she learned of his deception. As it stood now, he was still able to enjoy the pleasure of her friendship.

Mentally he ticked off a number of other reasons: the hell of living in such close proximity with her and not being able to hold her, to touch her; the strain of continuing his covert activities; the danger to him and others should she guess his identity; the fact she would, indeed, be safer in New Bedford. But, hell, even if he did not marry her, she would still find a way to circumvent her father's edict. In the long run he knew she would be somewhat safer if he could keep an eye on her.

Still, he tried one more time. "You professed to me recently how noble and honorable Armand was. Won't it bother you that you are violating the sanctity of his memory by allowing someone to take his place in marriage?"

She missed entirely the bitterness in his voice and replied with a simplicity that pierced him to his core: "No one could ever take his place."

Cristobal rose to his feet and held out his hand to her. "You've been up here long enough without a chaperone."

She let him pull her to her feet. Her gaze lifted to meet his. She clung to his strong hand even after he released hers. "Will you . . . will you marry me, Cristobal?" she whispered, humbled now, her mauve-blue eyes glistening with their desperation. "For the sake of our friendship?"

"*Sí,*" he replied, slipping back into the Spanish of his childhood. "For the sake of our friendship, Jen."

14

It was a simple ceremony without a *soirée de contrat* or *dîner de fiançailles* or any of the other prerequisites of a fashionable marriage in Brownsville's *haut monde*. Nevertheless, Jeanette's marriage to Cristobal Cavazos was just as binding, just as legal. She was richly dressed in an oyster gros de Naples gown trimmed with eggshell Honiton lace. A limp-brimmed bergère straw hat with a chaplet of orange flowers shaded her pale face as she descended the Cameron County Courthouse's steps with her second husband at her side, his hand solicitously at her elbow.

Behind the couple trailed Aunt Hermione, sniffling her happiness into a wet lace handkerchief. Cristobal ushered the two women on board the riverboat tied at the landing, blowing off steam, its big paddle wheel idle. The steamboat, one of the Kenedy-King packet, would take the three of them down the Rio Grande on the leisurely twenty-two-mile trip to the port of Bagdad.

"Now I can go to your father secure in the knowledge that I have fulfilled my duty," Aunt Hermione said tearfully.

Jeanette slid a glance at Cristobal, hoping he would say nothing to contradict her. "We had hoped to wait a more

decent interval, Aunt Hermione," she said, "but Father's
order left us no choice but to marry now."

"I've known all along you two would be a perfect match
for each other."

"I've been trying to convince your niece of that for
some time," Cristobal said, tossing a mocking grin in
Jeanette's direction. She stifled an urge to laugh, remembering how reluctant her friend had been. Wearing a
black frock coat and pantaloons with a gold-trimmed
chestnut-colored cashmere waistcoat, he was elegant as always.

The odor of hot oil drifted up from the boilers in the
engine room, and Aunt Hermione held the handkerchief
even closer against her red nose. Jeanette did not mind
the smell, finding it part of the excitement of riding such a
powerful machine. As the steamboat negotiated the sandbars and drifts that scored the muddy river, she leaned
against the gingerbread railing with the other passengers,
feeling the breeze rustle the curls at her ears. Many times
at night she had smuggled cotton across the river by ferry,
and she much preferred the river when it looked a serene,
dark blue rather than the frothy yellow-brown it was in
daylight.

But her pleasure faded as she gazed out over the waves
rippling back from the steamboat's bow. Too easily she
recalled the ocean's blue-black waves—and *him*. Was
there no respite from being reminded of the Frenchman?
Must that awful memory dampen even the simplest of
pleasures?

A warm hand covered her gloved one on the railing.
She looked up to find Cristobal at her side. His lips
formed a twisted travesty of a smile. "Aunt Hermione will
think it strange we aren't enjoying our conjugal bliss."

"Dear Cristobal," she murmured. Her free hand went
up to touch his jaw. "I am truly grateful for your sacrifice.
I promise you shall not want for anything at Columbia."

His lids drooped sleepily. "Even for the pleasures of the night?"

Her hand dropped as if it had been burned. "Well, I would not expect you to bring your—your gray doves to Columbia, naturally."

"Naturally," he said drily, his brown eyes now as muddy as the Rio Grande. As if by unspoken accord, the two of them directed their gazes away from each other toward the flat river bank flanked by twisted mesquites and occasional elm motts. "There are, of course, some conditions that should be discussed."

"By all means," she rapidly concurred. She lowered her voice to a husky whisper. "For one—we are husband and wife in name only."

"Secondly," he contributed solemnly, "I am to be permitted my . . . diversions." He quirked a silly smile at her. "A cockfight, a horserace, a game of cards, etcetera. After all, dear girl, Columbia is so far from everything and so accursedly boring."

She grinned at him. "I couldn't agree more." With him absent from Columbia, her activities would be that much easier to carry out. She stood on tiptoe to plant a kiss on his bronzed cheek and inhaled the scent of his men's cologne. "Our business arrangement is going to work splendidly, Cristobal."

"Oh, just splendidly," he echoed with a straight face.

In Bagdad several Southern refugee families, their household goods stored in ox carts, waited to board the *Honduras*, bound for English shores. Jeanette and Cristobal waved Aunt Hermione off on the Yankee frigate, with the old woman admonishing, "Take good care of Washington for me, dear. Be sure and talk with him so he won't get lonely. Oh, dear, I do wish Boston's weather were better suited to him. I shall miss the tootsie pie."

"I'll treat Washington like he was one of the family," Jeanette reassured her aunt. She took Cristobal's arm, adding with a love-stricken smile meant for her aunt's benefit, "Do tell Father how happy Cristobal and I are."

And she *was* happy, she realized with some surprise as she and Cristobal made the return trip by steamboat to Columbia. She had succeeded in remaining at Columbia, where she could continue her work for the Confederacy. From the steamboat's railing the two of them watched slip by in the twilight the vast Palo Alto Prairie's ranchos and their mesquite-fenced corrals. Any bridal jitters she may have had were dispelled by Cristobal's *mots d'esprit*.

Tales of his trips kept her laughing, and every so often she told a story of her own. "Did you hear about the rancher who tried to sell his wife's silverware for a block of salt?" she asked him, recalling the incident from a run she had made to Alleyton. "'It's worth forty dollars if it's worth a cent,' the rancher told the speculator. 'Then it's worth a cent,' the speculator said."

The story elicited that silly chortle of Cristobal's, to which she was becoming accustomed.

It was late when they reached Columbia. Tia Juana welcomed them with her broad nose tilted haughtily and a dark glare in Cristobal's direction, which he blithely ignored. Though Jeanette was grateful for the old black woman's presence that particular night, she was irritated by the belligerent attitude. Cristobal should be treated with the courtesy due her husband. Instead of requesting Tia Juana to show him to one of the guest bedrooms, she nervously led the way herself.

She halted before the door of one of the larger bedrooms, which placed Cristobal at the opposite end of the second-floor hallway from her bedroom. "Your belongings?" she asked, only then aware he carried nothing but his top hat.

"I'll have Henri send them over later in the week."

"But your night clothing—"

The light from the candle sconce on the wall flickered

over his dark face, highlighting the devilry that pirouetted at the corners of his mouth. "*La*, Jen, I haven't slept in anything in years. My long legs always get tangled in those cursed nightshirts."

She turned away to hide the blush that surely must have dyed the roots of her hair crimson. "Very well," she choked. "Have a pleasant night, Cristobal."

She retired to her bedroom, on the whole very pleased with the way the arrangements were working out. True, she thought as she removed first the net then the pins from her hair, there would probably have to be some adjustments. Would Cristobal need to notify Tia Juana when he would be having dinner at the house? Did he smoke— funny, she had never noticed. Did he plan to entertain his friends at Columbia? What kind of friends were they— gambling associates? What if she did not like them?

Wrestling now with the corset's laces knotted behind her back, she told herself that she would just have to adjust to her husband's idiosyncrasies—as he would have to adjust to hers. But what idiosyncrasies Cristobal had! His chief attributes seemed to be his good-humored foolishness and handsome looks, for he possessed neither financial assets nor the will to soil his hands or mind with honest labor. But then Cristobal probably thought her just as eccentric and frivolous. Yes, the two of them would work well together.

"Get out! Awk! Help! Get out!"

Jeanette jumped and whirled on the macaw. "I had forgotten you were here, Washington," she laughed. She crossed to the cage suspended on the stand and dribbled some nuts from the feeder into her palm.

Ignoring the proffered food, Washington tilted his short, arched bill at her in indignation at being overlooked. With a furrow of his scarlet and green plumage, he squawked, "Awk, rapist!"

"I think the wretched bird is referring to me," a voice drawled from the doorway.

Once again Jeanette spun about, spraying the nuts over the Westminister carpet. Unaccustomed to a man in the house, she had left the door open. "Oh, Cristobal!" she sighed, her hand at her throat. "You frightened me."

"Help! Help! Rapist!" the parrot yelled.

Cristobal, his shirt hanging out over his pants, crossed to the macaw and dropped the cover over the cage. "Enough of you, my fine feathered friend." He turned to Jeanette. "Gad, Jen, I think your aunt had high hopes when she taught Washington to talk."

Jeanette's voice pealed in laughter. "I've thought just that for a long time, though Aunt Hermione swears the bird already knew those 'vile' words. I suspect my dear aunt to be a frustrated old maid!"

Abruptly Jeanette colored under Cristobal's frank appraisal. There she stood with her gown gaping in the back and her hair tumbled about her shoulders like a fandango dancer's and unabashedly discussed the most personal of topics with him. At moments like this there was something about him . . . something that seemed to alert some dormant instinct within her. A hunch . . . a presentiment?

The sudden appearance of his foolish grin dissipated all apprehension. She had forgotten that with Cristobal she did not have to conform to society, since he himself did not. "I heard the yelling," he said sheepishly, "and like some Don Quixote came to rescue you."

He turned to leave, and she said, "Wait. I've gotten these laces all knotted. Would you mind?" She pivoted to display her back.

After a second she heard him walk up to her. She lifted the heavy mass of hair from her neck to reveal the mess she had made of the laces. His fingers began to work at the knots, and she could feel the give in the stays as he loosened each lace from its metal eyelet. "By the cuckoo's nest, I can't perceive why you wear these accursed torture instruments, Jen. You're much more—"

"What?" she asked, curious as to what he had been about to say.

"Don't utter another word, or you'll pop the laces," he warned instead.

She could feel his breath upon her nape, and she quivered at the pleasant sensation.

"Cold?" he asked.

Her eyes trained on the covered cage, she shivered again. Something about that rich baritone voice elicited an unidentifiable response from her. "A little," she lied.

She really should not be exposing her intimate undergarment to him. But Cristobal was her husband now. And she did know she had no worry about him making any kind of amorous advances toward her. After all, he had more than once made it quite clear to her that she held no appeal to him other than that of a friend.

His hands came up to clasp her shoulders, gently rubbing up and down her arms. "You've goose bumps, Jen."

She surrendered to the power flowing from the hands that ran lightly over her shoulders and arms. "Mmmm," she acknowledged. Her head lolled back on his chest, as she savored the warmth of his body against hers. Above her head, his breath stirred her hair. Her head drooped forward. "Massage my neck, will you, Cristobal."

One arm about her waist, bracing her, his strong fingers found the tension-rigid tendons in her neck and exerted just enough pressure to cause her to go limp in relaxation. It had been a long day, and she had been more nervous at the civil ceremony than she had the day she had married Armand. But then she had known Armand all of her life, and Cristobal had been gone for so long. He was almost like a stranger in some ways, for she had not shared all that had happened in his life in the intervening years.

"Oh, I wish you would do that all night!" she sighed.

Abruptly she was released and almost staggered without his arm to steady her. "But it's late—and I have a wager on some duel being fought at dawn." He stretched his massive frame and yawned. "'Night, Jen."

"Rape! Help!" cawed the covered Washington after the broad back of the departing man.

15

Jeanette arched her back and shifted her position on the wagon seat. She waited for the ferry to return to the Mexican side of the river. Her wagons were stacked high with crates of rifles, barrels of ammunition, and boxes of medical supplies that she had collected from the Matamoros warehouse the Frenchman used. Although it was nearing two in the morning, and her body and mind cried out in fatigue, she felt a sense of exhilaration at having completed another successful cotton run. After a few hours of sleep later that morning, she would begin preparing for the gun run north under the cover of night's darkness.

She was happier than she had been in a long time, since—she really couldn't remember when she had experienced the elation that suffused her daylight hours. A sense of being productive, a sense of fulfillment, a sense of purpose imparted by her underground work for the Confederacy. Even her bitterness over Armand's needless death, her anger at the general, the "Monster" Morgan, who refused him medical aid were diluted through her work.

Only on those nights when she was not occupied in running contraband did she experience despondency. The dark hours stretched interminably before her. Too much idle time to recall the Frenchman . . . and the marvelous way he had made her body come alive. It seemed almost a sacrilege that her body—and, yes, even her mind—could respond to a stranger in such an unladylike way when she had never abandoned herself to Armand like that.

Worst of all were her dreams, where she had no power to suppress her treacherous visions. The dreams bothered her the most when she knew the Frenchman was in port.

She would roll from one side of her bed to the other, punch her pillow for a better position, and at long last succumb to sleep's oblivion through sheer exhaustion. But she would awake the next morning, tangled in the sheets and mosquito netting, with the nauseating knowledge that even her unconscious had betrayed her in her dreams of the damnable Frenchman.

Bleary-eyed over a cup of Tia Juana's hot chocolate, she would remind herself that her life was better these days. She no longer had to deal with the Frenchman; neither did she have to worry about Aunt Hermione discovering her duplicity. She attributed her restlessness to Cristobal's frequent absences from Columbia that summer. She had come to enjoy his company. He temporarily kept away the gloom that night brought. She suspected that he sometimes slept over at the quarters he still kept in Brownsville rather than disturb her by returning in the morning's early hours.

Trinidad was waiting when she and the three *campesinos* drove the wagons up the dirt road that zigzagged from the river bank, where it was lined with canebreak, up the bluff to the chapel. "You're late, *sobrina*," he told her, when she threw on the wagon's brake. "I worried eet was another bandit raid."

She jumped from the wagon's seat. "No," she said and swatted her dusty hat against her thigh in disgust. "The customs agents wanted a greater share of the tariff before they would let the Frenchman's agent release the war supplies—claimed they couldn't be sure the arms weren't going to the French."

Trinidad grunted. "If eet's not the French, eet's the Juaristas, and if eet's not the *guerrillas* eet's the *Yanquis*."

She left him to oversee the concealment of the loaded wagons while she sought a few hours of much-needed rest. Tia Juana clucked over her like a mother hen, picking up the dirty boy's clothing Jeanette haphazardly discarded as she moved through the house to her bedroom. "Hot bath's what you need, missy. You gonna sleep better."

"I'll sleep like the dead no matter what," she mumbled, and fell forward across the bed nude. "Keep the water warm till later, Tia Juana," she managed to add before her lids dropped like shutters.

The heat of the July day beaded Jeanette's back with perspiration where her thick braid followed the line of her spine. From the open window wafted the scent of the summer roses and the humming of a bee busy pollenating. Her nose tickled, and her hand drowsily swatted the air. The pesky fly persisted in its attack. With annoyance she slit one lid to find a yellow rose waving before her nose. Groggily she rolled to a sitting position—too late! Cristobal sat before her in the reading chair. His hand held the rose that only seconds earlier had played upon her nose.

Immediately she rolled back on her stomach and grappled with the bedcovers, trying to pull them up over her exposed backside. "What are you doing here!" she demanded.

He lifted his booted feet and laid them on the mattress.

"Why, I came home to change clothing, Jen."

"In my bedroom, I mean," she strangled indignantly, still wrestling the tangled bedding past her waist.

"Oh—that." She could have sworn she heard laughter in his voice. "Tia Juana said you weren't feeling well. Seeing how your door was open, I thought I'd check on you. Do you need anything?"

"No. Yes. My robe."

"*La*, Jen, make up your mind."

"Oh, get out!"

"You know," he drawled, "you sound just like Washington. Glad you moved the nit downstairs. He was making sleep impossible."

"I tried to tell Mr. Cristobal you were too sick to be disturbed," Tia Juana said from the doorway.

Cristobal leaned over and placed a hand on Jeanette's forehead. "Anything serious, my dear? It's not like you to spend the day in bed—naked as a Thanksgiving turkey."

She groaned. There was nothing to do but go through with the farce. "Tia Juana, get me a cup of hot tea—for my headache."

The old Negress lumbered off, and Cristobal arched a brow. "Merely a headache?"

She cowered beneath the covers. "No . . . no, I think I may be getting—the dengue. It comes on every so often and lasts several days. I just need plenty of rest—and quiet."

Her obtuse husband did not take the hint to leave. "That tropical fever?" he echoed incredulously. "It's those deuced mosquitoes!"

"And there's nothing that can be done for it," she wanly added, really getting into her character of the dying Lady of the Camellias. She let her lids droop with the heaviness of serious illness.

It seemed Cristobal refused to take her performance seriously. "Oh, I don't know, Jen. I could always dance around your body naked and lash you with wet reeds as a cure."

"That's not a cure," she snapped. "That's a social event!" And then the corners of her lips danced in a smile in spite of herself. "Oh, Cristobal, it's just a headache. Let me rest a while, will you?"

He took his leave with an elaborate bow and his foolish grin.

The carriage passed by the dusty streets and alleys where Mexicans lived in squalor and entered the open black-iron gate of the Quarter Masters Fence, the brick wall which separated Brownsville from the fort. Fort Brown, the oldest United States garrison on the Rio Grande, sprawled in the sweeping curve of the river, isolated from the town by a large *resaca*. Above the fort, the stars and bars of the Confederate flag fluttered with the merciful evening breeze that rustled in from the Mexican side of the river.

The horses pulled the carriage across the parade ground and past the enlisted men's barracks to the largest building of the encampment, the post exchange and warehouse. Here a fashionable ball was being held by the Brownsville Needle Battalion to raise funds for clothing for troops in the field. Jeanette was exhausted and would have preferred to remain home. Only that morning she had returned from running the most recent shipment of guns to Alleyton. However, she felt it was important that she and Cristobal attend the ball in order to maintain her reputation as the typical female social butterfly who had nothing better to do.

She peeked up through the fringe of lashes at the handsome man who helped her alight from the carriage. His clean-shaven face was totally at odds with the handlebar mustaches and flowing beards of the soldiers in full-dress grays who entered the post exchange. Not once had Cristobal questioned her about her ten-day absence, and she could only assume he accepted at face value her previous statement that she intended occasionally to partake of the pleasures denied a widow.

In fact she asked him that morning in a pointed but light-hearted manner, "Did anything happen while I was gone?"

"Were you gone? So was I."

It had been a little deflating to her ego. But then that was what she had wanted from Cristobal—indifference to what she was about.

Inside, the exchange had been cleared of all merchandise and a blue-velvet-draped dais erected at one end for the five-piece military band and the Brownsville Home Guard Chorus. As this was their first appearance in society as man and wife, Jeanette was curious to see the reactions of Brownsville's elite to her precipitous marriage.

Surprisingly the distinguished women, the clever men, and the soldiers of exalted station formed a brilliant court about the two of them. Jeanette's smiles and Cristobal's sallies entertained the war-bored citizens far into the night. That evening acknowledged them as the leaders of fashion and style. Later their words and dress would be copied—Cristobal's lavender doeskin gloves (to complement his wife's eyes, he replied with a sleepy grin), Jeanette's golden hair powder (to resemble that of the Empress Eugénie, she answered carelessly).

If Jeanette's good-natured contempt for her husband's foolish yet funny repartee showed through her frivolous veneer, people smiled indulgently and regarded her marriage to the lazy peacock as supreme eccentricity on her part. As for him—well, a golden key is said to open every door, asserted the more malignant minds, referring to the attraction of Columbia.

Annabel Goddard was among the disgruntled, her over-blown lips pushed out petulantly; yet Jeanette noticed the long-limbed Cristobal's new marital status did not keep Annabel from clinging to his arm. When the Brownsville Home Guard Chorus opened their portion of the evening's program with "Troubadour," Jeanette retired from the sand-sprinkled dance floor with her present partner, the aging Deputy Collector of Customs. She rejoined her husband and Annabel in time to hear him drawl, "I go to the opera whether I need the sleep or not," followed by the blond beauty's high peal of laughter. Jeanette did not think the remark that humorous. Indeed, she was beginning to find it a little annoying that her husband seemed to lavish more attention on other women than he did on her.

Claudia, the one woman Jeanette would have enjoyed talking to, had not come because her husband had managed to obtain a leave. With the intermission the talk once more turned to war. A Captain Ffauks divulged that military spies in New Orleans reported, in addition to the Federal blockade operating off Brownsville, Louis Napoleon planned to establish his own blockade at the mouth of the Rio Grande.

"Old Louis plans to use his French Navy to capture the independent blockade runners bringing arms to Juárez's government operating now out of northern Mexico," the officer stage-whispered with a conspiratorial wink that included all those who had gathered about Cristobal and Jeanette.

Her detached interest suddenly became intense at the mention of the French. For days now she had been uneasy, knowing the Frenchman's steamer lay at anchor with only a few miles separating her from him. What would happen to the Frenchman once Napoleon's navies set up a blockade? Since the Frenchman's steamer was obviously a registered French vessel, he should have no trouble passing through Napoleon's blockade—unless the Frenchman planned to continue his sale of war supplies to Juárez's armies. But this made no sense at all, fighting against his mother country, France.

On the other hand, what if he chose to run the blockade out of some other, less dangerous port? And if he did, how then would she obtain her own arms and ammunition?

As much as she wished to see the Frenchman before a firing squad, her continuing need for war matériel was stronger. One day soon, she promised herself grimly, she would have both her wishes granted.

16

"The Yankees have landed!" Through the November drizzle the red-headed boy galloped his roan down muddy Elizabeth Street, shouting again, "The Yankees have landed. They're here!"

Jeanette paused at the doorway of the Yturria Bank, thinking that the boy sounded like something out of Longfellow's latest poem, "The Midnight Ride of Paul Revere." This was the second or third time such an alarm had been sounded, and she was not that concerned. She went on through the doors and took her place in the teller's line to purchase the usual sight draft to the agent acting for the Matamoros merchant whom the Frenchman used.

When she stepped outside again, the streets were filled with people running and yelling. She stood on the edge of the boardwalk and strained through the shroud of rainy mist to see the fort at the far end of Elizabeth Street. The boy had been right! Soldiers wearing the yellow stripe of the cavalry charged through the Fort Brown's gates like Attila's Huns. Behind them rolled supply wagons and caissons weighted with siege guns.

Jeanette thought of her cotton stored at the chapel.

What would happen to it? Forgetting to open her umbrella, she hurried toward the fort. Her skirts dragged in the mire, and the heavy mist plastered wisps of hair against her cheeks. Dodging the frenzied men and women who clogged the streets, she caught the bridle of a passing cavalryman. "What has happened?" she yelled.

"The Union General"—the soldier gasped out—"Morgan—he's marching on Brownsville—with seven thousand men!"

"Sweet Mary in Heaven!" she breathed. "Seven thousand against four hundred!" Then she turned cold. Morgan the Monster. Armand's executioner.

"We're preparing for retreat now," the soldier said. "General Bee is putting the torch to the fort. If you value your life and property, ma'am, git!" Before she could question him further, he wheeled his mount and rode away.

She tried to make her way back to her carriage, but the hysterical mobs buffeted her about the street like a leaf in a whirlwind. She found herself pushed along toward the single bridge leading to Matamoros. Everyone was anxious to reach the Mexican side of the river, which afforded protection from the invading Yankees. At the ferry she saw three men pull guns to force room for women and children. A worse sight followed as she watched soldiers dump the siege guns into the river. The Confederates were not even going to defend the city!

Suddenly eight thousand pounds of Confederate gunpowder exploded in a great roar. The ground beneath Jeanette's feet shook. She looked over her shoulder as orange and red tongues of flame leapt from Fort Brown. Firebrands showered down upon the town's roofs. She whirled about and began to shove her way back into the city. In the melee she lost her umbrella, and someone knocked off her straw bonnet.

The crowd grew less dense, but already looters were shattering windows, breaking into stores and houses. Soldiers were too busy firing government buildings to halt the plunderers. Smoke filled the air so that the sky looked black. Jeanette continued to plod through the mob of men and women who rushed past her like stampeded buffalo. At some point her hair tumbled loose from the chignon's pins. She pushed a wave out of her eyes and hurried on.

In the middle of Washington Street a detachment of soldiers set fire to a pyre of two hundred cotton bales rather than let it fall into Federal hands.

She must get back to Columbia and prepare it for the invasion! Shouldering her way through the frenzied crowd, she reached the Yturria Bank; her carriage was gone! It was too late to wonder if the horses had run away or the wagon had been stolen. She had to make her way out of the city before it went up in fire. Windows in the dry goods store across the street shattered from the intense heat. The store's wooden frame whoomphed in a torn curtain of flame. At that moment she heard a child's frightened cry. Through the whirls of smoke she spied a little girl standing paralyzed at the edge of the boardwalk before the blazing building.

Swerving for a runaway wagon, Jeanette dashed across the street and reached the girl. "Mama!" the child sobbed wildly. "I want my Mama."

"Ssshh," Jeanette consoled, kneeling to stroke the tot's sandy curls. "We'll find your mother."

When or where she did not know. She took the only feasible action that occurred to her, lifting the little girl in her arms and running toward the French quarter, which looked as yet untouched by the inferno. With any luck Cristobal would be there. Her damp skirts and the weight of the little girl, whose frail arms clung to Jeanette's neck, hindered her progress.

"Annie!" a woman called.

Jeanette turned to see a woman her age, arms out-stretched, hurrying toward her. "I thought I had lost her," the woman cried and took the child, who whimpered, "Mama!"

With tears of relief in her eyes and words of thanks on her lips, the woman hurried off into the smoke-filled street with her little girl. For a moment Jeanette stood still, empty-handed and alone. Where were her family, her children, someone to care about? Then she thought of Cristobal and hurried on toward her friend's—no, her husband's apartments.

Exhaustion slowed her legs. She had almost reached Cristobal's apartments when the entire wall of a livery stable crumbled. Instinctively her arms flew up to shield her face from the falling debris. A timber struck her back, and she staggered to her knees. Several seconds passed before she shook her head, trying to clear her befuddled mind— only to discover that her hair was on fire!

Through a haze of tears she started swatting at the flaming hair about her waist. A nightmare! Then someone was there, wrapping her in a coat, rolling her in the dirt. She thought she would suffocate. No! She would not let herself swoon! But blackness began to engulf her as she was lifted and cradled against a solid chest.

"*Chérie . . . chérie.*"

Her last thought was one of panic—the Frenchman!

"Tttchh, tttchh!" Rubia stood back to view her work, hands on hips.

Jeanette stared at herself in the oval mirror. Soot still smudged her left cheek and streaked a shadow over one arrowlike brow. But her hair—Rubia had clipped away the singed portion. Jeanette turned on the padded stool to better view the result in three-quarter profile. Formerly

straight because weighted by mass and length, her tresses
now curled and feathered about her shoulder blades. She
wrinkled her nose at the reek of the burnt hair scattered
over the hardwood floor.

"It is the best I can do with such a mess," Rubia said in
Spanish.

Jeanette realized the young woman had thought her grimace at the acrid smell was a criticism of her work. "Oh,
no, I like it." She ran blistered fingers through the soft
curling strands. "I like—the freedom from all that
weight." She dimpled a smile at the beautiful blonde who
looked at her in the mirror. "You should have cut it all
off."

"It would complete your boy's disguise, would it not?"

Crimson washed over Jeanette's face. "He told you!"

Rubia turned away to put the scissors in a bureau
drawer. "Kitt? No, he speaks to me of nothing . . . other
than that which is very dear between us."

Jeanette suffered a twinge of—she told herself it was
resentment; resentment at being numbered among those
women who shared the Frenchman's—Kitt's bed.

"I have put two and two together—your midnight visit
here. Another time I returned from the *Revenge* and
caught sight of a boy, with a face very much like yours,
talking with Alejandro."

"Kitt—he brought me here?" She had been wanting to
ask the question since awakening on Rubia's bed half an
hour earlier. She remembered very little after her hair
caught fire—being rolled in the dirt, carried somewhere—by the Frenchman, she presumed—and coming
to in the bed of a wagon. Recalling the wagon's jarring
motion, she put a hand to the back of her head. The
smoke-blackened sky above the bouncing wagon had presented itself to her view only temporarily before she lost
consciousness again.

"It was Solis who brought you in the wagon. When Kitt found you, the *Yanquis*—they were marching on Brownsville. He felt you would be safer on the Mexican side of the river. The *Yanquis* have already taken possession of the fort and mounted cannons on the earthen embankments."

So, she had had her opportunity to learn the mysterious Frenchman's identity but, just like a woman, had lost consciousness first! A man wouldn't swoon because of a little smoke and fire. Hell and damnation! Her feminine curiosity got the best of her. "How long have you known Kitt?"

"More than a year." Rubia handed her an ivory-lidded box of hairpins. "My husband's hacienda—it was attacked by the guerrillas who hide in the Burgos Mountains south of here while he was away. Afterward . . . after the bandidos were finished with me, my husband—he tolerated me." She shrugged. "For a while I sought refuge in the convent at Monterrey. But the sisters—I could see they thought I was *basura*—trash. I came here—to look for the only kind of work left for a woman like me."

For a moment Rubia's face softened. "Kitt was in the cantina. He arranged—for a better position for me."

"I see." A position on her back? Jeanette hated herself for her small-mindedness. Were it not for the small pittance of revenue from Columbia, with Armand's death, she could have easily been in the same predicament as Rubia. She grimaced as she began coiling her hair and inserting the pins. She *had* been in that position—Kitt had placed her in the predicament of making a choice. And she had chosen his bed. She and Rubia were sisters in sin after all.

She finished her chignon and turned on the stool to face the young woman who watched her. "You love him, don't you?"

"Love him?" Rubia asked and paused. "I don't know if I could ever love a man again." Her voice rasped as harshly as a fingernail on a file, then softened. "But I care very deeply for him. Very deeply. And you?"

She laughed abruptly. "Hardly." She guessed she must hate the Frenchman as much as Rubia cared for him. "I prefer a more considerate man."

Rubia glanced at the ring on Jeanette's finger. "You have married since last you were here?"

"Yes. And my husband is at least considerate enough not to force himself on me." She blushed, realizing what she might be revealing about her marriage with Cristobal. "My feelings are also considered," she explained carefully.

"I see."

Jeanette rose and straightened her skirt. "I thank you for everything," she said sincerely, taking Rubia's hand in hers. She felt a kinship with the Mexican woman. "If you should need something, please let Trinidad know. I would very much like the opportunity to return your kindness."

Rubia accompanied her to the door, saying, "I doubt that any stages are operating between here and Mata- moros, so I took the liberty of sending a boy to Columbia for Trinidad. He's waiting for you below. Be sure to keep on this side of the river when you return home."

"Thank you, I will."

Jeanette opened the door, but Rubia put a hand on it. "Something else, señora . . ."

"Yes?" Jeanette drew in her breath at the bleakness she saw in the woman's eyes. "Kitt has left a message for you."

Kitt. It was difficult for her to think of him in terms of a given name. He was always the anonymous "Frenchman." She steeled herself for the message Rubia was about to relay. "What is it?"

"He says that with the *Yanquis* controlling the left bank

now—and along with the French blockading the Gulf . . ."

"What?" Jeanette prompted when the young woman hesitated.

"That any further business negotiations with him will have to return to the original terms agreed upon by yourself."

❧ 17 ❧

"How long do you think you can continue to fool Napoleon's navy, Kitt?" Rubia demanded. "Sooner or later they will deduce your cargo is not headed for their French troops."

Solis propped his worn boots on the small table and sipped from the whiskey glass. From his chair in the corner of the room he could watch Rubia's face as she paced from the door, past the bed where Cristobal lay indolently stretched out, to La Fonda del Olvido's dust-filmed window, and back again. Her gentle demeanor was stirred by concern for Cristobal. How much concern? How much was she in love with his friend? Or was her concern more out of a deep gratitude?

Solis hoped it was. Because for Cristobal there was only one woman—Jeanette. Cristobal needed that fiery, more willful woman whose temperament matched his own.

Few besides Solis detected the sweet, soft core in Rubia. Yet he knew she could be determined and brave— he had seen the evidence in the way she proudly held her head, the way her gaze steadily met the eye, despite the shame he sensed still burned in her heart. And even now, with the French conquering one town after another in central Mexico and slowly moving northward in pursuit of Juárez's itinerant government, Rubia continued to work for the Juaristas, knowing full well that she could face a French firing squad.

Solis acknowledged it was more than concern that prompted his feelings for the woman whose sweetness, whose softness he longed to reach out to. He understood what it was to have to sell one's body for survival, and doubted if anyone who had never been forced to endure such degradation could ever understand. The one time he had done so—as a child—it had meant food for his mother and sister. The next time—*gracias a Dios*—the customer he approached had been Cristobal's father. That gentle-hearted man had refused and offered instead a position as a retainer on the family's estate. He owed Cristobal much.

"I agree with Rubia, Cristobal," he said now. "It is dangerous enough that you run the Federal blockaders without risking it against the French also. You could just as easily aid the Juaristas by commanding their northern forces."

"And what would we use for weapons—broomsticks?" Cristobal responded laconically, not bothering to open his eyes. He had spent forty-eight hours at the *Revenge's* helm during a nasty southwesterly gale, not trusting anyone else to bring the sloop safely to port, and he was exhausted.

He slit one lid. "Instead of making the long run to England, I plan to operate between here and Bermuda, and transship supplies out of Bermuda to and from Europe. With that neutral port listed as my destination on the manifests, even if the United States or French men-of-war haul us over, their courts will have a difficult time proving I am intentionally breaking the blockade."

"In the meantime you could rot in some Yankee prison for *Dios* knows how long," Rubia said, halting before the foot of the bed.

His hands cupped behind his head, Cristobal winked. "Somehow I think a prison safer than risking the wrath of our little cotton runner."

Rubia smiled, but her eyes were shadowed with bleakness. "I truly believe you and your wife are two of a kind, Cristobal—hopeless renegades."

Jeanette's eyes were even more bleak a month later at Fort Brown when she stood alongside Cristobal in the outer office of her bitterest adversary, Major General Morgan. The Federal general's aide-de-camp said, "Raise your right hand and repeat after me, please."

First Cristobal took the Oath of Allegiance in his distinctive, lazy voice; then Jeanette repeated the words. Brownsville was divided almost fifty-fifty in its loyalties, and she knew that many of her friends and acquaintances, loyal to the Confederacy, would turn against her. She had no doubt that she would be ostracized by the very people whose opinion mattered most. Yet she saw no way, with the Federal troops now controlling the Texas side of the Rio Grande, to continue running the contraband without arousing suspicion. Besides, she consoled herself, posing as a Union sympathizer, she could find out much about the Yankees' activities.

Even as Jeanette repeated the oath to the Union, she mentally swore to bring down Morgan one way or another. If nothing else, the Federal invasion afforded her the opportunity for personal revenge.

Still, it was no consolation when an hour later Cristobal escorted her down to the river's bank to say good-bye to Claudia and her parents. Though there were many who had refused to take the Oath of Allegiance to the Union, General Morgan hadn't singled out any Rebel family for retribution—until his soldiers intercepted Rebel mail. Among the letters was one from Claudia to her husband in Richmond with Lee, giving him detailed information about troop strength at Brownsville.

The "Sesesh" lady, a term used for patriots of the seceded states, and her parents were now being escorted to the steamer by a squad of Union police guards because of what Morgan called their "intolerable impudence." "Banishment to Mexico," was Claudia's punishment. Morgan was setting an example with one of Brownsville's most prominent families.

A group of friends had gathered at the landing to bid the Scharbauer family good-bye. As they perceived Jeanette's approach, one after another silently turned away, making a path for her. As if she had leprosy, she thought miserably. But could she blame them? She could understand their loathing for her. A traitor in their midst with no ethics, no principles.

Chin tilted rebelliously, she made her way through the silent group to Claudia. Behind her Cristobal followed, seemingly indifferent to the scornful eyes, the mouths curled with contempt. Claudia turned from kissing a friend's cheek, and Jeanette knew a moment's discomfort in facing her friend. Yet Claudia smiled sincerely. "Jeanette," she said warmly, reaching for her friend's hand. "I was so afraid I would miss you."

"That's because the Cavazos were busy taking the Oath of Allegiance!" Pauline Scharbauer said in a scathing voice.

"Mother," Claudia reproved in a quiet but firm voice.

"I'll miss you very much," Jeanette whispered, afraid she would begin to cry. "I did not know if I should come. I didn't want to spoil your leave-taking."

"You are!" Pauline said.

Claudia ignored her mother. "I understand—everything. Each of us has to do what we think is right in our own hearts. And I know—beyond a shadow of a doubt, Jeanette—that you are doing what you believe you have to do. That is enough."

Jeanette's throat was choked with tears. She squeezed Claudia's hands before releasing them, but Cristobal said in his deep, resonant voice, "You are a very gallant woman, Mrs. Greer. I feel it an honor if you would continue to count Jeanette and me among your friends."

Somehow, as Jeanette stood beside Cristobal and watched the steamer carry the exiled family toward a foreign shore, she found herself envying the respect that Cristobal had paid to Claudia. Never could she remember him considering any other human worthy of respect. Even himself he seemed to treat with a kind of amused self-derision.

She glanced sideways at her handsome husband. What would happen if that night she were to tell him of some of her thoughts? It had been a long time since she had shared any of the things she held deep inside. Her fears, her hopes. "Cristobal . . ."

He took her gloved hand and brought it to his lips. "I'm afraid I must desert you tonight, my dear, for a game of cards. With Morgan's aide-de-camp, no less. Pity taking money from those glorious soldiers."

"But . . . I was hoping . . ."

"Hoping what?"

"Oh, nothing."

"Trinidad'll see you safely home. Don't wait up for me." He grinned crookedly then. "As if I ever thought you did, Jen."

18

*"Lavender's blue, dilly-dilly . . . lavender's green,
When I am king, dilly-dilly . . . you shall be queen."*

Ignoring Annabel, who sang so badly in a pretty way, Cristobal watched Jeanette with heavily-lidded eyes. Across their parlor his wife flirted outrageously with the good-looking Mark Thompson, Special Agent for the United States Treasury in charge of all captured and abandoned property.

Cristobal knew gossipmongers whispered about her. She had emerged from that cocoon of mourning a bright, vivacious butterfly that seemed delighted to tease the dangerous flame of public opinion. Jen was rapidly earning the reputation of a Madame de Montespan. Polished, frivolous, elegant—Jeanette Cavazos entertained often. And gradually she was introducing Union officers into her fêtes. The presence of the formidable enemy at her parties kept at home only the staunchest of Confederate patriots among Brownsville's elite. And if that winter of 1863–64 Jeanette noticed the few snubs directed at her on the streets of Brownsville, she seemed not to care.

Thompson, a man in his early thirties with crisply cut black hair, leaned close to Jeanette now to whisper something in her ear, and Cristobal caught the provocative smile she turned on the special agent. How much of that smile was meant to gain knowledge of enemy movement—and how much was meant for the charming man himself?

Cristobal felt that old knot tighten in his guts. Even though he had made her his wife, she would never be his. Sometimes being near her and unable to hold her, or to kiss those tempting lips, was more than he could bear. Perhaps that was why, despite the presence of the Federal troops in Brownsville and the French and Federal troops blockading Bagdad against war supplies coming to either the Juaristas or the Confederates, he recklessly chose to run the blockade even more often than before.

When the Yankees had captured Fort Brown, he knew that running the blockade would be utterly foolhardy. And he knew also that Jeanette would continue to run the cotton and arms, regardless of the risk she was taking. He had thought that, required once more to share the Frenchman's bed in exchange for running the contraband, she would discontinue her underground activities.

Or had he hoped, a mocking voice nagged, to once more hold her, to make her his in spite of her passive acquiescence those times she did come to his bed? And what of those times he had thought he detected a response? Those moments when she clung to him, forgetful of her hatred, had been worth all the agonizing ones he openly played the fool to her flirt. If only the intensity of her hatred for the Frenchman could be converted to an equal intensity of its opposite. To experience such an overpowering emotion as love with Jen he would risk everything.

Whatever his motive for changing the terms of their business deal, he should have known better than to think she would give up so easily. Never, in all the years he had known her and loved her, had she surrendered without a fight—not in blindman's buff, or later in the debates they waged on everything from which of them had the fastest doodle bug to the shape of a cloud.

Though she had yet to visit the *Revenge,* he suspected that she continued to amass cotton bales. Her periods of absence from Columbia indicated as much. But so far the tail he had put on her in his own absence had been unable to ascertain where she was storing the contraband. What in the hell was she up to?

He let out a yawn, not an affected one but one brought about by a sleepless two-day run out of Nassau. He knew he needed to keep his wits about him; that General Morgan, the fiftyish man sitting stiffly at his side waiting for Miss Goddard to finish the wintry evening's repertoire, was a shrewd man. *The Matamoros Morning Call* had reported the falcon-faced Union general as stating he would put an end to the blockade running if he had to hang every suspected citizen in Brownsville as a collaborator. The strict military rule imposed by the Yankees on New Orleans convinced the Brownsville Confederates that Morgan would not be lenient.

Already the general had established a ten o'clock curfew on the streets of Brownsville—which meant, Cristobal thought with an inner groan of relief, that Annabel Goddard could not go on singing too much longer. Unless Jeanette had succeeded in wringing a special dispensation from the pockmarked general for the evening's party. Cristobal did not know, because he had not come in until late that afternoon—"time enough to shave your two-day beard and dress," his wife informed him, not bothering to hide her glance of contempt for his disreputable state.

He had forced a good-humored smile, saying lazily, "*La*, Jen, the cockfight lasted half the night."

Apparently Rubia's perfume had lingered about him, for Jen placed her fists on her hips and her eyes narrowed, but she smiled sweetly. "It appears you were fighting *with* the cocks."

Her barb had hit too close to home. He had been with Rubia until late in the night, reviewing the information she had gleaned from the cantina's French clientele. She no longer expected him to stay the night now that he was married, but the look in her eyes—he would rather face Morgan the Monster. He smothered another yawn. Living a spy's double life was getting him nowhere twice as fast.

And Jen as well. He noted she was thinner, but somehow more alive, more vibrant than a year and a half ago when he had first seen her upon his return to Texas. There was an elusive iridescence in her expression. In his eyes—and those of quite a few other males—she was a very attractive woman. And the irony of it all was that she did not even know it—nor of his love for her, *gracias a Dios*.

At last Annabel finished her song and rose from the piano, inclining her head in acknowledgment of the polite applause. Everyone prepared to go, and praises of a "wonderful evening" were delivered by the guests. Cristobal lolled at the door with Jeanette to see everyone off. General Morgan was the first to leave. The man, who possessed a small, cadaverous body, was even more dwarfed by Cristobal's massive frame.

Tia Juana presented Morgan with his military greatcoat, but when he reached into the inside pocket for his gloves his hand withdrew a scrap of paper. With a curious expression his talonlike fingers unfolded the paper.

Cristobal watched as the general's expression darkened

like a sea-gale sky. The brows lowered over the piercing pale eyes. The general looked first to Jeanette, then Cristobal. "Who's behind this?" he asked in a soft, raspy voice that had the edge of steel.

Cristobal arched a questioning brow at Jen, but she shrugged her ignorance about the matter. He took the note from Morgan. "A December sun in torrid clime gleamed on the Confederate band . . ." he paused in reading aloud the poem and glanced at the general. The man glowered for him to continue the doggerel couplet.

> ". . . *gleamed on the Confederate band*
> *who escaped the Yankee dogs*
> *by crossing the Rio Grande.*"

Cristobal's gaze dropped to the bottom of the note to the curiously drawn flower, with the words printed beneath it—"Lavender Blue."

He stifled the grunt of fury that exploded in him. So that was what his wife was up to—smuggling Confederate refugees across the border! As the fortunes of war turned in the Union's favor, more and more Confederate soldiers and their families were fleeing—usually into Mexico, where the French puppet, the Emperor Maximilian, who needed supporters for his shaky throne, welcomed them. Sometimes the Confederates traveled into South America—even as far as Argentina—to escape what surely would be harsh rule upon the South should the Union win.

"What's the meaning of this?" Morgan demanded. Beneath deeply hooded lids his falcon-sharp glare moved one by one over the faces of the Confederate citizens who shifted uneasily in the tensely silent room.

"Fie, General!" Jeanette rapped. "You don't think one of us would be foolish enough to leave that in your pocket? Why, wouldn't we have waited until later rather than chance casting suspicion on ourselves?"

"And this—" the general's bony finger jabbed at the drawing of the flower. He turned slitted eyes on the pale Annabel. "What exactly were those words you sang to-night?" he asked in a sibilant voice.

"A coincidence," she quivered. Scarlet dyed her complexion so that it was almost impossible to tell where her hennaed hairline began. "The words . . . lavender blue— they're from an old folk song. Nothing more."

Cristobal slashed a quick glance at Jeanette, but she laughed merrily. "'Tis nothing but a prank, I vow, General Morgan. The note could have been in your coat pocket since this morning, couldn't it?"

The general grimly allowed as much, but suspicion still lurked in the eyes when he took his leave.

Mark Thompson took Jeanette's hand, his lips lingering far too long on the fingertips of a married woman. But then everyone knew the Cavazos' marriage to be one of convenience—eccentricity on the lovely Jeanette's part, greed on the buffoon Cristobal's end.

Cristobal, seeming oblivious to the amorous messages Mark's hazel eyes flashed at his hostess, sported with Laurie Eubanks. The pale, thin girl blushed shyly at some lazy quip of his. Jeanette privately thought the lawyer's daughter wore too many hairpieces. The girl was much too young for Cristobal; was most unlike the brazen whores he preferred. Did he never take anything seriously? Her chagrin shortened her words of good-bye to the special agent more than she intended, and she hastily bestowed a simpering smile at the vexed gentleman.

When everyone had departed, she climbed the stairs to her bedroom, leaving Cristobal in the parlor to pour himself a drink from the well-supplied sideboard. Mentally she ticked off the successes of the evening as she prepared for bed. She had learned that in addition to Brownsville, the Federal Expeditionary Forces had captured the Texas ports of Corpus Christi and Aransas Pass, as well as effectively blockading Galveston; worse, the whole of Mississippi was now in the possession of the Union Army and Navy.

That did not concern her. What did were the words she had wormed from the special agent earlier that evening. What was it he had said? "The entire Confederate Government has been sustained by resources from Brownsville—feeding and clothing the rebellion . . . arming and equipping it . . . furnishing materiel of war." She was swelling with pride at her part in the effort when the agent added, "But we're here to put a stop to it."

With a little more pumping she had learned that General Morgan was intending to send forces up the Rio Grande in order to block any further cotton trade. And then Mark inadvertently revealed that the previous day the Confederate companies of Sloss and Spencer at Rio Grande City had disappeared.

That news was coupled with what Trinidad had learned —that the renegade Mexican, Cortina, had seized Governor Ruiz in Matamoros, holding him a prisoner, and that bands of robbers were prowling both sides of the Rio Grande—and suggested that a state of anarchy existed in the Rio Grande Valley. Now was not the best time to run the cotton. But she had little choice if Morgan intended to march up the river. His soldiers would confiscate everything in sight.

She did know soldiers were everywhere on the Brownsville streets. They had commandeered quarters while they rebuilt the fort the retreating General Bee had burned. Cristobal had mentioned peevishly that they had even taken over his own apartments and commandeered Henri as the officers' valet. It would be only a matter of days or weeks before Morgan's advancing troops marched past Columbia and discovered the cotton in the chapel.

She had to move the bales. Soon. But that would mean dealing with Kitt. She preferred to think of him as the Frenchman, to keep her past dealings with him on an anonymous level. To give herself to him even one more time—it was too high an emotional price to pay.

She slipped into her blue velvet robe and crossed to the fireplace mantel to wind the clock. With each twist of the spring's stem she reminded herself that the Frenchman was a mercenary, that he had used her, that he had no ethics. Still, as much as she hated facing the fact, she knew she was attracted to him. He had the same qualities that heated her own veins. He was reckless and bold but cautious. He delighted in laughing in the face of danger. She knew that same thrill each time she made a run . . . each time she had lain with him.

These were feelings that her husband would never understand. And in spite of Cristobal's pleasurable company, she found it difficult sometimes to restrain her scorn. As if the contemptuous thoughts of her husband had summoned him to her, he said from the doorway behind her, "Who do you think our Confederate poet is, Jen?"

She spun around. Cristobal lounged against the door-jamb, watching her. Rarely did he come to her bedroom. "You surprised me," she said.

"Our poet tonight surprised everyone. Who do you think he is?"

She turned her attention back to the clock. "Probably just a jokester, Cristobal." Her tone was light and insouciant. But her heart was racing. She never let herself forget that Cristobal, despite his laziness, was shrewd.

She should have known better than to use as a signet

the lavender flower he had told her grew around the Mediterranean shores. But it was the first thought that came to her mind when she decided to lay a red herring. The escaping of important Confederate families should give General Morgan something to think about for a while other than the imperative need to halt the running of contraband.

Annabel's song had almost ruined the scheme, but the note had been worth the risk. On Jeanette's last trip to Alleyton Colonel Ford had asked her, or rather the young Mexican man he thought she was, to help the Confederate family escape. She smiled to think that Cristobal never suspected the wife and three children of a prominent Confederate cabinet member lived in the attic for two days while they waited for an English ship to put into Bagdad. But then Cristobal had been away—off whoring, no doubt.

She set the clock back on the mantel and turned to him with a casual smile. "Why so intrigued by the note?"

He moved forward out of the darkness framing the doorway into the light cast by the Rochester lamp. She noticed that his indifferent gaze lightly raked her figure, displayed so vividly by the clinging velvet. Could she possibly arouse Cristobal's interest? It had never occurred to her.

"By tomorrow everyone in the Valley will be intrigued," he replied languidly. He leaned a forearm against one of the bed's four posters and crossed one highly polished Oxonian shoe over the other. His scarf lay untied about the open neck of his frilled shirt. His eyes roamed from her wildly curling hair, which since its cut she could no longer contain in a braid, down to the breasts that thrust unfettered beneath the robe.

"'Who is Lavender Blue?' will dance on the tip of every person's tongue," he continued. "Within a month children will no doubt skip rope to some couplet about the daring man—if General Morgan doesn't send him to the gallows first."

Jeanette shivered. She wanted to change the unpleasant subject. "You know, Cristobal, we have been married almost a year now—and you have yet to kiss me. Not just a friendly peck on the temple or cheek. I mean like a husband kisses a wife."

His lids drooped in a sleepy manner. "Gad, Jen, I thought you knew by now husband and wife don't normally kiss with anything akin to passion."

"But they do," she said, her feminine vanity stung that he could ignore her so easily. "It isn't just—gray doves who know the power of an impassioned kiss."

"Oh?"

Had he understood what she implied, or was he indeed obtuse to everything but gambling, drink, and whores?

"Where did you discover this bit of information?" he asked in a bored voice.

She could shock him and tell him of the rendezvous with a certain Frenchman. She moved toward him, her hands on swaying hips, her mouth curving in a smile that challenged his indifference. But his next words faded the smile.

"I suppose you and Armand enjoyed the passionate kisses of one another?"

She stuttered at the mention of Armand. "Why—of course."

Caught up in reflecting on the past, she failed to notice Cristobal's face close over like a mask. It had been so long since those first months as Armand's bride that she had forgotten the excitement he had aroused in her. She tried to recall the desire he must have stirred—was it ever the kind of frenzied need the Frenchman kindled deep inside her?

All that came to mind were those last comfortable months she and Armand shared before he went off to war. They both had known he would be among the first to volunteer. Those last nights together had been precious. But it was a shame, she thought, that love relaxed one so much that one fell asleep with regrettable ease.

As it was, the deep, warm companionship between her and Armand had served to quiet the occasional longings for something exciting that she knew surely must burn in every female. Or, Sweet Mary, was she so different from other women? Perhaps that was why Cristobal never saw her as anything other than a good friend.

She smiled at him, feeling suddenly shy. "There are other kisses than brief pecks between man and wife, Cristobal."

"Such as?"

She crossed the carpet to stand before him. Before she could lose her courage she stood on tiptoe and splayed her hands against the breadth of his chest. He did not move to assist her endeavor. Eyes closed, she pressed her lips against his hard, immobile ones. She remained so, barely moving her mouth against his. She could smell the cognac he had just drunk. After an interminable moment, she felt his large frame shudder beneath her hands. Were nice women—was the idea of a wife initiating passion—so repugnant to a male?

Abruptly Cristobal's hands shot out to grab her upper arms roughly. He jerked her against him and ground his mouth down over hers in a brutal, acquisitive kiss. Surprise held her frozen. Slowly the capturing caress changed to a searching one. His tongue quested the parting of her lips. Once again that feeling of *déjà vu*, of having experienced Cristobal's kiss before, swept over her. Then she became lost in the maelstrom of her husband's passion. The bottom of her stomach dropped out. Her knees buckled. She clung to the solidity of his shoulders for support.

Slowly, with great reluctance, he set her away from him.

"That, Jen," he said with an indolence he was far from feeling, "is the other kind of kiss."

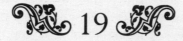

19

Jeanette sidestepped the cotton bales cluttering the narrow aisle. What little warm air filtered into the chapel was musty. She finished counting the bales. Enough for five wagon loads. She shouldered her way back outside and blinked against the bright February sunlight. "Can you have five *campesinos* ready to leave tonight?" she asked Trinidad.

The old Mexican shrugged deeper into his poncho. Though the day was not that cold, a good thirty degrees above freezing, his old arthritic bones warned that those blue northerners would soon be riding in. "You cannot wait a few days more, *sobrina?*"

She shook her head and pulled her cape closer about her. "Even if the chapel weren't bulging its sides with cotton, we still need to make the run. The soldiers in the field need supplies."

And not just horse blankets and saddles and rifles. If the reports in the *New Orleans Times* were accurate and not just Federal propaganda, Confederate soldiers were marching barefoot and coatless through winter blizzards. But amputations from frostbite and deaths from pneumonia were nothing in comparison to the savage fighting

159

in the recent battle of Lookout Mountain in Tennessee.
The *Times* reported that in that Federal victory a total
of eight thousand men on both sides were killed or
wounded.

Eight thousand men! Their lives wasted.

"You weel go back up the river to Rio Grande City
thees time?"

"Yes," she said firmly, knowing that the old man did
not approve the long, roundabout journey through bandit-
infested territory. But neither did he approve of running
the cotton across the border to Matamoros now that General Morgan's soldiers patrolled the Texas side of the Rio
Grande's banks from its mouth up past Brownsville. Trinidad had even spotted Yankee troops as far west as Columbia's easternmost boundary. Any day now they could
wander upon the chapel. She simply had no choice but to
make the run.

Trinidad reached a gnarled hand up to Jeanette's sunbonnet and removed a cotton tuft that clung to the
grosgrain band. "*Ay de mí*—you do not want Cristobal to
see thees."

"I doubt if he would notice," she said waspishly. Her
husband was still in town, his longest absence yet. The
nights he spent at Columbia he seemed more intent on
the working on his articles in his bedroom than on the
titillating conversations she was accustomed to enjoying
with him.

Three weeks had passed since that night he had kissed
her, and the memory of that kiss still lingered to pique
her feminine vanity. Did her independent nature lessen
her feminine appeal? And there was something else about
that disturbing kiss that she could not put her finger on.

The puzzle still nagged her like a toothache when she
slipped out of the house just after midnight dressed in her
boy's disguise. She always drove the lead wagon, if for no
other reason than to keep out of the dust. The wagons

bumped over rough cactus-peppered hills and through tangled chaparral on dry arroyos. The first night out the northerner that Trinidad's bones had expected hit, and Jeanette hunched around the warmth of the campfire with the rest of the *campesinos,* drinking steaming coffee out of tin cans.

These were the times when she was the happiest. The freedom in the open spaces—the unlimited reach of the star-spangled sky over her bedroll—the cry of a lobo wolf or shriek of screech owl to break the frosty night's silence. Other feelings, too, completed her happiness—the camaraderie of the men, the excitement of challenging a dangerous enemy, the fulfillment of doing something worthwhile.

More than once she chuckled to herself at her latest escapade. Another note for General Morgan from Lavender Blue. The day after she pulled out with the wagon train Trinidad was to leave the note in the offering box of the convent's chapel in Brownsville:

Five hundred bales of cotton escaped your hands; bound for blockade runners across the Rio Grande.

And below it a drawing of the lavender-blue flower. That should cause the general to froth at the mouth for a couple of days.

Oh, to see Morgan recalled, disgraced, and discredited, as Grant had recalled Burnside!

Rather than pay duty on the Rio Grande City ferry, she worked alongside Xavier and Andres to rope the cotton bales across the muddy river. From the other side Lorenzo, Felix, and the one-armed Pedro worked the ropes. Afterward the *campesinos* floated the wagons over. That night she lay a long time in the semitrance of her physical exhaustion. Despite the fringed leather gloves, her hands were raw from tugging at the rope, and her back and forearms ached. At last the croaking bullfrogs in the cozy river mudbank lulled her to sleep. She slept deeply, secure in the knowledge that one of the faithful *campesinos* always stood guard against possible bandit attack.

Monotonous days followed; days of leading the wagon train of cotton up one side of the river and back down the other, days of going long distances without water because sometimes it was impossible to get down to the river.

The laborious journey at least served to dissipate her preoccupation with her husband. Yet the nearer the wagons rumbled to Matamoros and Bagdad, the greater grew her apprehension. Soon she would have to deal again with the Frenchman. But it would be the last time, she swore. Once she paid the Frenchman his degrading price for the war supplies consigned at the Matamoros warehouse, she meant to seek out another avenue for her cotton; one she had just learned of earlier that week at a military tea given by the lonely Federal officers at Fort Brown.

A great many of Brownsville's citizens had shunned the invitation. But others came because the large Federal forces stationed there expended a considerable amount of money every payday on Brownsville merchandise (especially the saloons' mind-bending beverages). Naturally the shop- and saloonkeepers wished to continue to receive the military's patronage. Cristobal had escorted Jeanette and was his usual droll self. Between her charm, his repartee, and a spiked punch, they managed to entrance the guests and soldiers, who were far from home and bored with the rigors of garrison duty. In fact, at the end of a song performed by the military's glee club she sweetly persuaded the aide-de-camp to talk more freely of his duties. He was an intense man with gray eyes that never left her face, which made her uncomfortably aware of the direction of his thoughts.

"Despite our occupation of the lower course of the Rio

Grande," the soldier had said, "the only effect has been to change the point of entry to upper Rio Grande crossings; enough supplies are still getting through to supply the whole Rebel army."

That she knew, but it was the rest that he divulged which gave her an idea. "From the contraband caravans our spies have spotted coming and going out of Monterrey, it appears that Mexican city may be the new distribution point for Confederate war supplies." He took another swig from the punch cup before adding, "And the hell of it is, Jeanette—pardon me—Mrs. Cavazos, is that our hands are tied by the Monroe Doctrine."

"Politics!" Jeanette simpered. "You'll just have to explain it all to me, suh."

The aide-de-camp was quite pleased to demonstrate his knowledge and explained, "The Federal Government is pledged to support Juárez against French intervention into our Western Hemisphere. So—you can understand, Jeanette—these supplies of cotton and salt and other Southern goods, they could be meant for Juárez."

Yes, she could understand the Federal Army's predicament very well. And she could see that her next trip would be to Monterrey!

But first there was the Frenchman to deal with.

Alejandro watched Jeanette with a cockeyed grin. Nevertheless, she detected in his gaze a gleam of admiration for the young woman he had contemptuously thought of as a frail boy with all the courage of a startled jackrabbit. Her last encounter with him was the ignominious return to shore after her near-fatal injury to his captain. By then everyone on board the *Revenge* knew she was a female; fortunately, though, her identity remained a secret.

Facing into the winter wind that blew off the Gulf, facing the rapidly approaching great hull of the *Revenge*, she wondered where the courage was that had empowered her to make the dangerous runs through countryside rife with marauding bandits who would as soon kill as talk. She needed that courage now. No sweat broke out on her brow. Her stomach did not quiver like a mass of marmalade. Yet she was so terrified of the confrontation that loomed before her like the gates of Hell that at any moment she expected to swoon. And she would never forgive herself for such a lapse.

Solis waited for her when she swung her body over the ship's bulwarks and dropped to the deck. If she expected any recrimination from the Frenchman's right-hand man, she found none. Rather, she saw the light of compassion in the raisin-brown eyes. Surely the Frenchman planned no revenge so long a time after his shooting?

Then she understood Solis's look. Twenty feet away Rubia descended the set of shallow stairs from the quarterdeck. She was dressed in a pert mulberry-blue chip hat that matched her paletot, a knee-length cape of plush trimmed with gimp cord and Spanish lace. Her preoccupied gaze vanished as it crossed that of Jeanette. Jeanette, dressed in shabby dungarees and soil-blackened cowhide jacket with her disreputable felt hat flopping over her nose, wanted to sink through the deck. First Rubia, next her—the rutting Frenchman might as well be running a brothel!

The two women nodded civilly. "Hello, Señora Cavazos," Rubia said quietly.

"Good afternoon, Rubia," Jeanette said. She liked the young woman and tried to keep the anger, which was really for the Frenchman, out of her voice. She watched as Solis gently, almost tenderly, lifted Rubia over the railing. Envy for the woman who was fortunate to have finished her meeting with the *Revenge*'s captain battered at Jeanette. She repressed the cowardly urge to dash for the bulwarks and hurl herself over the side.

Squaring her shoulders, she waited for Solis to return.

Overhead the wind whistled in the masts, and the seagulls cried stridently. Waves slapped at the brig's broadsides. All around her was the smell of wet ropes, tar, and damp canvas. She noticed with something akin to hope that the crew, a motley collection of nationalities dressed warmly in duck trousers, heavy woolen jackets, and various colored stocking caps, were preparing to sail. Perhaps this . . . meeting would not take long after all!

Solis tied the bandanna over her eyes and the leather thongs round her wrists, this time leaving her hands before her—perhaps the Frenchman realized the extreme discomfort she endured at having her hands tied behind her back and was being more lenient. Lenient, perhaps; careless, no. For her wrists were bound more tightly.

She was almost afraid to hope that she would be spared the further indignity of once again bartering her body. Her heart thudded in tempo with Solis's rap on the heavy door. The door's hinges creaked. The cabin's warm air, pungent with the smell of tobacco, wafted over her, seeping through the bandanna that partially covered her nostrils. But her sixth sense, sheer instinct, informed her that the Frenchman stood before her. She could sense his enormous height, his solid breadth merely by the flow of air about them. Yet she would have known his proximity had they been in the vacuum of Galileo's galaxies.

Solis's hand at her elbow propelled her halting steps over the cabin's threshold. The door slammed shut on any hope of retreat. A long moment passed. Then large hands slipped under her arms, down her rib cage, over her hips. Feeling, she realized, for concealed weapons. It was a terrible indignity; worse when the hands moved up to briskly pat the inside of her thighs. She steeled her mind to a blankness. But when one hand slid beneath the jacket to cup a breast, surprise, followed by outrage, brought her to her full height, some thirteen inches short of the man who dared to touch intimately a bound and helpless woman.

She told him as much. "You jackanapes! You have not the courage to loose my hands! You know this time I would kill you, you—you scum of the earth!"

"Non, si vous désirez les fusils," replied the seductive baritone voice with a hint of amusement in it.

All she understood was the word for firearms. "Speak English, you cowardly cur!"

Rich, low laughter. And the soft but firm squeezing of her breast. The thumb and forefinger rotated the rapidly peaking nipple. She was so furious at her helplessness she wanted to cry! Instead she blindly spit in the direction of the rogue's face. Instantly her breast was freed. But his other hand still gripped her waist. She went rigid, expecting at any second the jarring impact of a fist slamming against her jaw. Like a frightened parakeet, her heart swooped and spiraled against her rib cage.

Again that damnable low laughter. Suddenly she was swept up high, high against the Frenchman's chest. Ridiculously, all she could think of at that moment was how far she would fall, with her bound hands unable to break the fall, should he drop her. She could hear the heavy, erratic pounding of his heart against her ear. Sweet Heaven, but this man was excited with passion! Despite his bedding of another woman only moments earlier! She had to give him credit for his prowess. She did give him credit, for she knew all too well the effect his lovemaking had on her. Damn him and double damn him!

Her last vestige of hope expired like a snuffed candle when her body sank into the fluffy mattress. The Frenchman meant to take her. When his hands glided her britches down over her thighs and ankles, all fight went out of her. She forgot to fight him—to fight the feelings he generated. She wanted to forget. For just once she wanted to surrender.

The thud of boots, a belt, the slither of clothes being shed. The bed creaked as his great body lowered to pin her small frame to the mattress like a butterfly pinned to a collector's board. But for that eternal moment in time she would forget that she was a collector's item, one of the many women the Frenchman took and mounted.

Her arms came up. She hooked the leather thong knotted about her wrists and hands behind his neck and drew his face down to hers. With a sigh she felt his lips, firm yet pliant, close over hers. The kiss seemed to last forever, a deep one that left her wanting more. His lips released hers and plundered a trail of soft, hungry kisses across her cheekbone, pausing at a heavily lashed eyelid, then moving to burn the shell of her ear. *"Ma chérie, mon coeur, mon âme,"* he rasped.

Beginning at her fingertips, she vibrated like a plucked violin string at the sensuous way his breath caressed and teased her ear. *"Pourquoi ne peut-il être comme cela toujours?"*

She neither knew nor cared what he murmured. Her lips parted to the pirate's tongue, which conquered her mouth as surely as any sword conquers the unarmed. But she was armed—with the passion she had to give him. And the conqueror went down in defeat before the lovemaking of the conquered. Wrists bound, her arms moved questingly over the width of the shoulders, lower along the spine. Her fingertips touched, then gripped, the firmly rounded buttocks, pressing them downward against her arching hips.

"Morbleu!" he groaned.

She ignored the oath, lost as she was in her need for this desperado who obeyed no law but his own. A self-proclaimed rebel, his kind knew no fear. But his kind would early in life know the hangman's rope. She would taste of the man—his skin, bone, muscle fiber; she would drink of his essence—while still there was life in him.

And in her. For some voice in the recesses of her mind whispered that she possessed the same temperament as the Frenchman. And that she, too, could soon face the gallows.

That knowledge slammed into her with a clarity that startled her, that left her breathless as a blow to the windpipe. She faced the abyss of death. She walked the precarious ledge that made life all the sweeter.

And so she abandoned herself to lovemaking, matching the Frenchman's passion with her own strong, heated desire. He nipped her neck. She shuddered and bit his nipple. The salty taste of a man's skin. It was an aphrodisiac. She thirsted for more!

"Kitt," she murmured in a voice husky with desire.

"*Oui?*" he whispered against a fleshy, milk-white globe heavy with the need for release.

Arms at either side of his jaw, she tugged downward. She arched her back to make her breast more accessible, and through the pressure of her arms directed his mouth to her turgid nipple. She nurtured him there, glad that she could not be disappointed by the sight of his face. He had to possess a strong face, not a handsome one necessarily, but one with the characteristics of the proud lion, the fierce eagle.

She gave up her speculations on the Frenchman's appearance as he suckled her breast, giving her an intense feeling of pleasure. "Kitt," she said again and hurried on before prudish Victorian shame would halt her words. "I want to taste of you."

She heard the swift intake of his breath. He understood her. A long moment passed. Then he shifted his position. She grew giddy with the realization of what she was about. Now he straddled her, his knees anchored at either side of her ribs. A faint, sensuously musky odor reached her and set off some primeval urge in her.

Her fingers touched with wonder the tumescent proof of his virility. She wished she could see. She had never really had the courage to look at Armand. Hard. Veined. Pulsating. Around its thickness her fingers barely met her thumb. Her hand moved to cup the rough-textured sacs that were as heavy with need as her breasts and was rewarded with his grunted, *"Merde!"*

A blind person's touch sometimes reveals more than sight would. She smiled, delighted that she had found the courage, at least for the moment, to shed her female inhibitions. But then wearing a blindfold lent false courage. She would never in a million years be able to look the Frenchman in the face should she chance to meet him in a crowded room. Never! Oh, God forbid that the Frenchman frequented the parlors of Brownsville!

A hot flush washed over her, and she groaned with anxiety that such a thing could possibly happen. Her fingers slackened their inspection. Yet the vessel she held begged to be emptied, tickled her lips as his hands cupped her cheeks and guided her. And she drank of this man who quenched her thirst as Armand never had.

20

The sunlight shafted down from the Protestant church's high stained-glass window. Its beams coalesced the air's dusty particles into an ethereal halo about Jeanette's lovely head. No woman, Cristobal thought, could look more angelic—and behave in such a devilish fashion. Too well he remembered their parting scene aboard the *Revenge* nearly six weeks earlier and the vehemence of her hissing epitaphs. Choice Spanish curse words no doubt learned from the *campesinos*.

He could almost swear she enjoyed the act of lovemaking as much as he, that her delight was no performance; yet when the time had come for him to sail, she had coldly left his bed. Averting her bandannaed face as he dressed her, she had spat, "I shall yet see you swinging from a rope!"

He thought he knew her well enough; that her anger was directed at herself and her weakness in wanting a man she perceived was using her. Perhaps he was—he knew that he was also weak; that he could not pass up the opportunity to hold her, to bury himself in the woman he had always loved and always would love. He was taking

uncalculated risks now, in order to hasten his voyages, in
order to return to this one woman.

> "*Amazing Grace, how sweet the sound—*
> *That saved a wretch like me,*
> *I once was lost, but now I'm found,*
> *Was blind but now I see.*"

Jeanette's voice broke on a last shrill note, and
Cristobal shuddered. The damned. macaw sang better
than his wife. Ah, his fair love was not perfect! Thank God
she wasn't, or he would not have enjoyed her so much
over the years. Never had she bored him. Living with
her, he was certain, must be like visiting Bedlam. She
flicked him a sheepish sideways glance, and he was unable
to hold back his grin.

Even at that moment he could see she was trying to
stifle a fit of giggles. From the pew's far end Brownsville's
matriarch, Elizabeth Crabbe, jutted her gray eagle's head
around and cast a severe frown at the two. Compressing
her lips, Jeanette seemed to be trying to concentrate her
attention on the minister in the pulpit. Cristobal smiled
broadly at Mrs. Crabbe and nodded. The matriarch
sniffed and swerved her head forward.

The dreary sermon suffered through, he stood and
made way for Jeanette's umbrellalike skirts. As she passed
near him, he inclined his head and whispered, "At least in
the Catholic church, we don't have to sing."

She shot him a murderous look. But he thought he detected a recalcitrant grin lurking in the curve of her lips.
Oh, those luscious lips! At the church's double doors he
and Jeanette converged with General Morgan. Henri reported that Morgan was disciplining his soldiers unmer-
cifully for failing to locate Lavender Blue.

The general executed a formal, half-military bow over

Jeanette's proffered hand. "Mrs. Cavazos—Cristobal," he
said. "Such a pleasure to find citizens attending church
who still support the Federal Government."

Jeanette acknowledged the ambiguous tribute with a
vapid smile and presented her gloved hand to the special
agent, who stood at the general's side. "Mark," she said,
using an insipid tone that made Cristobal want to shudder
again, "you and General Morgan must come to Brownsville's April Fool's Ball."

She turned back to the general, who was much shorter
than either Mark or Cristobal, and smiled sweetly. "That
is—if you're not too engaged chasing that infamous Lavender Blue."

Cristobal groaned inwardly. He spoke several languages
but could not master the tongue of his wife! *Jen, you little
fool! What is it that prompts you to take such needless
risks? But then, what is it that goads me to do the same?
We are cut from the same cloth, my dearest friend . . .
witless, mad humans we are, who enjoy living life to the
fullest.*

The general's steely falcon eyes fastened on the lovely
face. The freckles were misleading, making the woman
seem more like a child. But the man had always been
careful not to let appearances deceive him. That was why
he had reached the rank of general at such an early age—
and that was why he was sure he would succeed in catching Lavender Blue. He meant to retain his rank until he
could no longer sit straight in the saddle. He had no family but the military. It was mother, father, and, yes, even
God to him. For the military no sacrifice was too great, no
duty was too mean.

He smiled, a friendly, benign smile that might have
graced the face of the minister. "Oh, I shall find Lavender
Blue sooner or later. Even if it means turning the town
inside out for the renegade—even if it means playing

King Herod and destroying the innocent in order to locate the guilty. I shall do that, too."

Jeanette witnessed a demonstration of the general's grim adherence to his code of duty the following week when a continuous roll of muffled drums drew curious spectators to the quartermaster's wall, as it was meant to.

Pup tents splotched the grounds now, and the Union Jack waved desultorily in place of the Bonnie Blue. The bugle notes of "Boots and Saddles" summoned the fort's detachments to the parade grounds. Into the suddenly silent mass of civilians and soldiers walked the short general. He was faultlessly dressed in the single-breasted dark-blue woolen uniform, its brass epaulettes gleaming in the winter sun, and jack boots that clinked ominously with rowel spurs.

Behind him two soldiers dragged a fighting brown-skinned boy of perhaps nine. The child was dressed in little more than rags. But then, since Brownsville's mercantile trade with the outside had been shut down by the Federal Army's occupation four months earlier, poverty was more obvious about the city. The women were wearing old gowns made new by beribboned trim. Food was scarce and dear when available. Brownsville's glorious days as the back door to the Confederacy were ended.

In a thundering voice at odds with the small body, Morgan said, "For trying to steal government-issued beef from the fort's commissary, I hereby order ten lashes for the offender."

A burly sergeant tied the boy, still struggling against his captors, to a hitching post. With whip in hand the sergeant took his station behind the urchin, whose bare back exposed protruding shoulder blades and a prominent rib cage. Morgan grasped the saber sheathed in the steel scabbard by its brass hilt and raised it high. The blade,

deeply curved like a Turkish scimitar, reflected the sun's
angry light. The roll of the drum began again.

"Scalawags!" spat a woman to the right of Jeanette.

Farther down the quartermaster's wall a thin woman,
whose bowed head was covered by a black mantilla, wept
loudly. *"Qué ayúdale, Dios!"* she pleaded. "Help my
son!"

Jeanette turned to Cristobal. His usual droll countenance was gray. Coward, she thought. You should be
fighting. Perhaps if more despicable men like you did,
that child would not have to steal beef. Maggoty beef at
that. "Can't anyone do anything?" she hissed.

His hand tightened about his ornate walking cane until
the knuckles were white. But the voice was light, affected. "What in the cuckoo's nest would you have me do?
Would you have half the town whipped for a scrapper who
most likely has lifted more than one purse? He no doubt
deserves the punishment."

That child could have been himself—a dirty, ragged
Mexican-American boy who picked fish bones off Nantes'
wharf when his mother's job as a scullery maid did not
earn the food for the table.

"Barbarians!" Jeanette muttered. "All of you!" She
thought she was going to be sick, right there in front of
everyone.

Cristobal withdrew a handkerchief from his lace cuff
and languidly waved it before his nose. "My dear, please
don't include me in the same category as those uncouth
savages." Dared he risk one for many?

His wife stepped forward, leaving him no choice. His
hand shot out to encircle her wrist and hold her back. His
strong, rich voice rang out across the parade ground. "Ho,
there, General!"

The drumroll faltered. In the deafening silence all
heads swiveled toward the dandy leaning nonchalantly
against the wall. The man must be deranged! Cristobal

straightened and lolled across the dusty parade ground toward General Morgan. Purple veins throbbed in the general's temples, but he curbed his impatience. The fop and his vapidly pretty wife were his only sources of amusement in that hellhole of a frontier post. "Yes?"

Indolently Cristobal swung his cane up to his shoulder. "I'd take an oath this is the same urchin who pilfered my gold watch last week, General, and I demand the satisfaction of laying the lash myself."

A cold-blooded fish the dandy was, but his type of man. No lily-livered knave to go sick at the sight of blood. "I'm afraid this is a military concern, Cavazos."

"But I am a civilian, and that—" he jabbed his cane in the direction of the trembling boy who watched fearfully over one shoulder. His dirty cheeks were streaked with tears. "That smelly wretch of humanity," Cristobal continued lazily, "no doubt lays claim to being a civilian."

Morgan's patience was shredding. He wanted to get on with the whipping. Around the wall the citizens, straining to catch some word of the conversation, were shifting restlessly. He didn't want to have to quell some rowdy demonstration. "But Brownsville is under military rule, Cavazos," he said with finality, "and I mean to set an example. The military is supreme here."

"But think, General," Cristobal rattled on blithely, unperturbed by Morgan's shortness, "what an example it would set for one of their own to administer justice."

Morgan's lashless lids narrowed until they seemed almost closed. The man may have something there. An example set—with the public opinion trained against the dandy rather than the military. He looked over his shoulder and nodded his head at the sergeant. "Give Cavazos the whip," he rapped.

The stocky soldier's beetle eyes almost bulged their surprise. Then the wide-lipped mouth flattened in resentment at being deprived of the enjoyment of the task at hand. However, he obeyed the order and lumbered over to pass the whip to the elegantly dressed man whose nose wrinkled in distaste at the soldier's odor of sweat mixed with months of accumulated dirt.

When Cristobal stepped before the hitching post, a gasp of outrage swept through the crowd like wildfire over a dry prairie. The man meant to whip the child himself! "Beast!" murmured one mother with a tot's curly head pressed against her neck. "Stinking mucker!" cursed the old bootblack who plied his trade a block over from the fort. Jeanette stood paralyzed with shame. Regardless of the vile act Cristobal was about to perpetrate, he was her husband. She would not speak out against him now. But later . . . her hands clenched at her sides until her nails cut half-moons into her palms.

Cristobal passed his cane to the waiting sergeant and shrugged out of his black frock coat before he took up his stand before the post. The lad's small rib cage heaved with fright. The whip's leather lash swept upward. The crowd's indistinguishable words of anger began to rumble through the still morning air. Cristobal's pause seemed a calculated insult, and more than one man felt the bile rise blackly in his throat. But none had the courage to step forward.

Morgan thought uneasily that his soldiers still might have to quell an unruly mob. The lash snapped, cracking loudly on its downward course—and entirely missed the boy. "What the—?" the stocky sergeant cursed, when the lash gouged the dust dangerously close to his boots.

A faint titter arose from the crowd.

"Sorry," Cristobal said. "Not used to applying such a long whip. Prefer the quirt myself."

Once again the whip slashed and snaked and sliced through the air. A gasp rose from the crowd when Cristobal, ineptly following through with the swing of his arm, lost his grip and fell forward. The whip sailed through the air. Its butt struck the sergeant in the stomach. At the man's surprised grunt, smothered chortles erupted from the civilians and soldiers alike.

"Cavazos!" Morgan barked. The dandy was making a fool of himself, not to mention a complete mockery of the military.

Cristobal hefted his ungainly frame upright. "I shall do better next time, Morgan," he muttered, meticulously brushing the dust from his trousers.

Impatience mingled with chagrin to ruddy the general's complexion. "You are bungling the whipping, Cavazos!"

Unperturbed, Cristobal wiped the dust from his hands. "My methods of punishment are more subtle, General. I vow I could worm the whereabouts of my watch from that urchin if you would give me half an hour alone with him."

"Just take the little heathen and leave!" Morgan nodded curtly at the bugler and rapped out, "Dismissed!" to his troops.

Cristobal took his coat from the bristling sergeant and grinned drolly. "Sorry to strike you, old man." Before the sergeant could muster a retort, Cristobal added to the general, "And, Morgan, I shall let you know if my watch turns up."

"Blithering idiot!" Morgan muttered and stalked away.

The bugler's notes were drowned out by the crowd's boos and laughter as Cristobal grabbed the boy's ear and pulled him along with him. The boy kicked and flailed, finally breaking loose to dash for freedom through the press of people.

Cristobal shrugged his broad shoulders and ambled off toward the black-iron gate, carelessly swinging his cane. The men and women made way for him, all the while hooting at the buffoon that he had made of himself. Jeanette stood her ground, but he saw burning in her eyes a contempt no longer tempered by her friendship for him. The freckles across her nose leapt out from the deathly pallor of her skin. She said not a word when he took her elbow.

They walked a block toward the center of town in tense silence before he raised a hand to hail a hack. "I had no idea the exertion of applying the lash could be so wearing," he said, handing her up inside the carriage. "While you finish your shopping, I think I shall lift a draught of refreshment."

"Oh, by all means do!" she retorted and jerked her hand from his grasp.

"Now, Jen, you're not going to be one of those wives who nag about a little drink?"

She drew a shuddering breath. "Madame Dureaux's Millinery," she told the driver.

Cristobal watched the hack roll away before he turned his footsteps toward the Matamoros ferry. During the twenty-mile stagecoach ride from Matamoros to Bagdad he contained the misery that pricked at his soul. He stretched out his long legs diagonally to avoid the bony knees of the drummer across from him, and closed his eyes. But the contemptuous curl of Jeanette's lips haunted him, and his eyes snapped open, unseeing of the mesquite-studded hills and sandy marshland that rolled past the coach's window.

La Fonda del Olvido was packed with sailors of every nationality waiting out the afternoon's rough sea. The room was hot with the press of bodies and reeked of stale beer, pulque, and *aguardiente*. Cristobal's eyes searched the smoke-congested room to find Solis in a far corner with three more of the *Revenge*'s sailors. Cristobal could not face such camaraderie at that moment. Solis looked up and lifted a swarthy hand in greeting.

Cristobal shouldered his way to the table. "A boy was almost whipped for theft at the fort," he said tersely. "I want you to find his mother and see that the family is well cared for."

Solis nodded, but his finely arched brows rose in curiosity that his captain would concern himself for one boy in particular.

Cristobal offered no explanation but left them to weave a path to the long bar. "Brandy," he grunted when the white-aproned bartender approached.

He took the mug and headed for the stairs and the room he kept.

But the mug remained on the bureau, the brandy untouched. On the bed's edge Cristobal sat with his head buried in his hands. Was the need for deception worth the anguish of what he had lost? A friendship that overrode the bounds of sexuality. Never could she despise him more. But that was not completely true; her loathing would be as sharp as a machete—and as deadly, should she ever discern his masquerade.

Sometime during the evening Rubia entered. Her pale hands lowered to cradle the weeping man against her stomach. Desolate, his arms went around her hips. "Hush, Kitt, love," she consoled him. "Everything will be all right."

21

The cawing of a blackbird announced that soon blood-red bars of sunlight would finger out from the Gulf's eastern horizon. The denuded branches of a nearby salt-cedar mott, grotesquely bent by the prevailing winds, all pointed toward the west. Concealed within that mott, Felix, Xavier, and two other *campesinos* huddled about a hay-mounded, high-slatted wagon for protection against the chilly March dawn. They waited for their mistress's signal. Every few minutes another type of signal came from the tall, brick tower shrouded in the Gulf's ghostly fog.

Jeanette's eyes strained through that thick fog. She timed the intervals between the lighthouse's signals through the heavy gray curtain. Two and a half to three minutes or thereabouts. Enough time to overpower the pickets on the entrance side. Another three minutes to disassemble the lighthouse's lens—if the keeper offered no resistance—and get away.

Colonel Ford, who only that week had retaken from the Federals the Ringgold Barracks farther up the Rio Grande, had thought the plan suggested by her, or rather the boy she disguised herself, a good one. The same night she heard of the fort's capture, she had ridden the eighty miles out to Ringgold Barracks.

"A darkened lighthouse," she told Ford in simulated broken Spanish thirty-six hours later, "will make it easy-like for *los* blockade runners to put in *por la costa*."

In the poor lantern light, Ford's sharp blue eyes, the eyes of a born marksman, squinted at her. For one long uneasy moment she feared he had guessed her masquerade. But he shook his head and rubbed those eyes with a gunpowder-stained hand, saying, "I'll approve your daring attempt with the stipulation that you hand the lens over to us for safekeeping."

Getting that lens safely away from the lighthouse presented a much more difficult task than simply smashing it in its frame. But she would worry about that problem once she made it to the lantern room. The beam passed over her. She raised her hand, silently beckoning the *campesinos* to follow. Her worn boots sank into the sand, but the smashing of the breakers against the distant shore muffled the crunching noise. The picket, a shadowy blue figure, paced regularly before the lighthouse's wooden door. "What—hey!" the man exclaimed when she jammed the revolver's muzzle against his backbone.

"Not another word!" she snarled. At once her *campesinos* surrounded her. With soundless efficiency they bound and gagged the picket, whose eyes bulged with fright at the specters who had appeared out of the soupy fog.

She left two on guard and took two with her. Quickly, quietly, they climbed the stairs that wound through a series of rooms to the lantern room at the top. The grating of the lens swiveling above them in its frame covered their shuffling footsteps. They paused at the open door of the glass-sheltered room. In the room's center on a railed gallery about the lanterns, a crusty-looking sailor half knelt, puffing at a corncob pipe. Turned three-quarters away, he rotated the crank that set the revolution of the lens in motion. Perhaps his peripheral vision alerted him to the intruders, for he wheeled to his feet. The pipe dropped from his weather-seamed lips. His hand grabbed for a flat-edged bar to his right, and at once Xavier and Felix hurtled toward him.

They wrestled the keeper to the floor and knotted the hemp rope about his hands, while he abused them with a variety of colorful oaths. "You lubberly sons of a sea cook!" he managed to hurl at them before they at last stuffed the handkerchief in his open mouth.

Jeanette spun away and put her effort to the lens. It was barrel-shaped, some four feet high and three feet in diameter. How to remove it from its frame without shattering it? And quickly! She studied the old wooden screws and determined that once they were loosened it was simply a matter of raising the thick, multi-prismed lens that encircled the lanterns.

"Señora," Felix said and handed her the flattened edge of the bar with which the keeper had attacked them.

Swiftly she loosened the screws. It took Felix and Xavier to help her raise the immensely heavy lens drum. The keeper twisted and rolled on the floor while the three carefully edged their way down what seemed to her a mile of steps. The lens's metal-rimmed base cut into her fingers, and her spine ached from descending the stairs at a stooped angle.

Once they reached the bottom, the other two *campesinos* stepped out of the dawn's semilight and relieved her of the burden. She massaged her numbed fingers, took a last look at the trussed-up picket, and followed her men into the salt-cedar thicket. They buried the lens in the depth of hay, both to cushion it against the jarring from potted roads and to conceal it against the prying eyes of possible Federal troops.

The precaution turned out to be a necessary one, for as she drove the wagon toward the outskirts of Brownsville a detachment of cavalry could be seen against the horizon. She rapped an order to her *campesinos*, and they immediately pitched face forward in the hay.

Within minutes the detachment surrounded the wagon. Each of the soldiers, who all sported flowing beards, trained their bayonets on the five Mexicans. Fear prickled her neck, and she experienced an immediate need to relieve her bladder. The urge was followed by a rolling feeling in her stomach.

"*Qué pasa?*" she asked the lieutenant who rode forward.

"Speak English, boy," he commanded. He twisted in the saddle and ordered the eight waiting soldiers, "Search the wagon for firearms."

She watched in horror as the soldiers moved their horses forward and their bayonets came up to prod the hay. "My brothers," she jerked out, "they are seeck. I take them to the doctor. Yellow jack."

She vividly remembered her mother's last day—the black vomit, it was a sure sign of imminent death from yellow fever. The churning in her abdomen—she felt like throwing up again. She clung to the side of the wagon, waiting for the stomach spasm to pass.

The bayonets halted. The soldiers looked from one to the other in apprehension. The lieutenant reined his mount back sharply. He jerked his chin over his shoulder. "Get a move on it, greaser!"

When the wagon was safely away from the patrol, she laughed weakly, releasing the tension that had steadily built since she set out for the Point Isabel lighthouse. Wait till General Morgan found his next note!

Word of the daring escapade reached Brownsville citizens in the *Weekly Ranchero* two days later.

The Gulf Coast shores will be dark this year,
now that the lighthouse lens has disappeared.

Cristobal paused in reading aloud the couplet and looked over the top of the newspaper. His honey-brown eyes fixed on Jeanette across the breakfast table. "It's signed, of course, Lavender Blue."

"Lavender Blue!" squawked Washington from his cage and jabbed his hooked beak at Jeanette. "Help! Rape! Lavender Blue!"

She wrinkled her nose in disgust at the macaw. Now wherever did the cursed bird learn the words Lavender Blue? Shrugging her shoulders, she said firmly, "I'm tired of listening to anything to do with the war, Cristobal."

She wished she could tire of him. Beneath the concealing shadow of lashes her eyes flicked to her husband. Dressed in his *robe de chambre* of black-and-silver-printed cashmere, he disregarded her statement and continued to read aloud the news. His swarthy face was arresting with its arrogant nose, high slashing cheekbones, and thickly lashed eyes. Yet her contempt for what he was bordered on sheer revulsion; then, why did she find herself seeking her husband in the midst of a crowded room?

And she knew the answer. Because everyone else bored her. Everyone but Kitt. Oh, hell and damnation! Neither man was worth Armand's little finger. Yet, damn their black souls, each appealed to her in a different way. Kitt, through her body; Cristobal, through her intellect. Disgusted with her inconsistencies, she dug her spoon into her grapefruit. The grapefruit's bitter taste prompted her as usual to reach for another pinch of sugar.

"'. . . and with the discovery of the ribbon in the lantern room, it is believed that Lavender Blue could possibly have a female accomplice, though neither the picket nor the keeper sighted a woman.'"

Shock sucked in Jeanette's breath, and the wedge of

THE KEEPER HAD TO HEAR — P. 182

grapefruit lodged in her throat. "A ribbon?" she choked. She had been unable to find a leather thong to bind her braid and had hastily substituted the blue velvet ribbon. Later, when she helped unload and hide the lens at the chapel, she thought she had lost the ribbon. How careless of her!

"A blue velvet ribbon, General Morgan's aide-de-camp states," Cristobal added. Over the shallow Dresden bowl of swollen hot-pink roses that Tia Juana had picked that morning his sleepy eyes watched her. "Perhaps Lavender Blue's accomplice is Annabel. She did sing a song with those words that evening, Jen."

"Oh, surely not!" As little as she liked Annabel, she did not wish to see her end up being questioned in "Monster" Morgan's office. Jeanette shuddered at the thought. The general would not be a pleasant man to deal with.

"Perhaps Lavender Blue is even a woman."

Too swiftly she inhaled and the sweet, heavy scent of the roses filled her nostrils. She glanced up sharply, but Cristobal was already lost behind the pages of the newspaper. "What makes you say that?"

"What, hmm?" He lowered the newspaper to sip at the Mexican chocolate.

"What makes you think Lavender Blue could possibly be a woman?"

"Merely an idle comment, Jen."

Her husband's blatantly sensual gaze dropped to the low V-neck of her pale-ivory, satin *déshabillé* and flagrantly lingered there despite the way her hand moved to nervously finger the lacy border. She felt the hot flush of color creep up over her collarbones toward her neck and face. The kiss Cristobal had last bestowed upon her leapt unbidden to her mind. She had actually enjoyed it, though to this moment she had been unable to acknowledge the fact. What kind of woman was she that she could take pleasure in a kiss from a man she so utterly loathed?

What kind of woman was she that she could take pleasure in the act of copulation with an unknown man? But
that was not completely accurate. She knew every sheath
of smooth muscle and every area of roughly textured skin
of that unknown man. She knew his scent, masculine,
musky with salt spray and sweat, not tainted with the cologne Cristobal wore. She knew his rich baritone voice,
with none of Cristobal's affectations.

Still, shyly, in an almost virginal manner, her gaze went
to her husband's bronzed hands. What would it be like for
those supple fingers to trace the patterns of love on her
naked body?

She must be utterly mad!

Above the roses her gaze locked with Cristobal's. Did
he see the sudden yearning that possessed her? Oh, how
she hated this new side of her! She had never been like
this before she took up the damnable farce. But she had
been like those roses—a bud, swollen with life contained
too long. The Frenchman had picked the bud, had kissed
it with his lovemaking so that it bloomed into a full-blown
rose. She had opened herself to his sunlight—to the sunlight of everything. Of life. Would she truly want to fold
up her petals with the night and deny life's excitement
that was as heady as the roses' heavily sensuous odor?

"Jen . . ." Cristobal began.

She missed the pleading in those dark eyes but heard
the odd tone in his voice. There was something about that
voice. For one crazy moment she could have sworn it
sounded like the Frenchman's. How absurd! She really
must be losing her mind!

She put the back of her hand across her eyes. "I—the
early morning heat. I think I'll go back to bed for a while,
Cristobal." In truth she really did not feel that well; as Tia
Juana lectured, she was running herself ragged.

With brooding eyes Cristobal watched his wife leave

the breakfast room. Jen was treading on dangerous ground. The fatigue of carrying on her own masquerade was making her careless. He let the newspaper drop on the table. Listlessly he rose and, stretching his massive frame, turned to the bay window where the macaw's cage was suspended. "Lavender Blue . . . you must be careful," he mused aloud.

"Lavender Blue!" Washington echoed. "Lavender Blue!"

22

Plaster showered the floor. A second fusillage of bullets zinged erratically about La Fonda del Olvido's stucco walls. Rubia flung herself back from the window where she had been watching the fighting since dawn—this time too late. Dazed, she looked down at the crimson streak where the stray bullet had burrowed along her arm.

A French bullet most likely, she thought, as she rummaged in the chest of drawers for something to staunch the copious bleeding. Under the Mexican Imperialist general, Tomas Mejia, the French had taken Monterrey and were besieging Bagdad. The fighting was nothing new to the Mexican towns. They had known revolutions and guerrilla attacks throughout their unstable histories. Only the men fighting that morning were different. Not just Mexicans this time. On the streets below the motley clothing identified the other nations—Polish, Austrian, and Hungarian mercenaries. But the French Foreign Legion troops predominated. Those *Régiments Étrangers* stood out in their brilliant blue and red uniforms and the kepi hats with the white suncloths that shaded their necks.

Rubia located a lace-edged handkerchief, one her Castilian grandmother had crocheted. She sat down on the edge of the bed and tried unsuccessfully to wrap it about her arm. Blood was everywhere now—splattered on the royal-blue velvet draperies, dribbled across the muslin sheets, smeared across one breast and her stomach. With a detached interest born of the shock from the wound her hand touched her stomach, still flat but penciled with stretch marks. The marks left from pregnancy. But would anything erase the marks left on her soul and imprinted on her mind? The image of her infant daughter, scarcely eighteen months, raped in the same room even as she was raped, flashed before her eyes.

She shuddered and was surprised to find tears spilling off her cheeks. Never had she cried. Not then, or later when her blue-blooded husband shunned her as dirt beneath his feet. Oh, how wrong her grandmother had been to insist that she marry nobility. And Don Bartolome Hinojosa had been the only gentleman there in the wilderness of the Mexican state of Tamaulipas whose family was of noble Spanish birth, untainted by Indian blood. Yes, her husband was noble, noble enough to keep her as his wife, despite her soiled body.

Another battery of gunfire ripped through the room, yanking her back from her reverie. Somewhere a cannon boomed, and the walls and floor vibrated. More plaster flakes drifted down around her, incongruously like the peaceful snow that fell on Spain's mountains. Behind her the door burst open, as if blown by the powerful blast of a hurricane. The French? The Juaristas? The fear arrowed through Rubia's mind in the second that she whirled, pulling the sheets up about her nudity.

His dark, flat face looking savage, Solis stood in the doorway. He was panting with the dash he had made from the beach, through the streets rife with crossfire, and up the staircase to her room. The words that had been on his tongue—about how the *Revenge* had just put in, the sight of the smoke hanging like a pall over the city, Alejandro's confirmation of the French invasion—the words and the overwhelming fear for her safety faded at the sight of the aristocratic young woman whose beauty was inadequately concealed by the thin sheet.

"Solis," she breathed.

Her sleep-tumbled, spun-gold hair curled over one shoulder; her pale hazel eyes, lined by thick, sun-tipped lashes, were wide with fear—and pride. A goddess, he thought, bemused.

Then he saw the red splotch that stained the sheet, just above her breast. Without thinking, he crossed the room in two strides and yanked the sheet from her. She screamed. Fists pummeled at his face and shoulders. "No! *Dios*, no! Not again!" she cried.

He understood. Her fear of rape. He tried to catch her flailing hands. "Sssh!" he murmured. "It's all right, *mi amor*."

But she would not be quieted. Hysteria contorted her delicate features. It wasn't the hysteria but the blood that he saw pouring from the wound in her arm that made his palm snap across her face. Her head jerked with the impact and her body splayed across the bed.

Immediately Solis crawled over to kneel at her side. He could see by the glazed pupils that her hysteria had been replaced by a numbed curiosity. He forced himself to forget the small, exposed milk-white breasts that rose and fell rapidly, contrasting so with the swarthy pendulous ones of the Indian women he had known. For the briefest of seconds his observant gaze skimmed over the apex of her legs mounded by a golden moss. Then he turned his attention to the wound in her arm that looked as if it had been gouged by a slicing rapier.

He ripped the sheet down one edge, saying softly, "The French will soon occupy Bagdad." Talking, maybe it

would calm her. "If not by tonight, then tomorrow most
certainly." He lifted the dead weight of her arm and began to wrap the wound with the muslin strip. "You can't
stay here. Sooner or later you'll be identified as working
with the Juaristas. Kitt can take you on the next run out—
to Bermuda, Cuba, the Bahamas—anywhere you wish."

Her eyes blinked. Sanity restored? "No. I belong here.
I was born in Mexico. My daughter was born here. And
died here. I will die here, Solis."

A child? How had her daughter died? Some fatal childhood disease like the pox? It took eighty-six percent of the
infants in the Indian villages like his.

He knotted the strip, and she winced. "You will live to
be a very old lady and tell about the French intervention
before you die," he said gently. "But in the meantime you
must leave. You can come back after the fighting is over."

"Will Mexico's fighting ever end?" she asked in a distant voice. Then her eyes focused on his intense face, just
above hers. Unconsciously her hand slipped up to stroke
the hollow beneath one high cheekbone. "No, I will fight
in my own way, Solis. These wars—these revolutions—
the guerrilla *bandidos*—they must come to an end one
day. So families can live peacefully."

Without thinking what he was doing, he turned his face
so that his lips brushed the fingertips of the grand lady.
Afraid to see her response, her repugnance at the audacity
of his intimate action, he rose and went to the door. With
distance between them, he trusted himself to look back at
her. There was a curious look in her eyes. He could not
identify it. But at least her lips, naturally pink without the
adornment of the rouge pot, did not curl with their contempt. They were parted—and soft.

"I'll be outside the door until dusk," he told her. "Kitt
is with the Juarista commander now. But at nightfall he'll
return. We're leaving then. All three of us."

*   *   *

"Sweet Mary in Heaven, but you look bad!"

Cristobal paused in the bedroom doorway and rubbed his unshaven chin ruefully. His pinstriped trousers were streaked with dust where he had elbowed his way across a dusty street with bullets winging over him. "I had the misfortune to be visiting a—"

"Don't tell me," Jeanette said from the bed, "a brothel." She laid aside the newspaper she had been reading. It carried the latest news of General Sherman's devastating march through Georgia, his Federal troops destroying everything like a plague of locusts. Atlanta, the Confederacy's military depot, lay in his way. The question was how long the city could hold out against Sherman. How long could Brownsville hold out against General Morgan? How long could Matamoros hold out against the French?

How long could she hold out against the Frenchman?

"Well, yes," Cristobal drawled, "as a matter of fact, it was a brothel. That's what I wanted to talk to you about."

He paused, and she raised a brow. "Yes?"

"Why the devil don't you wear a nightcap, Jen?"

Self-consciously her hand went up to her hair where it lay upon her soft pink nightdress. She shoved it back behind her shoulder. "That's totally irrelevant to our conversation."

"Right, of course. Well, curse it, Jen, this is a highly irregular conversation. But, this brothel's across the river in Mexico." He glanced sheepishly at his scuffed boots. "And I was—uh, there when the French overran it this morning. You heard the fighting?"

"Yes. Do get on with it, Cristobal. I'm tired."

"It's my friend—"

"A woman, no doubt."

"Well, yes—anyway, Jen, I'm concerned about her safety."

"I would think your friend would be thrilled about the

fortune she could make servicing the French soldiers."

An unholy light flickered in Cristobal's eyes. A demonic grin played on his lips. "Indeed, Jen, Frenchmen are rumored to make marvelous lovers, aren't they?"

She blanched. Did he know about the blockade runner? "Are they?"

"Armand was a Frenchman." He stepped into the room. "*You* tell me."

At his approach she pulled the bedcovers up to her chin. "That's none of your business!"

He halted next to the bed. "So it is." His fingers played with a tendril that had strayed from her hair. "As I was saying," he murmured softly, "I'm concerned for my friend's safety. I would like to bring her here for a few weeks, until everything settles down."

"What?" She sprang upright in the bed. "Install your doxy in my house? Have her here for the two of you to— to—"

"To parrot you—what we do is none of your business."

Her fists crimped the sheets. "It's my house, and I won't have—"

He caught one of her fists and, with the slightest pressure at the underside of her wrist, forced her to release the sheet. She tried to yank her hand away, but he brought it to his lips. "I seem to recall that nicely folded billet Mark Thompson passed you in front of Kleiber's Drugstore. If I don't mind you meeting with your paramour, you certainly shouldn't—"

"He's not my—there's a difference." That conceited bore and his ridiculous note suggesting an assignation! "I don't meet him in my house. Any more than I'll allow you to—"

"Jen, dearest, it's only for a few weeks. It's her safety I'm concerned about—more than her body. I thought you were above being small-minded. Don't tell me I have married another Elizabeth Crabbe."

He released her hand, and she rubbed her wrist, as if his grip had hurt her. That was something he never wanted to do. Hurt her. But he knew he was doing so, and she would know it, too, when the war between the French and Juaristas was over and his masquerade was revealed. Alas, at the moment he had more important things to worry about. First Rubia's safety. Then Alejandro. In no time the French would track down the boy who had aided the Juaristas. He would make Alejandro his cabin boy. But Rubia—he was counting on Jen's innate generosity.

"All right," she said grudgingly. "But there must be a hundred whores in Matamoros. Surely you aren't going to bring all of them here, are you?"

"Of course not. And she's from Bagdad. Said she's been aiding the Juaristas in some way. I couldn't help but offer Rubia asylum, could I?"

"Rubia?" Jeanette gasped.

Cristobal lifted a brow. "You know her? Surely not."

"No . . . no," she stuttered. "It's just a rare name for a Mexican."

"Oh, she's quite blond, I can assure you that."

"I'm certain you can," Jeanette said drily. She should have realized that Cristobal would eventually bed one of the most beautiful prostitutes in the Valley! Rubia could identify her as the boy blockade runner. And if Rubia was working for the Mexican liberals, the Juaristas, then she was in actuality aligned with the Yankees—and against the Confederacy. Which made the two women enemies.

Yet somehow Jeanette knew she could trust her. Instinctively she liked her, despite the irony that Rubia shared the embraces of the two men in Jeanette's life.

"Yes, you may bring her," she agreed, unable to fathom her reluctance. Surely it did not bother her—that Rubia shared Kitt's bed. Certainly no more than it bothered her that Rubia shared Cristobal's bed!

* * *

"Even a pelican has better manners than you, Washington."

Sitting in the wing-back chair, Jeanette lifted her gaze from the altar cloth she embroidered to fix on Cristobal. With the utmost unconcern for his nipped finger, he once more inserted his hand through the cage's open door. "That's it, Washington," he gently coaxed. "Step aboard. Walk ye ol' gangplank."

The badly knotted embroidery work dropped to her lap while she watched in surprise as the macaw actually permitted Cristobal to remove him from the cage. Traitorous bird, she thought. The macaw pecked her hand into a sieve whenever she tried to remove him from his cage.

Cristobal, wearing the elegant plum-colored jacket that he had donned earlier for dinner, set the bird on his shoulder. If only Washington would leave bird droppings on the jacket. Jeanette still smarted from Rubia's installation at Columbia earlier that afternoon. Oh, the young woman was polite and gracious and, judging by the idle conversation at dinner, seemed well educated. Not at all what one would expect from a—

Jeanette blinked and tried to return her attention to the embroidered mess. She wished she wasn't so small-minded about Rubia. She knew that under other circumstances she would have liked her very much. And the woman had not betrayed her recognition of Jeanette; rather, she had given her a reassuring wink at the introduction.

Jeanette told herself that it was simply all the attention being paid the lovely wounded refugee. Both Trinidad and Tia Juana hovered over Rubia, awaiting the slightest wish from the soft-spoken woman. And the woman was not really a cousin—not really related in any way to Trinidad Cervantes.

Why, Trinidad and Tia Juana had never showered that

much concern on her! It was bad enough that her husband devoted an inordinate amount of attention to Rubia. Even now—with the ungodly bird perched on his shoulder—he swept a bow before Rubia, who reclined on the sofa. With a delighted laugh she clapped her hands, murmuring, *"Bravissimo!"*

That was the core of the problem. Rubia was involved with both Cristobal and the Frenchman. Jeanette jabbed at the altar cloth, tangling the thread. She was jealous of Rubia! Now shame did wash over her. Why couldn't she be different? Why couldn't she be content to be a lady? A true lady. A grand lady, as she intuitively suspected Rubia was.

The door knocker interrupted her thoughts, and Tia Juana waddled over to the door. A moment later Mark Thompson appeared in the parlor's doorway, his hat tucked courteously beneath his arm, his military bearing ramrod stiff.

"Help!" cried Washington, poking his beak in the aide-de-camp's direction.

Mark ignored the macaw. Instead his keen-eyed glance took in Cristobal sitting on the sofa's arm near Rubia. "You seemed surprised to see me, Lieutenant Thompson," Cristobal drawled.

Mark arched one contemptuous brow. "Quite, Mr. Cavazos. We were under the impression that you spent your leisure time elsewhere."

"And no doubt you came to keep my wife company?"

Jeanette glanced sharply at Cristobal, not quite certain she had interpreted correctly the saber edge in his voice. Before Mark could reply, Cristobal continued, "I do wish you would check on Jen now and then. I worry about her being alone in my absence— I write articles, you know, and perforce must travel."

"And I'm sure you do an extraordinary amount of research," Mark said, not bothering to hide his sarcasm.

"Oh, yes. If I could tell you all the places my research takes—"

"Cristobal," Jeanette intervened before he could launch into some colorful account of his afternoons spent in cantinas and cathouses. She knew very well that he would take great delight in discomforting the officer. She laid aside her embroidery, saying, "We have a guest who should be introduced to Mark."

In the midst of making the introductions, she missed Cristobal's narrow-eyed reaction to her free use of the officer's given name. Mark bent over Rubia's fingertips with a polite phrase of acknowledgment, then turned to Jeanette. "Madam, one of our units—the Thirty-seventh Illinois Infantry—has decided on the spur of the moment to have a starvation party tomorrow night."

More parties. The starvation parties were the latest fad of the elite who had sacrificed luxuries since the war's inception. With rumors and reports of losses and defeats on both sides flying like birds of omen, people seemed obsessed with gaiety, very much like Paris at the height of the French Revolution.

"I would like to invite you," Mark finished. His glance swept over Cristobal. "And your husband and guest, of course."

Something perverse made Jeanette hasten to reply, "How marvelous! But I'm afraid Rubia has been ill. And, naturally, my husband has other plans. Isn't Tuesday night your—er, card night, dear?"

"Quite so," Cristobal replied carelessly. "But do enjoy yourself, Jen. Whatever do you serve as refreshments at a starvation party—water from the Rio Grande?" His chortle made Jeanette wince.

"Hardly," Mark said, relaxing now, his smile contemptuous. Jeanette's husband really was a mucker. "We've managed to secure several kegs of bay rum."

Cristobal stroked the bird, who nervously walked the

length of his shoulder. "No doubt from the stores of block-ade runners your ships have captured."

From experience Cristobal knew that the thirst of Southern politicians waxed greater those days. Meat des-tined for starving Southern families was allowed to spoil on island wharves and wounded soldiers went without quinine and chloroform, while blockade-running captains carried sherry and cigars and silks.

"Captured—and confiscated," the special agent stated.

Sensing more verbal combat was underway, Jeanette took Mark's arm, steering him toward the door. "Do count on me to come, Mark." She leaned closer into the man, adding softly, "It seems months since I've danced."

She might glean much from the starvation party. She would like to know how soon before the Union soldiers finished the narrow-gauged railroad they were building from Brazos Santiago to ease their transportation prob-lems.

When she returned to the parlor Cristobal was busy talking to Rubia while he stroked and petted the irascible macaw. Despite her husband's surface charm, he really was detestable. What Rubia saw in Cristobal was beyond her.

23

El Valle de los Gigantes. The Valley of the Giants. The giants were the 7,800-foot-high *Cerro de la Mitra* and the 5,800-foot-high crests of the *Cerro de la Cella,* or Saddle Mountain, which totally surrounded the provincial city of Monterrey, Mexico.

When the first scattered jacales of Monterrey's outskirts came into sight, wavering in the hot blast of the summer sun, Jeanette halted her wagon along a rocky arroyo that barely trickled with water. She relaxed her grip on the British Enfield for what seemed like the first time since she left Columbia. For more than five days she and her *campesinos* had traversed the 135 miles of savanna, wind-whipped desert, and fertile valley, constantly on guard against Mexican renegades, French troops, and Juarista bands.

Several times a day they passed other caravans laden with contraband—long files of trotting, jingling pack mules, broken-down hay carts, and ox drivers who whipped their bony animals ahead of them. Because of the scarcity of water, Trinidad had exhorted her to look for water holes rimmed by animal tracks, but unpolluted by their corpses.

Sand gritted in her eyes and abraded her tongue. Despite her hat, the sun baked her skin. How would she explain her burned skin to Cristobal? That she and her latest lover had spent days frolicing in the sun? But then he never bothered to ask about her absences, as she kept quiet about his.

Merely to share the same house with the cruel, worthless representative of the human race was often more than she could endure. If only for that reason she had sacrificed attending the starvation party. One more week in the house with Cristobal and Rubia would have been too much. Instead she had elected finally to make the cotton run to Monterrey.

More than once she wondered if the journey to Monterrey was worth the agony. The excitement she always experienced before departure paled beneath the hot sun, evaporated like the countryside's dry water holes. But she had only to remember Armand—the Confederacy—Robert E. Lee—Morgan. Mere words, yet they carried emotional weight for her. She could—and would—do no less than the thousands of gallant men. When the war was over, perhaps she would return to the staid life of a woman.

The idea appalled her.

She flexed her stiff fingers, then took off her sweat-stained hat. Her braid tumbled free to bounce against the small of her back. She leaned against a cotton bale and fanned herself while she waited with the *campesinos* for Juan to return from his scouting of Monterrey. The Old World city's cathedral spires glinted in the distance like beckoning fingers of gold. Why then did cold ripples of foreboding lap at her feet? Surely the danger of dealing with the mercantile houses of Monterrey could not be as bad as the horror of debasing her own body and mind that she had undergone in dealing with the Frenchman.

"*Señora!*" At Pedro's call, her gaze swung in the direction he pointed. Wisps of dust smoked the air between them and the city. Not enough dust for a band of horses to kick up. And drifting too slowly even for one horse. A relieved sigh escaped her cracked lips. Most likely the burro Juan had taken. In the twenty-odd minutes more she waited for Juan she made up her mind that once the negotiations were finished she would rent a hotel room, take a long, leisurely bath, and consume a heaping plate of Monterrey's spiciest enchiladas. And she would sleep off the replete evening while her *campesinos* made their rounds of the cantinas. Tomorrow would be soon enough to start back with the supply of firearms and medicines.

Juan's handlebar mustache drooped with a heavy coating of sweat and dust when he slid off the burro and crossed to her wagon. Respectfully he doffed the sombrero, though she doubted she resembled a woman in any way at that moment. "French Legionnaires—they corral at every street corner, señora."

"But what about the British firm—Knight & Knight?" she prompted, curbing her impatience.

"The *Ingles*—they have no firearms, no one does. The firearms go out as quickly as they come in. But the *Ingles*, they have gunpowder. They will sell us the gunpowder for the cotton."

She rifled through her memory and recalled that two powder mills operated out of San Antonio. Not that much out of the way from the Brownsville–Alleyton run. "Let's dump the bales on Knight & Knight."

Jeanette led her caravan into Monterrey toward Plaza Zaragoza, the center of town. The façades of the centuries-old homes they passed faced shyly backward, toward their patios. She shifted uneasily on the wagon seat. Even the burros seemed restive and tossed their heads nervously as they plodded past the Baroque cathedral and

down one of Monterrey's narrow old streets bordered by
the two-story colonial Spanish homes that blocked the
sunlight. Once Jeanette had to rein the wagon flat against
a time-darkened, gray stucco house in order to allow a
diligence to edge past.

Just beyond the residential section mercantile warehouses crowded both sides of the wider cobblestone
streets. She and Juan went inside the corrugated-roofed
establishment of Knight & Knight, of Charleston and
Liverpool. Heat suffused the warehouse piled high with
crates, boxes, and barrels labeled misleadingly with contents such as dry goods, combustibles, and lard, which
she had learned was usually packed with Boston pistols.

She was grateful for the dim interior as she approached
the desk stacked with ledgers and sheaths of letters. A
balding man looked up over the wire-rimmed glasses
perched on the end of his nose. "Yes?" he asked in a
clipped accent.

Resorting to broken Spanish, she quickly negotiated the
deal. A Mexican clerk, small and as impeccably dressed as
the Britisher, hovered in the background, recording the
transaction into Spanish for the government's records.
Jeanette should have been pleased that she had obtained
the astronomical price of ninety-five cents per pound of
cotton against the gunpowder, but something in the way
the Mexican clerk's nut-brown eyes studied her made her
even more uneasy—uneasy enough to postpone that
thought of a hot bath and dinner and a restful night at the
Gran Ancira Hotel. She sensed she would sleep better
that night on the desert with the howling of the *lobos*, the
great Mexican gray wolves, for company than in one of
Monterrey's sheeted beds.

The sun was rocking over the western peaks when she
snapped the whip over the burros' backs and headed the
wagons out on the dusty road north to Matamoros and
Brownsville. Even after dusk descended across the alka-

line desert, she drove steadily onward. A silly feminine notion, she told herself, that uneasy feeling that grew steadily worse in the Knight & Knight warehouse in Monterrey. The British speculator was faultless in his negotiations with her, regardless of whether he believed her to be a dirty Mexican boy representing a substantial American firm or a young *bandido* who stole the contraband. Yes, it was a silly feminine notion.

A sliver of a moon lit the camp that night. Jeanette ate little of the tinned jelly with biscuits and highly salted smoked bacon. Neither did her *campesinos*. They sat around the orange tongues of the campfire, talking desultorily. "Ahh, she was a flashing-eyed dark beauty," Emilio said of the maiden he had glimpsed in a Monterrey doorway. "I tell you the Monterrey cantinas offer the highest monte stakes," Xavier proclaimed knowledgeably, though the young Mexican had yet to enter one.

She sat off by herself, leaning against a wagon wheel, and half-listened to the yarns they spun. For once she did not want to join in their camaraderie. Instead she cradled the Enfield in her arms and peered into the darkness beyond the comfortable perimeter of firelight. She still could not shake the feeling of foreboding. When it came time for the men to turn into their bedrolls, she stationed two more guards about the camp and elected to share the first watch herself.

But it had been a long, arduous trek from Brownsville with no layover for rest. The physical and mental strain dropped each guard's chin against his chest in slumber. Her own lids slid closed, and her hand dropped from the rifle stock. The Enfield's barrel dangerously nosed the sand when the ping of the first shot creased the air.

She snapped to her feet. Her knees almost buckled from the numbness of sitting in one position so long. Too late she swung the rifle up to her shoulder, her gaze sweeping rapidly about her. Even as she encountered the

glittering eyes of a hundred or so shadowy forms encir-
cling the camp, a hand jerked the Enfield from her hands.
Arms encircled her waist. Then shouts of confusion, oaths,
and commands broke out all around her. She screeched
her ire and kicked and flailed her arms and legs at the two
men who sought to constrain her.

"Híjole una mujer!" shouted one when her hat tumbled
off and her braid swung loose—at the same instant another's fist clipped her jaw. Blues and reds and greens
splintered kaleidoscopically behind her eyes. The stab-
bing pain vanished with her consciousness.

Wild gusts of wind, carrying sharp grains of sand, pelted
the men and animals that straggled across the desert.
Tumbleweed bounced against the wagon wheels. Jeanette
pulled the cork from her canteen. When she turned the
canvas-covered container upside down, a few drops wa-
tered the rim. The Mexican, who had been put in charge
of her wagon, sniggered. His yellow teeth gleaming
against the bristly beard, he hauled in on the reins and
offered her his canteen. She shook her head in repulsion.

"You no wanna drink after stinking Mexican, eh?" he
grinned. "But tonight—you lay beneath one." He snorted
again. "You lay beneath many. Well, you stink, too. So it
will not be so bad, eh, woman?"

It would be unbearable. But she had borne one man's
rape, though she doubted the Frenchman would call it
that. Could she not bear several? She wondered. She had
heard of women hemorrhaging after multiple rape. She
shivered despite the full blaze of the sun that left her head
pounding and a fever running through her body.

She avoided the leering man beside her and kept her
gaze trained on the motley line of Mexican gunmen strung
out ahead of her wagon. She knew she was safe, even
through the night, until the caravan reached the Sierra
Madre Mountains and the Huasteca Canyon of which the

pistolero had spoken. Before then the band of Juaristas could not afford to halt for fear of running into other depredators who wanted gunpowder as badly as they—namely the insidious revolutionary bands or the French troops who scoured the countryside looking for Juárez's government, which was in hiding somewhere in the desolation of northern Mexico. And soon she would know where.

She had been right about her foreboding. She knew now the Mexican clerk must have tipped off the Juarista band about her caravan of gunpowder leaving Monterrey. The Juarista who now drove her wagon told her as much. "He is our—*intelligencia, entiendes?*"

Yes, she understood. The man took *mordida,* a bribe, to notify the Juaristas whenever wagon loads of supplies that the Juaristas needed left Monterrey. The Juaristas had given her teamsters the choice of joining the band or crossing the barren desert on foot. The memory of sun-bleached bones along the desert route had quickly decided the teamsters. Her, they had given no choice. She was to provide their amusement.

The approach of nightfall did not halt the Juaristas. But the Sierra Madres loomed dangerously closer for Jeanette. Just in front of her a Juarista's horse stumbled and would not rise. The Mexican driving her wagon swerved the large wooden wheels around the prone animal, and a few seconds later she heard the crack of a pistol shot. She shuddered and squinched her eyes, but behind her lids her imagination conjured up too vividly what must have happened. She feared she was going to be humiliatingly ill again.

Although the sun had long since dropped behind western peaks, heat still shimmered up off the desert. Overhead even the stars seemed to burn hot. Now she wished she had drunk from the Juarista's canteen. The tip of her tongue darted out to moisten her cracked lips. "Water—

please." The words whispered from her parched throat.

"Ah, maybe now you will be good to me, eh?" He threw an arm around her shoulder and his hand groped among the ties of her buckskin shirt, seeking entrance. His callused fingers found her breast.

What did it matter? Another man had touched her, and she had survived. What was one more—or ten more—as long as her lungs continued to expand with the precious breath of life? Then she pitched forward.

Cursing, the Mexican maneuvered the wagon's reins with one hand while he shifted her back against the seat. He had felt the heat rising off her breast. Sunstroke. Awkwardly he flipped the cork from his canteen and held its lip against her mouth. She really wasn't that pretty. Burned skin, matted hair, blistered lips. Except for the eyes. Whenever the *puta* lowered herself to glance at him. Unusual color. She coughed, choking on the brackish water. He grinned. She would live. Long enough at least for him to empty himself into her later that night.

During the long night the caravan of wagons snaked upward through the canyons of the Sierra Madres filled with straggly pine trees. Every so often the Juarista peered through the dark at the woman who slumped against him. Her soft moans and shallow breathing informed him that she continued to live. But when they reached the Juarista camp high in the pine-shrouded mountains and he lifted her from the wagon, her skin scalded his hands. She muttered deliriously. English words he wasn't sure he understood:

"Kitt . . . the Frenchman . . . our baby . . ."

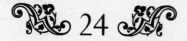

24

Music. Cool nectar. For one flashing moment it seemed to Jeanette that heaven had swung wide its pearly gates for her. Gradually her vision cleared. Above her the emerald ceiling slowly coalesced into pine fronds. Their fresh, resinous scent filled her nostrils. Instinct prompted her tongue to lick her lips. She tasted the nectar, cool droplets of water. And the music—she could distinguish it now as the most pleasant of sounds, a gurgling waterfall somewhere nearby. She tried to turn her head, but the effort pinched nerves that tapped with nauseating persistence at her temples. Cautiously she moved her hand, encountering pine needles. Evidently she lay on a bower someone had prepared for her!

Her gaze left the ceiling to sweep carefully about her. A wall of trees. Then at the perimeter of her vision a figure stirred, rose. A man's broad chest and head blocked out all else. She must still be delirious!

She closed her lids and opened them again. "Cristobal," she rasped, her voice as scratchy as the pine needles. Disbelieving, she lifted her fingers to touch his jaw. It was real. Flesh and bone. Shadowed with the dark stubble of several days' growth of beard. Only then did she notice that her fingers were wet with her husband's tears. Cristobal—crying? The self-centered, cavalier Cristobal Cavazos shedding tears for someone? For her?

Weak, her hand slipped down to her concave stomach. She knew now she had been with child. Did she still carry Kitt's baby?

"Jen." Cristobal's voice sounded as cracked as hers. His hand slipped behind her neck, and he raised her head to meet the tin mug he held to her lips. "I was afraid the sunstroke left you comatose. Three days now! *Sacré tonnerre, vous . . .*"

Her lids fluttered closed. She wanted to hear what else he was saying. But she was so tired. He was saying something in French. She really must master the language.

"Well, you have decided to awaken."

The voice, a gravelly one, addressed her in the most elegant Spanish. She tried to focus her eyes. A bronzed, stony-faced Indian, clothed impeccably in gray frock coat and striped trousers, shimmered then solidified before her. He stared unblinkingly at her for a moment, after which he turned to utter something to someone beyond her range of vision. Her gaze slid from the Indian, past the tent's canvas wall, to the massive figure that stepped out of the shadows.

Cristobal! Then he had not been a dream. He knelt beside her cot. His hand brushed away the hair clinging to her cheek. At that moment she realized her hair had been unbraided; it spread out over her shoulders and breasts, which were covered in a white cotton gown. Her brows knitted. Who had dressed her—no, undressed her? Cristobal? The fever, Monterrey, her husband, the attack—they were a discordant swirl of wind-whipped leaves.

He sensed her disorientation. "One of the Juaristas,

Jen—he recognized you. Immediately after the attack, he rode to tell me. I came as quickly as possible."

Questioning, her gaze lifted beyond him to the Indian, and Cristobal said, "My friend—Mexico's President, Benito Juárez. Benito, my wife . . . and my friend."

She would have denied the last. But hadn't Cristobal acted as befitted a friend? Had he not ridden more than a hundred miles to her bedside?

"Señora Cavazos, *mucho gusto*," the dignified Indian acknowledged the introduction gravely. "My headquarters, such as they are, will be your home until you are well enough to leave with your husband."

She had always considered Juárez just another of many Mexican chieftains, a pure Zapotecan Indian whose role she did not quite understand. But meeting him, she realized he was one of those people who are larger than life.

Benito Juárez was the constitutional president of the Mexican people, but he was more. The leader of a social movement to which his people were devoted, a president without a capital, a highly educated man—on the run. And a friend of Cristobal? How?

Everything was so utterly confusing. She opened her mouth to ask, but Cristobal laid two fingers across her lips. "Later I'll explain everything more fully, Jen. For now—rest. We'll be leaving soon. Tomorrow or the day after—as soon as you're better."

She had rested too long as it was. Although her body was still weak, her mind twisted through the puzzling maze of the last few months. Something nagged and rattled in a tiny compartment at the back of her brain. It had been back there, demanding to make itself known, for some time now. And now she sensed that whatever it was, it wasn't pleasant.

Later Cristobal entered the tent with a bowl of stew. Through her forest of lashes she watched him set the bowl

on the crate, a makeshift stand, and pour a cup of wine
from a wicker-covered flask. More lucid now, she realized
that the Cristobal to whom she was accustomed barely resembled the man who moved before her now. He still
possessed the same lithe grace, the same arrogant good
looks—perhaps it was the clothing. He wore common
denim pants and a rough, linsey-woolsey shirt. A dirt-
stained sombrero hung from his neck by a leather thong.
Then she saw what it was that was so incongruous.

"The .45 strapped to your leg—when did you start carrying a revolver, Cristobal?"

The cheap wine sloshed over the cup's rim. He straightened the cup, then grinned. "*La*, Jen, these desperadoes
are dangerous curs."

Her gaze narrowed. "If ever I saw a dangerous-looking
desperado, it's now." And it was true. Cristobal's infu-
riatingly lazy smile only made him seem that much more
wicked. Her fingers nervously plucked at the multicolored
blanket. She much preferred her foolish husband to this
stranger who had ridden over a hundred miles to claim
her. "I thought you told me the Mexican president was
your friend."

He laughed, that whimsical chortle, and she relaxed
some. "Benito is. That doesn't make him any less dangerous. These Mexicans are all a dangerous lot."

"You're a Mexican," she pointed out.

He sat down on the cot beside her and dug a rusty tin
spoon into the stew. "I was also born on the United States
side of the Rio Grande, and spent the majority of my life
in France—and elsewhere."

Something clicked inside her brain, but in that split instant before she could collate the information, he spooned
the stew between her lips. Obediently she chewed and
swallowed the stringy beef, tough vegetables, and broth.
The isolation of the tent in a mountain range in the middle of nowhere made her acutely aware of her husband.

His virility was no longer mitigated by foppish apparel. Funny, that she could feel the faint stirrings of desire for him in spite of his despicable, worthless nature.

When he reached for the cup of wine, she put a hand on his wrist. His brows arched questioningly over his dark eyes. "What?"

"You were crying—that first time I came to. There in the forest. Why?"

His eyes stared into hers, looking for the answer within her. Could he risk telling her the truth? She would laugh hysterically were he to declare his love. And for the truth of his duplicity she would hate him forever. As it was, someday—when the war ended perhaps—the privateer, the Frenchman, Kitt, could die also. Maybe, as Cristobal, he could re-establish all they had lost. He settled for a half-truth. "I was afraid you might die. I'd miss your charming company. And besides, you know how I would hate being stuck with the petty business details of running something like Columbia."

She snorted her disgust and changed the subject. "I need a bath."

"You've had enough baths to last you a week. Your body temperature was hotter than a sloop's engine room. For three days I kept you at the falls, hauling you in and out of the icy water." He shoved another spoonful into her mouth.

The word body threw her, embarrassed her. Worse, Cristobal had seen her without clothing. What a little prude she still was! Incredible, considering the kind of sordid life she had been trapped into leading over the past two years. She did not know what to say. Keeping her lids demurely lowered, she concentrated on chewing the gun-metal-hard meat.

The next day she was strong enough to stand. Protesting that she at least had to wash her sweat-matted hair, she persuaded Cristobal to let her bathe. He looped his arms beneath her back and legs. Ignoring the stares of the gun-toting men and the camp women, the *soldaderas,* they passed, he hefted her all the way to the secluded glen. Her arms clung to the thick column of his neck. For once she liked the feeling of being catered to. But she didn't like those discerning brown eyes watching her.

She lowered her lids against the intrusion of the gaze and asked to be put down. "Now go away," she told him when he set her on her feet, her bare toes peeking beneath the hem of the cotton nightdress.

"You don't think I'd leave you to the mercy of some lecherous Juarista?" She looked just like a child, he thought. A wasted child. The dual life she was leading had worn out her body. It had made her susceptible to sunstroke. "I'm staying here to watch you."

His smiling eyes, his air of calm assurance, infuriated her. "You wouldn't!"

"I would."

Obviously he wasn't to be dissuaded. "You're going to?"

He grinned foolishly and shrugged. "I've got to."

She turned her back on him and majestically sailed down the leaf-thicketed path toward the sound of the waterfall. In the twilight of the deep forest her senses were inundated by earthy smells, the faint perfume of the wild orchids, the sheen of rain-washed foliage. She had split-second glimpses of disturbed wild creatures scurrying through the underbrush—a large dinosauric-looking lizard, a chattering squirrel.

The nearer she drew, the louder the thunder of the cascading water became. But she was unprepared for the sight of the thousand-foot gorge that abruptly opened before her. Extraordinary, bizarre-looking rock formations jutted out to form the funnel for the explosive fall of water. The view made her dizzy, and after an awe-inspiring moment she turned away, directing her feet along the path leading farther upstream to the river that fed the waterfall.

The noise was still ear-shattering, but at least the rushing, crystal-clear water was more accessible, only a few slippery yards down a pebbled bank. From the appearance of the ill-kempt band of Juaristas, soap was a commodity obviously lacking in the camp. Jeanette resigned herself to washing her hair without the benefit of soap as she knelt on the knee-gouging pebbles at the water's edge. Her cotton nightdress soaked up the damp beneath her knees. She slid her forearm behind her neck and brushed the length of her hair forward over her head. Her hair muffled somewhat the volume of the waterfall. Still, something made her sense Cristobal's presence.

She looked over her shoulder and discovered him haunched immediately behind her. He proffered a dried, ochre-colored shrub. "Yucca root," he said, his breath tickling her ear. "It makes suds."

She nodded her understanding and took the shriveled plant. Still her husband did not leave. She sighed and, dipping the root in the water, began lathering her hair. Halfway through her task, she glanced out the corner of her eye. Cristobal, nibbling on a twig, watched her, a peculiar light in his eyes. They burned with something smoky and dangerous that she did not quite understand. At that moment she wished again for the old days of their friendship. But other things crowded between—her unaccountable desire for him that mixed impossibly with her contempt for him. The two feelings were incompatible. So how? Why?

When she had rinsed her hair and wrung out the excess water, Cristobal stood, spit out the twig, and bent to scoop her up. Another time, another place—a man had carried her so. The Frenchman. What was it that. . . ?

Cristobal did not let her pursue that train of thought.

"What were you doing out in the middle of a Mexican desert, Jen?"

She had hoped to postpone that question until she could conspire with her *campesinos*. She sighed. "It's a long confusing story, Cristobal."

"I gathered it would be," he said drily.

Quickly she glanced up, but his face was bland as he made his way back along the overgrown path. The best defense was a counteroffense. "How did you know the Juarista who rode to tell you of my capture?"

"I've faced him over a dirty pack of monte cards before," her husband replied easily. "He must have seen you with me in Brownsville."

"Have you talked with any of the captured teamsters?"

"Hardly." But then he didn't need to. He already had his answers. "They're not the sort I mingle with unless it's over a game of cards or in a cockfight arena."

"Well," she began, "I was out riding—with a . . . ummh, male friend." Her gaze skittered up to his. "You remember our agreement—that we each could go our own way?"

"Quite." He was hard pressed to keep the amusement from his voice.

"Anyway, my friend—uh, has a hacienda just south of Matamoros. We were out riding that evening, too far really, and chanced upon this caravan of goods."

"You ride dressed—like a boy?"

"There's no society matrons at his ranch to disapprove," she retorted.

"What happened next?"

"He—my friend—was haggling with them over a—an article he wanted to purchase, when Hannibal and his elephant horde swarmed down on us. Luckily my friend was able to escape." Pleased with her improvisation, she grinned. In the pine forest's fragmented light the freckles danced across her nose. "Really quite simple, after all."

"Rather."

She caught the derision in his voice and glanced up sharply, but he was watching the path ahead. "We'll leave tomorrow, if you're up to it. I have an engagement two days from now. Rather important one."

"Cards, a cockfight, or a woman?"

He looked down at her through the thicket of curly black lashes. "Don't tell me you're jealous, dear girl."

Was she? Impossible! "To quote you, Cristobal, hardly."

25

Cristobal flicked the lash over the burros' backs with all the expertise of a mule skinner; hardly compatible with the man who spent his days and nights in darkened grogshops and gambling houses. Her glance skirted over the profile of the man on the wagon seat beside her. The faint lines about his eyes, lighter than his teak-shaded skin, were laughter lines; but in another man they could just as easily have come from squinting long hours at a far horizon under a harsh sun. She had always thought his foolish smile made his mouth weak, but studying it now, she detected a pride etched there, certainly; and a sensual quality.

Below the hat that dipped low in front and back, fitting his head as if he had always worn it, Cristobal's eyes crinkled in a slumberous smile. "Have I suddenly grown a wart at the end of my nose?"

Embarrassed, she turned her gaze to the infinite stretch of emptiness. "I find it difficult equating the man driving this wagon with the Beau Brummel of Brownsville," she tossed off flippantly.

"I might say the same of you. Dressed in those boy's clothes, you hardly resemble the Madame Pompadour of

Brownsville parlors. And those calluses." His large hand caught hers and turned it over, palm up. "The Jeanette St. John I remember would as soon be struck by lightning than sport these."

"I told you," she said waspishly, "I forgot my gloves when I went riding."

He quirked a brow. "More than once?"

Her booted foot beat a nervous tattoo on the wagon's floorboard. "There were other things to think of."

"Oh, I'm sure there were."

Quickly she looked at her husband, catching the sardonic twist of his lips. Unsure of how to interpret his expression, she asked, "You aren't jealous, are you?"

He glanced at her before directing his gaze back to the dusty wagon tracks that crawled north over the desert toward Matamoros and Brownsville. After a moment, he said, "And if I were?"

She laughed then, a light musical note that had always appealed to him. "Fie, Cristobal. I know you better than that."

"Do you?"

Beneath the noonday blaze of the sun she scrutinized her husband for any sign of subtlety. But his handsome mouth wore its usual foolish grin. She really was fortunate that her misadventure had turned out as well as it did. True, she had to forfeit the gunpowder to Juárez's men rather than admit her proprietorship and jeopardize her cover. But she had escaped the attack unharmed, thanks—incredibly—to her usually ineffectual husband's intervention. And Benito Juárez had benevolently freed the teamsters, her *campesinos*, with a warning to choose a less risky commodity to transport.

She had issued a warning of her own. The previous evening she had hastily searched out Felix. She found him with the other *campesinos*, swapping stories around a campfire, and warned him that the teamsters must adhere to the story of her capture she had fabricated for Cristobal's benefit. Trinidad's big apelike son had screwed up his mouth. "I weel tell the others. But, señora, there ees sometheeng—" He shook his shaggy head and trod away, saying, "I do not know . . . sometheeng not right."

In the hours that followed Jeanette tried to pinpoint what it was that bothered Felix—and her. But she was still weak, and the mere effort of concentrating on anything for any length of time produced a nagging ache at her temples.

Cristobal insisted she rest in the back of the empty wagon when the sun reached its zenith. And he called an early halt that night, drawing the wagons into a horseshoe formation against other marauders. He easily assumed command, as if he were used to it. Had she not been utterly exhausted, she would have been impressed with the efficient way he handled the caravan—and the solicitous way he waited on her that night, preparing her plate of slum gullion himself.

When the time came to sleep, she made no protest that Cristobal shared the wagon bed with her; instead, with the cold air sloughing over the desert floor, she gratefully curled up in the arms he wrapped about her. She buried her nose in the warm curls that matted his chest above the V of his open shirt. After a moment, she wrinkled her nose and said, "Your hair tickles!"

In the darkness of the wagon he chuckled. "All right. Flip over." His hands grasped her shoulder and waist and rolled her so that her back was against him. Which was worse. For only a short while later she recognized the unmistakable sign of sexual arousal. It pressed against her, taunting her. All fatigue vanished in the knowledge of Cristobal's desire for her. A heady stimulus. Now her breathing was labored, as if she had been running. Like that first Eve she was tempted. After all, this *was* her husband.

The wisdom of her mind bickered with the natural urge of her body. Her husband was but a caricature of the type of man she admired. Yes, he had tenderly cared for her, but he was a worthless scoundrel. True, but she enjoyed his wit and intelligence. And he *was* strikingly attractive. But good looks were not reason enough for a woman to give herself to a man. There had to be that commitment of abiding love—and that reminded her of Armand. She had a commitment to him; to his memory.

And so she tried to inch away from the man who was now her husband. His hand, flat against her stomach, hauled her back against him. She steeled herself against the thick, flesh-stiffened brand that burned tantalizingly into her buttocks, and she prayed for the relief of sleep's unconsciousness.

"Notheeng but bones!" Tia Juana proḻounced, a disapproving curl to her full-blown lips. She had been frantic about her mistress's prolonged absence from Columbia, but Jeanette never would have known by the way the old Mexican woman plopped the cup of chocolate down on the night stand with a final "Hhhmph!" before she lumbered out of Jeanette's bedroom.

Jeanette sat up in the bed and looked down at the way her pelvic bones protruded through the nightgown's soft satin. No wonder Cristobal whisked himself away as soon as he had safely ensconced her in bed. His important "engagement" was probably another woman with more enticing curves. At least it wasn't Rubia this time, for at that late hour the young woman was already asleep.

A moment later Tia Juana rumbled back into the bedroom with the bird cage held high. "That bird—never would shut his beak from gabbin'. I don't talk to no birds. No suh, it don't make no sense talking with sump'in that can't answer yo question. You talk to him."

While she sat the cage on its stand, she told Jeanette

what had happened during the mistress's ten-day absence. "Da people are flocking to Matamoros like Moses and the Exodus. Not a soul left to haunt Brownsville. 'Cause dhere's talk dat de Union soldiers are gonna leave Fort Brown. And destroy Brownsville when dhey does."

"Morgan retreat?" Jeanette muttered. "Never."

"And I tried to buy a pound of tea—why ol' man Mc-Clellan wanted five hundred dollars, chile!"

Jeanette sighed. "That's because the gold dollar is now worth two thousand of Confederate currency."

Tia Juana plumped a pillow and put it behind Jeanette. "When you gonna stay home where you belong?"

"One day." The candle flickered sleepily in its socket, and Jeanette slid down in the bed, closing her eyes. It looked as if a child would finally force her to do just that. Besides, she was weary of her subterfuge. She missed the friends who had forsaken her as a turncoat. It would be fun to go rowing again with Cristobal, maybe plan a picnic now that summer was here. But what would Cristobal have to say about a child that wasn't his? Not much, probably.

"Aawwk. Rape! Lavender Blue. Aawwk. *Sacré tonnerre!*"

Jeanette's lips flattened in annoyance at the voluble bird. Then her lower jaw dropped in increments. Her hands began to tremble. A thousand thoughts hurled down upon her mind like a hurricane upon a ship at sea. Slowly her hands tightened upon the bed's counterpane, bunching it. Astonishment was followed by a fury that raged greater than the force of any hurricane.

Washington let only Cristobal touch him. Washington now spoke French. Cristobal did not—but Kitt did. The two were one and the same!

She swept the counterpane from her and sprang out of the bed. Her hands tore through her wardrobe until she found the pants and shirts. Her heart labored like a wheezing ship's engine as she rapidly dressed and tugged on the boots. There was not enough oxygen in the air to support the rage that fed on her lungs like some devouring sea monster. She stood on the brink of explosion. Her mind threatened to shatter into a thousand splinters.

Tears blinded her ride down the darkened military road. Armand. Shame. Cristobal. Betrayal. The Frenchman. The words drummed in tempo with the pounding of her horse's hooves. She wanted to turn the revolver's cold metal against herself. To end the hideous nightmare. But more, she wanted to see Cristobal lying at her feet, his blood staining the ship's wooden deck. Oh God, if only she had succeeded that first time! Her tortured mind cried for revenge. How perfect—how befitting that Cristobal's sloop would be called the *Revenge*. She meant to have hers. Her smile was as grim as the skull on the pirate's flag.

Foregoing the ride to Brownsville for a ferry, she forced the bay into the Rio Grande at the point five miles east of the chapel. At that point the water was some six feet deep. The horse shied and tossed its head, but Jeanette's knees pressing steadily at its flanks urged it on to ford the river.

The lights of Matamoros loomed in the distance. In the center of town, the sonorous cantina music could be heard echoing about the plaza. The Mexican town was just waking up at eleven o'clock at night. Spanish dons, Mexican pistoleros, French soldiers, sloe-eyed women with their faces discreetly veiled by black mantillas—all stopped to watch the boy on the horse gallop down the dirt streets as if the Master of Hell were hot on his heels.

Jeanette prayed. Whether to the Master of Hell or the Almighty above, she did not know. Her words repeated themselves—over and over on the twenty-mile ride to Bagdad. Don't let the *Revenge* have sailed. Don't let me be too late.

Why hadn't she connected the derivitive of the Spanish name, Cristobal, with Kitt? Why hadn't she noticed the similarities between the two men? Why hadn't she connected all the coincidences? Oh, what a blind, arrogant fool she had been!

The horse pounded through the shanty-lined streets of Bagdad. Its hooves sank into the sand as it labored toward the beach. Jeanette's eyes strained through the darkness. More than two hundred ships now crowded the harbor. Although France now controlled Bagdad, all blockade runners serving the Confederacy were allowed to ply their trade since the Rebel government and France were mutually aligned. And, of course, the French would naturally assume that the French-registered *Revenge* would be aiding either France and/or the Confederacy.

Jeanette slowly let out her breath. There, tugging at anchor, was the *Revenge*. Even at that time of night lighters scurried to and from the sloops, hastily loading and unloading contraband, for the moon was disappearing. Tossing the reins over the bay's head, she slid from the saddle. She pushed her way through the multitude of men working along the shore, her eyes searching among their darkened forms for Alejandro. Keeping her head lowered, she moved from one mound of contraband to another. Caps and balls. Cheese and wines. Calomel and saw blades. Nearly a quarter of an hour later she spotted him, heading toward a beached lighter with a crate hunched on his shoulders. She curbed the anger that raged and foamed in her throat like some corralled stallion. "Alejandro!"

Beneath the weight of the crate the boy turned slowly. "I need to see your captain," she told him. "Immediately."

He shifted the crate, which was labeled SALT in block letters, to the other shoulder. "The lighter—it will not be loaded for another hour or so. You will have to wait."

She shrugged. "I can wait, then."

She followed him to the bargelike boat and plopped in the sand while he slid the case into position with the others already stacked toward the rear. Insouciantly she crossed her arms over her knees, but her fists knotted and unknotted. She struggled to contain her impatience. Alejandro turned and wiped the sweat from his brow. "You have not come in a long time. The captain will be glad to see you."

"I'm sure," she managed thinly.

At last he trudged off. Quickly she scampered to her feet and began to push against the lighter's side. The splintered wood tore into her palms and held solid to the sand like barnacles to a ship's hull. Her boots dug into the sand for toeholds. It would take two strong men to even budge the lighter. How did Noah get the cursed ark off? It would take a monsoon's rain to lift the lighter.

"Hey! Señora!"

She whipped around to confront Alejandro. He loped toward her. *"Qué pasa?"* he demanded.

She pointed to the shoreline. "The tide, Alejandro. Soon it will run out." And indeed the laggard current was running seaward. "If we hurry we can catch the tide before it goes out."

Alejandro peered up at the darkened heavens. The bridge of his short nose furrowed with indecision.

She capitalized on it. "Here, give me a hand, Alejandro."

She turned back to push on the lighter. A tight smile of satisfaction creased her lips when, yielding to the authority in her voice, he fell in beside her. Together they managed to inch the lighter toward the lapping surf. *Hurry!* she wanted to shout. *Faster!* What if Cristobal decided to come ashore?

Then, miraculously, the lighter caught the tide's ripples

and bobbed like a Halloween apple. She waded in past her knees, still shoving, until the lighter was afloat. Grunting with the effort, she levered herself up over into the barge and, gasping, collapsed face first on the rough wooden planks. The smell of tar filled her nostrils, and the seawater salted her lips. Beside her, she heard Alejandro's labored breathing, muted somewhat by the rhythmic slap of the waves against the lighter.

Like some giant sea monster, the *Revenge* loomed closer and closer until its funnels blocked the stars from view. The *Revenge* had an odd, squarish shape. Then Jeanette realized the vessel's decks were crammed with bales of cotton mounded in tiers.

Alejandro cupped his hands to his mouth and yelled up, *"Oiga!"* Soon a dim face appeared over the bulwarks, followed by the lowering of the ladder. Deftly Jeanette scaled the swaying ladder and swung over the side. Lantern light at first blinded her.

"Alejandro?" the sailor asked, puzzled.

She jerked her thumb back over her shoulder and rattled in Spanish, "Behind me. I have a message for *el capitán.*"

The squat potatolike man hailed two of the many sailors who moved feverishly about the deck, coiling ropes and hoisting the sacks of coal that would permit the vessel to steam to its first ports without any calls for refueling.

Jeanette seized the chance and faded backward into the darker recesses of the ship. Her heart pumped erratically as she lightly ran down the narrow companionway, up another set of shallow steps, and halted before the heavy wooden door of the finest white oak timber. Blindfolded, she had made her way along this route many times before. She knew she stood before the captain's quarters. Without waiting to gather her courage, she shoved open the door.

From behind a massive desk Cristobal looked up from

the logbook opened before him. Slowly he lowered the pen and rose to face the wraith framed in the doorway.

"You slimy bastard," the wraith hissed through clenched teeth. His soul seemed to sigh deep within him like the fluttering of Death's wings. The play was over. He had lost her.

26

The revolver, a French pistol this time, was leveled at him. There would be no missing at that range. He laughed. There was nothing else to do to ease the great pain that ripped at his heart. He saw that his laughter shook her. The barrel wavered slightly, its gleaming metal winking at him like some cycloptic eye in the cabin's lantern light. His lips curled in a wicked smile. "Yes, Jen, I am all that, a slimy bastard. But I would have you any way I could take you. You see, I am not like my honorable friend Armand was, am I? *Un preux chevalier, sans peur et sans repoche.*"

"You're not fit to ever have called him your friend!" she cried out. Her finger twitched dangerously on the trigger, but the need to vent her wrath delayed the moment of reckoning.

He moved steadily toward her. "But I'm fit enough to take his place in your arms, aren't I?"

"That's not true! I didn't know . . . I had no choice!"

He laughed lowly, and he saw the small shudder pass over her slight frame. "Your body had a choice—it didn't have to respond."

"No!" she cried out. Anguish contorted her face into a

death mask. The revolver jerked spasmodically. With serpentine swiftness his hand curled about her wrist. The revolver clattered to the floor. He jerked her up against him. Her back arched as she struggled to get away. Her legs slashed the air, landing painful kicks at his shins. Her fists struck in blind fury against his chest and face. Knuckles caught his mouth, and he tasted blood.

Tears coursed down her cheeks. "I'll go to Mejia!" she raged, the tears choking her voice. "I'll tell him who you are." She gasped for air. "The Mexican Imperialist general will make certain you never show your face in Mexico again!"

He hardened himself to what he had to do. He could not let her go. Not now. Not until he found out what strategy Mejia was mapping for the French invasion of northwestern Mexico, where the rich mineral mines were located. Not until he could deliver more war supplies to Juárez. And that meant at least one more run between Havana Bay and Bagdad—unless Jen revealed the subterfuge of his French citizenship to Mejia and exposed him for the Juarista he was.

He dropped her and shoved her face forward against the wall. The breath whooshed from her. With one hand he pinned both of hers above her head.

"Oh, God, I hate you," she screamed, but her voice was muffled by the wall.

"Don't move," he warned, "or you'll hate what I do even more." With a needless thoroughness his hands began a search of her. They started beneath her armpits and rapidly moved down over her rib cage before slipping forward between her breasts. For a fraction of a second they hesitated in that valley. Her gasp of rage was like a spewing teakettle. In spite of himself he smiled. Jen had always been a little termagant.

Briskly he finished his search, his fingers lightly sliding down the outside and up the inside of her thighs. She trembled, and he could almost feel her fury, pulsating off her like heat off an engine's furnace. "To think I ever thought you a friend!" she cried bitterly.

Goaded out of his usual self-containment, he grasped her by the shoulders and spun her around. Her hat tumbled to the floor and her braid swung over her shoulder. "I have been your friend more than you know, Jen!"

"You call friendship marrying under false pretenses?"

"You asked me to marry you," he reminded her drily, "I didn't ask you."

He saw the flush of shame wash out the freckles that bridged her nose. But her lips curled scornfully. "At least I asked you in the name of something worthwhile."

"In the name of the Confederacy?" he scoffed.

"Yes!" Her eyes glittered at him with hatred. "But then you wouldn't know anything about values such as patriotism and honor and love and—"

His fingers gripped her shoulders. "And Armand did, didn't he?" His hands fell away. He pivoted from her and crossed to the cabin's bay window, darkened by night. His shoulders slumped. "God, there have been times when I almost hated my friend," he said in a voice raw with self-loathing.

Animal-alert, he detected behind him a sudden rustling and whipped around. Tears streaming down her face, Jen hurtled herself against him. Her fists beat ineffectually at his chest. "You have no right to call Armand your friend!" she sobbed. "You used his wife, you used the Cause—all for your own selfish needs!"

He caught her wrists and held her away from him. It was as if he had suddenly donned the Greek mask of comedy. His lips twisted in a travesty of a smile. "Sí, Jen. I'm selfish. Selfish enough to take you by force, fraud, or farce. Selfish enough to want you more than any damnable cause. Could you have said as much for Armand?"

"You're not half the person he was!" she spit.

His smile should have warned her. "And you are? A woman who sells herself for a price?"

Her hand lashed out. He made no move to dodge the stinging blow. Her eyes widened when she saw what she had done. Gingerly he fingered the red imprint on his jaw. "Your social graces leave a lot to be desired, Jen."

Expecting retribution, she faltered back a step, but he moved past her and crossed to the door, saying, "Make yourself comfortable in my cabin. It's time to weigh anchor."

"Wait!" She hurried to him. Her hand clutched at the soft cambric of his sleeve. "What do you intend to do with me?"

He grinned, but it was no longer the foolish grin that the hidalgo, Cristobal, had worn. "Take you with me on the run to Havana."

For a moment Jeanette remained rooted before the cabin door, unable to believe what had happened to her, what *was* happening to her. But there was still time to jump ship! She flung open the door. Solis stepped before the doorway. An apologetic look crossed his ravaged face. "You would never make it to shore, señora."

Helpless, she stood with him in the doorway and listened as the heavy iron chain slid with a splash out of the water. Four bells rang in the engine room and the sloop started forward. A moment later she heard Cristobal shout, "Hard-a-port!"

The sloop seemed to gain extraordinary speed. With hands braced against the companionway wall to steady her, Jeanette made her way out to the upper deck and crossed to the railing. Like a shadow, Solis followed close behind. She loved the feel of the fierce night wind blowing against her face, whipping strands of hair free from her braid. If only she could be free.

But there was no hope of that as the lights of the shoreline rapidly faded into glimmering specks and then vanished. At that same moment she heard somewhere out beyond the *Revenge* the beat of paddles upon the water. But sound in darkness was so deceptive that she could not tell from what direction it came.

Suddenly a warning calcium flare skyrocketed into the night sky. *"Merde!"* Solis cursed. "The blockaders are riding our wake!" He grabbed her wrist. "Into the cabin, señora, and for the love of God, stay there!"

He half pushed her back down the companionway and into Cristobal's cabin before hastily leaving her. She ran to the window. Kneeling on its cushioned seat, she strained to see through the darkness. If only it were the French men-of-war patrolling the Mexican shore who sought to haul over the *Revenge!* She could prove to Mejia that the cargo of cotton was to be exchanged for arms and ammunition—destined for Juárez! Then she could watch Cristobal crumple before Mejia's firing squad!

But what if the Federal blockader succeeded in hauling over the *Revenge?* Cristobal might be able to prove he was running supplies to Juárez, allies of the Federals. With dawning horror she realized that it was she who could be in danger. Cristobal could easily identify her as Lavender Blue. Surely the United States Government wouldn't shoot or hang a woman, would they? But had not the Confederate spy Belle Boyd been sentenced to an execution squad before she escaped?

Thunder roared outside the window and the ship's timbers vibrated at the same moment that water geysered hundreds of feet high directly before her. A man-of-war was shelling the *Revenge!*

A second later the sloop rocked violently with the after shock, and Jeanette clutched at the rough-textured abaca curtains to keep from being flung to the floor. The terror of drowning, of sinking to a dark and watery grave, ripped

at her stomach like shark's teeth. The thunder, the spray
of water, and the rigorous shuddering repeated themselves. Again and again. The ship's timbers groaned their
distress.

Jeanette huddled in a far corner of the window seat.
Prayer trembled on her lips. *God, spare the* Revenge. *I'll
devote myself to good works. I'll live a life beyond reproach.* Foolish promises but nonetheless sincere ones.

Throughout the night the bombardment continued,
though the interval between each shelling lengthening. In
contrast to the heavy iron-clad men-of-war, the *Revenge*
had been built for speed. But the *Revenge* was weighted
down with three hundred tons of cotton. To forget her
fear Jeanette tried to focus on more pleasant thoughts, but
only Cristobal filled her mind. She was in his cabin. The
Frenchman's cabin! He had made love to her here—her
eyes strayed to the wide bunk crouching in the corner.
There—in that bed. She hid her face in her hands and
groaned, and the ship's timbers echoed her agony.

She recalled the words of contempt she had flung at the
Frenchman in English, thinking he did not understand
her. Oh, how he must have laughed at her! Cristobal—
the dandy, the fop. Kitt—the Frenchman, the man to
whom she had given herself with such wild abandon. One
and the same. Ohhh! She opened her eyes to escape the
image of her body stretched beneath his, her legs and
arms entwined about him, opening herself to his lovemaking.

But even then she could not escape Cristobal. On the
massive desk before her lay his nautical instruments—a
polished brass telescope, a glass barometer, a brass-bound
sextant, an hourglass. And papers and maps strewn everywhere with his powerful handwriting scored across them,
giving evidence of his dominion. As she did.

Shame, embarrassment, anger coursed through Jean-

ette. She wrung her hands. God grant her revenge, she
importuned, completely forgetting her earlier vow to live
a life beyond reproach.

A gray dawn filled the window. Still the *Revenge*
plowed steadily through the rolling waves in its bid to out-
run the blockader. At least the blockader had ceased its
shelling. Perhaps the Federal vessel had even given up.

Jeanette, lavender smudges beneath her lavender-blue
eyes, left her watch to make her way to the quarterdeck.
The deck vibrated beneath her feet. Torrents of black
smoke poured from the *Revenge*'s funnels. All about her
the deck was piled with bales of cotton. Sailors were
pitching bales into the sea, counting on Yankee avarice to
stop and pick them up, for the cotton was worth five or six
hundred dollars a bale now. Jeanette understood more
clearly the desperate effort the *Revenge* was making to escape.

A sailor, his face blackened by smoke, emerged from a
hatch, and she crossed to him. "Your captain—where is
he?"

Exhaustion denied him immediate speech. He jerked
his head over his shoulder toward the hatch and muttered
something about thirty-minute shifts before staggering
past her.

The smoke burned her eyes as she carefully felt her way
down the steep, narrow steps. It was as if she were descending into the fires of Hell. The heat intensified. By
the time she reached the engine room, sweat beaded her
face and rolled down the valley between her breasts. In
the fire room a silent, shadowy crew of figures, Stygian
wraiths, shoveled coal into the devouring furnace. Its red-
hot mouth illuminated the room with an unearthly light.
Now she understood the thirty-minute shifts. No human
being could stand it down there longer than that.

The piston rods rose and fell with quiet strokes. Yet the
engine room seemed to dance under the vibrating blows

of the screw so that standing was nigh impossible. Jean-ette staggered against the wall. The hot metal rib burned her fingers and she gasped with pain. A hand seized her wrist and dragged her up out of the hellhole. The fresh salt air hit her. Her face tilted upward, and she greedily gulped in air like a beached fish.

"You were told to stay in the cabin," Cristobal gritted at her side.

Without waiting for her reply, he hauled her back up the companionway stairs toward his cabin. She tried to tug loose, but he shoved her inside and stood with fists on hips, coolly surveying her as if the two of them had never come together in the intimate act of love. The mouth she had always thought of as handsome but weak was stretched into an implacable line by the grooves of fatigue at either side. Soot blackened the hollows of his jaws, and sweat sheened his swarthy skin. His dark eyes watched her with a grim-ness that frightened her.

Would he demand of her what she had so easily given him? Worse, would he betray her to the Federal Govern-ment if she refused to comply? She could not bring herself to believe the friend of her childhood would do such a thing. But then, did she really know Cristobal at all? A lot could have happened to him since he and his family left the United States—many things could have changed him and molded him into another man. Certainly, she thought wryly, Cristobal had turned out to be a multifaceted man.

"Well?" he demanded. "What was so important to bring you out?"

She held her ground. "You're jettisoning the cotton bales to halt the blockader's pursuit. Put me in a longboat. They'll be forced to stop for me."

His lids drooped over hot brown stones, imparting that sleepy look. "No."

"Why not?" she cried. Then her eyes narrowed. "You said you were my friend."

His eyes flickered warily at her sudden woman's tactics.
"I am, Jen."

"Then release me," she begged piteously.

"I can't. A hundred things could happen. Our wake
could swamp the longboat. The blockader might not stop
for you. They might gain too much on us."

But the truth was that even if he could safely set her
loose, he would not. He wanted her there with him,
where he could feast his eyes upon her, for God knew
when and if he would ever see her again.

"If you were truly my friend you would let me go!"

A slow grin creased his lips. "I am afraid, Jen, that my
friendship for you is overridden by my desire."

# 27

Steadily the *Revenge* sailed for the Cuban harbor of Havana. Once Jeanette, still ensconced in the window seat, uncapped Cristobal's telescope to search the far western horizon for the blockader. But the Union Jack flag was at last lost in a cloudbank. For the moment the *Revenge* was safe, as was Jeanette. The demands of eluding the blockader had forced Cristobal to leave Jeanette temporarily.

All day the *Revenge* glided on, swaying on the gentle swell of inky water; for that was all Jeanette could compare the water to—a deep-blue ink, transparent blue, changing to a living green where the ship's bow quickly divided its glassy surface, and to a creamy white where the bubbles in the wake crushed each other in their whirling race after the rudder.

Some time after noon Cristobal returned to his cabin and, with only a cursory glance in her direction, flung himself across the bunk and fell into a heavy sleep. She thought about bashing in his skull with the heavy sextant, but where might that land her with his crew? Besides, she thought, looking at the unruly mass of dark-brown hair that tumbled over his brow, she could not do it. She, who would have killed a man for attempting to steal her wagonload of contraband, could not harm Cristobal—despite the cavalier way he had used her.

She sighed and, with knees pulled up against her chest, returned her attention to claims of the Caribbean. Her forehead drooped on her knees. Much later she stirred in her cramped position. She became aware of another presence and turned her head to find Cristobal, his jaw supported by one fist, watching her intently from the bunk. "Hungry?" he asked at last.

"I want you to let me go."

"After the run is completed."

"Then you had best kill me, because I swear, Cristobal Cavazos, I'll tell every French authority I can about you."

He swung his long legs over the side of the bunk and rose to stretch his massive frame. His self-assurance infuriated her. "And what of Lavender Blue?"

She clamped her lips shut and turned her face to the window where night was rapidly shading the horizon. "I don't want to ever see your face again at Columbia," she said tonelessly. "I want a divorce."

"Not as long as I live, Jen."

Her head swiveled around to meet his gaze. "Then may God put a swift end to your life!"

The normally droll smile was replaced by the serious set of his lips. "I've wanted you for too long to give you up now. We are married in the eyes of the law, Jen."

He left her then, and she stared absently out into the night. It was lit by thousands of phosphorescent insects. It seemed to her that the *Revenge* sailed on the Milky Way rather than the Gulf of Mexico. Ah, such a night.

Her bemusement must have shown on her face, for half an hour later Cristobal was at the doorway, saying, "One can easily understand why men claim the sea as their mistress; why they cling to her, fickle though she might be."

"Were that she was your mistress instead of I."

He sat a tray down on his desk and crossed to her with a cup of steaming coffee. "Tsk, tsk!" he mocked. "Such sentiments from my beloved wife."

She steeled herself against the fury he inspired in her and took the cup, saying sweetly, "Then you know my sentiments for a mercenary, a man like yourself without principles."

Unperturbed by the contempt in her voice, he hitched a leg over the edge of the desk and picked up a slice of salted beef, popping it in his mouth. "Are my principles any less because my loyalty lies with the Juaristas rather than the Rebels?"

"Loyalty?" she jeered, jarring her coffee precariously near the cup's rim. "What does a man like you know of loyalty? Married to one woman and consorting with another!"

A dark brow quirked in bewilderment and she blurted, "Rubia!"

"Ah, so it is a question then of faithfulness rather than loyalty."

Carelessly she swallowed a mouthful of the hot coffee. It seared every inch of her esophagus, and her throat screamed out in silent agony. But she managed to shrug indifferently. "Call it what you will."

He laughed lowly. "I call it jealousy."

"Ha!"

He leaned forward, a forearm braced on his knee. "Then we'll call it faithfulness. But tell me, were you any more faithful to Armand, taking a lover as you did?"

"I told you, it's not the same!"

He came to his feet and crossed to her. "But it is, Jen. I am conjecturing that you never loved Armand any less—"

"In all those years Armand was never unfaithful to me! After less than three months of marriage you were already bedding—"

"You never loved Armand any less," he continued, "despite the pleasure you found in my arms."

"I never found pleasure in your arms!"

"Oh, Jen, what a little hypocrite you are!"

Seething at his accusation, she grudgingly took the biscuit and slice of salted beef he passed her. Was she truly a hypocrite?

After the repast Cristobal left her, and she found herself pacing his cabin, fidgety as a schoolboy on a spring day. She was accustomed to being occupied, if not with the demands of the plantation then with the dangers of running contraband. She plopped down on the bunk, arms crossed behind her head. She tried to will herself to sleep, but her eyes stared at the smoke-darkened ceiling. The steady swish of water against the sloop's hull reminded her of her dual captivity—a captive of man, a captive of nature.

She experienced a terrible desire, almost a mania, to see dry land, to smell the earth, to fill her lungs with other than salt air, to stretch out on some green bank and watch the summer sun filtering streams of light through thick foliage. At that moment her resentment of her captivity was so great that, when Cristobal entered and began to tug off his boots, she snapped, "You smell like the bed of a camel!"

He laughed and, to her dismay, crossed to the bunk and leaned over her, planting his fists on either side of her ribs. "And you, my dear Jen, do not smell like any bed of roses."

His play on words brought a reluctant smile to the corners of her mouth. "That's better," he said.

The smile faded. "No, it's not, Cristobal! It's inconceivable that you would hold me here against my will!" His smell was a decidedly masculine smell—why couldn't it be a nauseating one? Why did she have to be stirred like some cow a-bulling?

He came to his feet, saying, "Sorry to have to point out the fact, Jen—but you forced your way aboard the *Revenge*." He began to unbutton the tight-fitting, doeskin britches. "Just be patient and I'll deliver you back to the comfort of Columbia. Until then you can be my *compagnie de voyage*."

"But when?"

He pulled his soot-smudged shirt up over his head, muffling his reply of, "In a month or so."

"A month or so!" His very nonchalance in the face of her plight—a situation he was responsible for—irritated her beyond caution. She sprang to a sitting position. "Get out. You're not sleeping here!"

He blinked his surprise. "This is *my* cabin. Surely you aren't going to be unreasonable at this time of night?"

"Get out!" she yelled shrilly, all self-control gone. It was going to be another of their confrontations. But this time, in contrast to all their childhood clashes, she meant to get the upper hand. "I demand the privacy accorded a lady," she said primly.

He hooted. "A lady!" He crossed to her and grabbed her upper arms, pulling her from the bed. "Look!" he said, positioning her before the small, tarnished shaving mirror that hung above the built-in chest. "Look at yourself, Jen! Is that dirt-streaked face and wild-tumbled hair the mark of a lady? Would a lady be caught dead in boy's pants that blatantly reveal her curves? Or those hands?" He grabbed up one. "Callused palms and broken nails?"

He spun her around to face him and caught her face between his large hands. "But, Jen, I wouldn't have you any other way. You're real—vital—alive!"

She shook free. She didn't want to hear his tender words. They confused her, diverted her from her purpose in life. Oh, why couldn't she think clearly! It was the confinement of the small cabin. "I don't recall having asked you to have me in any other way—other than in name only. Yet you used me abominably, Cristobal!"

He began to strip off his pants, and she whirled to face
the window. Never had she seen a naked man. Even she
and Armand had undressed in the dark and performed the
ritual of lovemaking beneath the concealment of blankets.

"I knew I would take you any way I could have you," he
said lightly, as if that taking were of no consequence.

"Rape," she said bitterly. "Oh, you might call it refined
rape, Cristobal, since I did have a choice of sorts. But it
makes you none the less despicable in my eyes. I could
never come to love you as I—"

"I know—I know. As you did Armand." His boots were
plunked down on the floor. "But I'll settle right now for
your arms."

She heard the soft squish of the mattress, and yanked
about. "Oh, no, you don't, Cristobal Cavazos. I told you
that was my bed."

He crooked a lopsided grin. "Want to wrestle me for
it?"

She snorted in disgust. "No! I should have realized long
ago you obviously were no gentleman." She discarded her
boots, first one, then the other, and came to the edge of
the bed in her stockinged feet. "But you stay on your
side. Our marriage conditions still hold."

When she had settled herself on the mattress with her
back to him, he leaned over her shoulder and whispered
teasingly in her ear, "I'm a patient and persistent man,
Jen. Eventually you'll see the error of your ways."

"Ohh!" she gritted. "Your conceit knows no limits."

He feigned a wistful sigh. "My one failing. But I'm trying to learn to be humble, dear. It's awfully hard when I
have a wife who secretly worships my body."

She squinched her eyes shut and prayed for sleep.

But just as she would begin to drift off, Cristobal's
warm breath would tickle her ear or his arm would pull
her close and awaken her. When his hand continued to

snake around her waist to palm one full breast, she snapped, "Apparently it's *my* body that is being worshiped!"

"Let me pay your lovely body the full homage due it," he coaxed.

The way his thumb and finger cajoled her nipples into pert little peaks, the way her lower abdomen ached for the same attention—she was so badly tempted to yield. "You said you were my friend," she reminded him. "Why don't you leave me alone?"

"I try, Jen," he chuckled in the dark. "Really I do. But all my good intentions vanish when I get near you, and the lusty beast in me takes over."

The proof of his own desire nudged her impudently in the small of her back. Oh, she did worship his body—that was the agony of it all. Never had she and Armand performed the intimate acts of lovemaking she had initiated with Cristobal.

When Cristobal's hand slipped under the waistband of her britches to satisfy the yearning of her woman's secret parts, she twisted around to face him. Her hand locked over his, halting its progress. "Cristobal, can't you see?" she rasped. "Can't you understand that if I yield now, I yield everything? My honor, my self-respect—that I dishonor the love I bear Armand?"

He jerked his hand from hers. "Dammit, Jen. That's just it. *Bear!* Present tense. Armand's dead! When will you get that through your stubborn head? I can't compete with a dead man!"

"You're not trying to be reasonable!" she charged.

"There's nothing reasonable or logical about love. By God, I wish there were. Then I could just reason you out of my mind."

He pushed her imploring hands from him and crawled over her and out of the bunk. As he slid into his britches, the soft moonlight that dappled the walls and floor illuminated his massive body. It gleamed with the movement of well-honed tendons and ligaments undulating beneath brown velvet skin. She stared. She drank in his masculine beauty. Her lips opened to call him back to her side, to tell him of their baby. But she changed her mind.

Her want of him was overshadowing logic. She must not let herself forget that Cristobal Cavazos, for whatever reason, had become a coldly calculating rogue. When he couldn't take her body in payment, he had taken her money. When he was bedding her, he was also making love to Rubia.

The child. She knew she would never tell him. The child would be hers—with no ties to bind her to Cristobal. Once she returned to Texas, she would immediately divorce him. It was too late to wish she had never set eyes on Cristobal Cavazos. But at least now she had a child to love; someone to care for. Now she could understand why the Aunt Hermiones of the world would suffer dependence on relatives. At least they had someone to care for.

28

The monstrous, forbidding Morro Castle, a fortress built by the Spaniards in the early 1500s, guarded the bottleneck harbor of Havana, Cuba. In its shadow stevedores worked feverishly on the docks, loading and unloading the contraband bound for both Mexico and the Confederacy. Even the Alameda de Paula, the promenade along the shore of the bay, was backed up with speculators, hucksters, merchants, agents for Mexico, France, the United States, and the Confederacy—all anxious to capitalize on the wars being waged by those nations.

"I've spent almost three days in this cage of a cabin," Jeanette protested. "At least let me go ashore with you."

He turned from the mirror, his face lathered with shaving foam, and coolly surveyed her—from her tousled hair down past the boy's shirt that stopped short of a pair of well-turned knees.

It was times like this when she felt she did not know her childhood friend at all. That feeling of comfort, of superiority even, that she knew with the dandy Cristobal vanished in the presence of the Frenchman Kitt. The way he arched a sardonic brow or smiled a lazy, infuriating grin made her light-headed. He might love her, as he pro-

243

fessed, but she suspected she could not control him through that love.

"Haven't you heard of pirates, Jen? They abduct white women and sell them along the Spanish Main for enormous profits."

"You look like a pirate!" she said with a grimace that curled her mouth in disgust.

He threw back his head and laughed at her candor. But he did look like one, she thought, resenting the amusement she seemed to inspire in him. Swarthy, with flashing dark eyes and a brace of pistols at his waist; his hair longer now, curling at his nape. All he lacked was an eye patch and an earring.

"How about a gentleman adventurer or a cotton privateer?" he asked rhetorically. "Oh, Jen, most women would be cowering in the corner and weeping at their predicament. But not you. You were always anxious to taste of life. Come along then—but, *por Dios*, put on your britches and keep that wild mass of hair tucked in your hat. And, oh, keep those lovely lips closed—until later tonight."

She would not let his vile humor provoke her that morning. She was too excited about going ashore. Obedient as a manservant, she followed Cristobal, who was dressed in a finely cut, camel-colored frock coat, from the longboat along the dock. The wharves were crowded with Negroes and Hispanics working shoulder to shoulder. She had to almost skip in order to keep up with Cristobal's long strides as he made his way through the narrow streets lined with stone houses with tiled roofs.

He turned into a small, narrow building bearing the box-lettered placard, W.E. CROWEL & CO., SHIPPING AGENTS. A small bell rang when they entered the office. A fair-complected man with wheat-colored hair entered through a side door to greet Cristobal, who presented his *carte de visite*.

"You have managed to bring us another consignment, Don Cavazos?" he asked, smiling and shaking his head, as if the feat were incredible.

"Cotton—salt—Mexican beef," Cristobal replied laconically and seated himself in the chair the agent pulled out.

Fuming at Cristobal's rudeness, Jeanette was left to stand at his side. He seemed not to notice her presence and smoothly continued his conversation. "You, of course, have the order filled?"

The tall, reed-thin man removed a sheath of papers and placed them at the corner of the desk before Cristobal. "Percussion caps. Rum. Molasses. And the Enfields. The last of them for a while. It's almost impossible to get them out of England right now with such an increase in demand for them."

Cristobal nodded, glanced over the papers, and picked up the pen. "The supplies are being unloaded now for transfer to your dockside warehouse." He scrawled his name, looked up, and said, as if it were an afterthought, "By the way, is there still a traffic in white slavery?"

The agent frowned his disapproval. "Why . . . yes, though at the moment, as you must know, the profits are a good deal better in contraband running."

Cristobal inclined his dark head toward Jeanette. "I have a cabin boy here that I think would prove of interest to certain people in the market."

Jeanette gasped. "You wouldn't!"

The agent looked dismayed at the feminine pitch of her voice. "That kind of boy? I see." The color that flooded the man's fair skin indicated his discomfort with the entire conversation.

"Actually not." Cristobal cast an acquisitive eye at her, saying, "I have kidnaped a young virgin that I thought would bring a good price."

"Cristobal! Stop this immediately!" She didn't really believe he was serious; she suspected he enjoyed taunting her. Still, one never knew about Cristobal. Had she ever really known him?

A look of distaste passed over the agent's now-red face. "We really prefer to deal in goods other than human flesh, Don Cavazos."

Cristobal sighed. "I was afraid of that. Besides, the girl has proved to be recalcitrant. I doubt if she would bring a good price."

While he concluded the transaction, she fumed in silence. After they left the agent's office, she caught up with Cristobal and jerked on his sleeve. He looked down at her stormy expression with mild surprise. "Don't expect me to be amused by that performance back there!" she said. "It was disgusting—utterly disgusting!"

"Oh, but Jen, I was so tempted. Think! I wouldn't have to worry about you blowing my ruse to the French. No one, not even my own sailors would question me about your disappearance. And think about the money I would stand to inherit—and Columbia. Yes, I admit it crossed my mind. But, alas, good conscience forbade me."

"Bah, what do you know of good conscience!"

He resumed walking and she fell into step alongside him. "Let's say, then, that I would find it extremely difficult sleeping at night knowing some other man might be indulging in your—uh, delectable attributes."

She wrinkled her nose at his mocking grin. "That you will have to worry about the rest of your life, Cristobal Cavazos, because you certainly will never again enjoy my favors."

"Don't count on that, Jen, dear."

She glanced up at him quickly, but his expression was bland.

Before she could retort, he halted to purchase two mangoes from a raggedy Negro vendor pushing a cart loaded with an assortment of tropical fruits. He passed her one of the mangoes and sank his teeth into his own before he resumed walking along the crowded street. "Have you ever stopped to think, Jen, that perhaps you could be misjudging me"—he swallowed a bite—"and others?"

The delicious juice coursed down her throat. "I doubt it." She wiped the back of her sleeve across her mouth. "I think I know you very well. Too well."

"And Armand?"

She fixed him with a freezing look. "I prefer not to discuss him with you."

He tossed the mango core into a pile of refuse on the cobblestones and said lightly, "I'm tiring of always hearing about what you prefer."

Caught off guard by the statement, she slid a glance up at her husband. He was gazing distractedly down at the shimmering turquoise bay that was studded with more ships than Bagdad's. Yet the forbidding set to his lips warned her she should be careful not to take his words as lightly as he stated them.

While he supervised the reloading of the cargo, she spent the rest of the day with Alejandro and Solis. Sitting on a crate, she helped the two tally the bill of lading. The mestizo treated her with the utmost respect despite her disreputable garb. And Alejandro seemed to regard her with a certain awe. He took the cigarette butt from his mouth and flipped it into the trash-littered water below the wharf before asking: "Is it true that you ride a horse astride—like a man?"

She chuckled. Giving in to the urge that had been pestering her ever since she set eyes on the boy, she pushed back the shaggy black hair that hung into his eyes. "Yes, it's true."

His bird-bright eyes widened. "And it's true that you shoot like a man—that you really did shoot *el capitán?*"

She sobered. It startled her to realize that being compared to a man was not all that flattering for a woman. "Yes. But it was an accident. I was angry. But people who can't control their anger—their emotions—they lose in the end." She sighed. "But I don't suspect I'm making much sense."

From behind her Solis said, "What you say makes sense, señora."

She colored, abashed at being overheard, and bent her head low over the column of figures she had been totaling.

Toward evening, an affable Cristobal invited her and Solis to dine at the Louvre, a large café outside the city walls. Her reluctance even to speak to her husband warred with her desire to escape the confines of the ship. "Like this?" she asked, and indicated the soil-blackened buckskins.

He grinned. "It's the only way I'd trust you among all those lecherous men."

Solis bowed out, muttering he had other things to do. Whether he'd planned a night of drinking at the local grogshop or was merely making a polite gesture in deference to her and Cristobal, she was not sure. But Cristobal certainly made no effort to dissuade his friend.

With its bull's-eye windows and mahogany booths, the Louvre closely resembled an old English pub. A dark-skinned young woman with short, wiry hair placed tankards of stout and meat pies before Cristobal and Jeanette. The inn had a warm ambiance, and for a while the two of them ate in silence while all around them men joked and laughed and talked.

To break the silence that grew ever more tense, she asked, "What did you do all those years you lived away, Cristobal?"

"I survived."

She glanced up from the thick, crusty bread she was breaking. In the seclusion of the booth his face was dark and guarded. "Yes?" she prompted.

He set down the tankard of ale. "The thousand acres my father owned—they were seized by the United States courts. After they were distributed among a hundred and fifty or so lawyers, we were left with nothing. We were poor. As poor or poorer than Alejandro."

"I didn't know," she breathed. "I was just a child. No one ever bothered to explain—"

"We emigrated to France where my mother had cousins," he continued tersely. "Life was not much better. My father died working as a machinist in a shipyard at Nantes. My mother had to support my sister and me. I applied for my father's job and was hired. And I grew up. Quickly."

She saw the tightness in his features. "Why did you come back to Texas?"

He hesitated. The truth? For her? He thought of the thousand and one nights he had lain awake in hovels—on ships, even on the hard earth—dreaming of the saucy minx who had stolen his boy's heart. To achieve that it had been worth the deception. He answered truthfully. "Partly for revenge."

"Ah, yes. That explains your ship's name. And for what other reason?"

"For my mother country. For Mexico. She needed—and still does—the help of her sons."

Perhaps Cristobal was right; perhaps she had misjudged him. Perhaps her love for Armand had colored all else. In light of what Cirstobal had told her, could she blame him for some of the things he had done? His deceptions—had she not practiced her own? Something in her softened toward the boy she had known. But the man—she still could not deal with him. Not this new man. Yet had not both the boy and the man been recklessly daring and ingeniously resourceful?

"But the United States is an ally of Juárez," she said, wanting to get away from the personal direction the conversation was taking. "Why, then, would you even indirectly aid the Confederacy?"

He tossed off the last of the ale. His mouth twisted in a semblance of a smile. "Juárez berates me with the same question. The truth is that feelings I have for a childhood friend overrode all rationality."

Uneasily aware of Cristobal's brooding eyes on her, she disregarded the statement and attacked her food. Like an ostrich burying its head in the sand, she hoped that by ignoring him she could ignore the sexual tension that licked at her nerve endings.

The barmaid refilled Cristobal's tankard. He ignored the open invitation in the buxom young woman's dark eyes and crimson lips, and proceeded to down the ale. Jeanette forced her attention on her food. But a little later she looked up from her plate to find his gaze playing on her lips before dropping down to the faint shadow of a cleavage in the open neck of her buckskin shirt. His pupils were glazed with obvious desire. Watching the way his lips touched the rim of his tankard, she knew exactly what he was thirsty for.

She felt that same sensation herself. That heat that flamed in the center of her belly. The itch that Cristobal seemed to cause. God help her, what kind of woman was she—wanting to bed with the man who had betrayed her time and again?

But a little voice whispered it could not be wrong—after all, he *was* her husband.

She took another drink of the dark stout to quench the fire that burned inside her. The drink really did not have such a bad taste, after all. With her tongue she licked the foam from her mouth. His smoldering eyes followed the movement. She felt a moment of feminine superiority—until that gaze rose to lock with her own. Its intensity could almost have knocked her over. "I know what you want," she said weakly.

"And you don't?"

Her teeth gnawed on her bottom lip. "No."

"Liar."

She wanted to wipe the self-assurance from his handsome face. His male superiority was challenging her. Her eyes smiled coolly. "I won't deny that you can arouse me. But then I have found that ability is not peculiar to you. Mark Thompson is also quite capable of stirring passion in a woman."

Frost opaqued his eyes before his lids half-drooped over them. "Good. Now that I know your . . . passions can be stirred, I feel it my duty as your husband to satisfy those passions."

Across the width of the table his hand caught her wrist and dragged her from the booth. "What do you think you're doing?" she hissed. All about them, men looked up from their drinks or plates to stare.

With his free hand Cristobal tossed a few coins on the table. "I intend to make you my wife—in every sense of the word."

29

Heedless of the stares of the Louvre's patrons, Cristobal pulled Jeanette along behind him.

"You can't do this," she cried.

He halted at the door and looked around him before meeting her enraged gaze with a quizzical lift to his brow. "I don't see anyone making an effort to stop me."

All the way back to the wharf, during the longboat trip back to the *Revenge,* while he hauled her up to his cabin, she pleaded with him, entreated him not to go through with his threat. He slammed the door behind them and faced her. How had she ever thought that smile inane? Why had she never seen its mockery? "But I mean to know you—in the Biblical sense, Jen."

"You have!" she shrieked.

He grabbed the hem of her buckskin shirt and yanked it up over her head as if he were a parent undressing a reluctant child for bed. "I knew you as the Frenchman knew an object he had bought," he pointed out calmly. "There is a difference. I mean to know you as a husband knows his wife."

She shook her hair free in the manner of an angry bull tossing his head when about to charge. "Then that's something you'll never know! Because I have only one true husband, and it's not—"

"And Armand's dead!"

Furiously he jerked down her pants. She stood passively, hiding her fear, while he knelt before her exposed body and removed her boots. She would not give in to him. She would not cringe now. To do so would invalidate all the times that had required her courage. Could she be any less brave now because she was being attacked as a woman?

He swung her up against him and stalked to the bunk, where he deposited her with something less than gentleness. In the darkness of the cabin he purposefully stripped. She waited, her breath shallow. She knew Cristobal was inebriated—but not enough to do this sordid thing, not enough to rape her. If she did not fight him, if she tried to reason with him, maybe she could make him understand.

Nude now, his long, lithe body obviously aroused, he bent over her, his dark face grim. "It's not Mark Thompson I'm competing with, is it, Jen?" he asked harshly.

She shook her head in the dark, forgetting that he could not see her clearly. "No," she murmured.

"Always it's been Armand," he grunted to himself. Then to her, "I mean to make you admit tonight that Armand is dead. Both to yourself and me."

She met his threatening gaze with a calmness she was far from feeling. In the airless cabin perspiration erupted on her, adhering her body like India glue to his sweaty one. "That's something you'll never understand, Cristobal," she said quietly. "My husband, my true husband, lives on in me—in my mind, in my heart. Neither you— nor your jealousy—can ever change that. Now—go ahead. Get your raping over with."

His anger leapt into white-hot flame. His mouth slammed against hers. Beneath the force of his conquering mouth, her lips were forced apart. She felt his teeth, then his tongue besiege her fortress. Her tongue parried the slash of his. But too late she discovered his offense was only a diversionary tactic. From another front he breeched her defenses, his knee subtly prying open her legs, his hand storming that soft vulnerability. But when he encountered the dryness of fright, his fingers halted their assault.

His head lifted from where it had nestled between the faintly veined globes of her milk-white breasts. In the darkness his glittering eyes delved into hers. "You willingly gave yourself to me before—"

"To the Frenchman," she corrected tersely.

"What's the price now?" he continued.

"There's no price great enough."

He took her then, thrusting in her with a savage force that made her arch up against him in pain. "No!" she screamed out finally. Fear sizzled through her. Not just for herself. But for the child. Her fingers dug into his upper arms, clutching, shoving at the thing that hurt her, that tore at her. It continued to pump and plunge like some diabolical engine, oblivious of her cries. The pain that ripped through her abdomen cut short her breath. "Cristobal. Listen. No! God, no! The child!"

The Bermudas had been awakened from centuries of somnolence, of sponging, fishing, and turtling for its livelihood, by the advent of blockade running. The people of the islands were strongly in sympathy with the South and the blockade runners; so much so that on at least one occasion the U.S. Consul was attacked in his office. The sentiment on behalf of the Confederacy was further heightened by the increase in revenues blockade running brought to the people.

Life was gay and easy on the islands. St. George's was a boom town in every respect, not only for officers and civilians but for common sailors as well. They overflowed the drinking places and filled the streets. Ladies of easy virtue flocked to the town from Atlantic Coast ports, and Shin-bone Alley boasted scores of bawdyhouses and iniquitous dives.

Magnolia Hill, the home of Mrs. Owen Williams, wife of the chief Confederate agent, was always open to South-ern supporters. Overlooking beautiful St. George's har-bor, it was constantly filled with Confederate agents and naval officers. Nubile girls of the islands entertained visit-ing young Confederate officers with all sorts of balls, dances, and festivities. St. George's had become not only a way station between Europe's ports and the Con-federacy, but a harbor of refuge for the blockade runners, a pleasant resting place after the excitement and fatigue of a voyage.

It was to St. George's—to Magnolia Hill and its beauti-ful mansion built of pink coral blocks—that the blockade runner Cristobal Cavazos brought his ailing young wife.

Barbara Williams sat beside the bed where Jeanette Cavazos slept. The Caribbean sunlight that streamed through the white eyelet cotton curtains was not kind to Barbara. It revealed the faint lines about her eyes and the deeper ones just beginning to show on either side of her wide mouth. But the eyes were a pale blue, like the tropi-cal waters that played about the sandy coves, and just as lovely. And the lips held a soft sensuality.

But her mind was sharp, practical. A woman of forty, she had known the humiliation of being called white trash. Her father sharecropped cotton on what was little more than a farm outside Atlanta. She had also known she would escape the humiliation of poverty at the first oppor-tunity. It presented itself the day she turned fifteen, when Owen Williams rode into the redneck tenant's yard filled with her dirty, half-naked brothers and sisters. Owen, nearing forty himself at that time and stocky, had asked directions. Barbara calmly gave them and just as calmly told him she was leaving with him.

She was half afraid he would laugh, but his kind eyes looked down into her dirt-smeared face, and after what seemed an interminable moment he had consented. She had never let him regret that moment. And she had never regretted it herself. Owen's business acumen and fairness had made him an affluent merchant; so successful was he that the Confederate Government had appointed him as commercial agent to Bermuda.

Barbara now had all she had lacked as a sharecropper's daughter. All but the erotic passion her husband was incapable of. But she found that in the occasional visits of Cristobal Cavazos. For these times she waited. She knew she would risk all she had, including her husband's love, to go away with the roguish blockade runner if he asked her; but he had never asked her.

And now she knew why. Gazing down at the small-boned woman before her, she could understand some of what Cristobal saw in his wife. Despite the mauve shadows about the long-lashed eyes, despite the pinched lips and pale, washed-out skin, Jeanette Cavazos was a very attractive young woman. Not the standard Southern beauty. Even sleep could not rob the face of its strong character, contrasting so with the young woman's delicate build.

Jeanette opened her eyes now, and Barbara noticed with a start their extraordinary shade. "Where am I?" The words were rusty, low.

"You are at Magnolia Hill in St. George's, Bermuda. Your husband brought you here this morning."

Jeanette blinked back the tears. "Who are you?"

"I'm—I'm a friend of your husband's."

Bitterly Jeanette turned her face toward the wall. One more woman who had shared Cristobal's bed.

The old man who sat on the other side of the bed leaned forward. "I'm Dr. Magee, Mrs. Cavazos. You have been ill—for nearly two days. You were hemorrhaging. You—" he laid a hand flecked with gray hair on the small, knotted fist, "you lost the child."

"Cristobal," Jeanette murmured bitterly.

"You must understand, Mrs. Cavazos," the doctor cleared his throat and continued, "intercourse does not normally cause a miscarriage. You must not blame your husband's . . . attentions. In fact he revealed that you recently suffered a heat stroke. Your body's poor health, stress, any number of reasons could have caused you to lose the child."

Jeanette closed her eyes. "I want to be alone."

In the evenings, when the sun was still high above the blue line of the Caribbean, the Williamses and their guests would sit on the wide piazza while tea, cakes, and ice cream were served by hovering Negro boys. The women would play croquet on the lush lawn, and the gentlemen would smoke the Havana "long nines" and talk desultorily of cargoes, contraband, and the Confederacy.

That particular evening there were just the two guests, with the men doing most of the talking. "There," Owen said, jabbing his forefinger at a copy of *The New York Times* that was only two days old. "The Chief Justice of the United States Supreme Court says—" he held the newspaper at arm's length and read: "'The ships are planks of the same bridge, and necessary for the convenient passage of persons and properties from one end to the other.'"

"In other words," Cristobal drawled, "transshiping cargo from ship to warehouse to ship is now looked upon as intentional breaking of the blockade."

"And subjects your ship once again to capture," Owen finished.

Barbara would like to have heard more of the actual
running of the contraband—of the exciting escapes. Cristobal's reputation held that he was a cool and resourceful
leader in moments of acute danger, that he boldly accepted and then expertly overcame risks others wouldn't
consider.

But the conversation continued to revolve around the
mundane—cotton and its cost—with the two men volley-
ing their ideas between each other and enjoying the exchange. Two shrewd minds. The rubicund Owen, the
rakish Cristobal. And Barbara was shrewd enough to keep
her remarks to herself. She influenced Owen's opinions in
a more subtle way.

Jeanette Cavazos, dressed that particular evening in a
charming daisy-yellow dimity that Owen had procured
from one of his warehouses, had hitherto remained quiet.
She had convalesced rapidly over the week she had been
at Magnolia Hill. Mornings spent sitting in the sun had
restored her golden color, the sea breeze her health. Yet
the lavender-blue eyes were dull and flat as slate. Except
when her gaze locked with that of her husband. Then Barbara saw the spark ignite, the blue eyes take fire. Something was wrong between the two.

Even at that moment Jeanette's eyes blazed into an inferno at what her husband was saying. "The Confederate
States Government has made a serious error."

"How so, Cristobal?" Owen asked.

"That first year of the war President Davis and his financial advisors made no move to use their one salable
commodity, cotton, to finance their war."

For the first time Jeanette spoke, her voice sharp as a
fine-edged Bowie. "Why should they have? The North
needed our cotton; the mills of Lancashire in England—
and those in France and the rest of Europe—needed it.
Jefferson Davis knew if we held cotton off the world mar-

ket until the need reached a critical stage, the result would be a fantastic increase in the price."

"She has a point," Owen said, though his ruddy face was careful not to betray his surprise at the young woman's outburst.

"Furthermore," Jeanette said, leaning forward in the white wrought-iron chair, "Davis hoped that Queen Victoria and Napoleon III and others in Europe might find it worthwhile to recognize the Confederate States of America—if Europe expected to continue to clothe its people in cotton fabrics."

Slowly Cristobal exhaled cigar smoke. "But the foreign governments haven't recognized the Confederacy, have they, Jen?" He disregarded the storm that brewed in his wife's eyes. "Now the Confederacy's coffers are empty of gold, its currency is suspect, and there is no credit with which to collect and transport cotton for export."

Barbara diplomatically intervened. "The air is getting slightly chilly. Perhaps we should go inside. Besides, it's nearing dinner." She caught the glance of appreciation her husband threw her.

Cristobal's gaze was shadowed. He took his wife's elbow to assist her up the shallow flagstone steps and felt her body actually withdraw from contact with his.

30

The voluminous skirts bunched and anchored about her waist by her dress's sashes, Jeanette wandered along the white, sandy beach. She recalled that evening she watched the Ethiopian Minstrels perform. She had wished—no, ached to feel again. Now she did. With a startling clarity. She saw—really saw—the moonlight that ribboned the sea with silver. She really noticed the water that rippled about her ankles, how deliciously cool it was. And she felt the pain that knifed through her soul.

Cristobal was responsible for restoring these sensations.

His very presence seemed to trigger something in her. Like the argument earlier in the evening. The two of them could not be together without provoking a response from each other. She had always thought that she and Armand had been forthright in their conversations. But, reflecting on their stimulating talks, she recalled now that never had they touched upon anything intimate. Always impersonal issues. Had she ever dared to utter what she truly felt about herself and others? Only Cristobal had been capable of goading her beyond the most superficial of subjects.

Heated debates were typical in their conversations. And their lovemaking had been just as heated.

The result of their lovemaking—her hand dropped to her stomach, mounded now with her bunched skirts. She had not thought that the loss of the child could make her heart hurt so much. The days and nights she had lain in the Williams' bedroom, recovering—she had tried to tell herself that the miscarriage had been for the best. With a child, Armand's child—she would never have attempted to break out of the mold prescribed for the proper woman. But, oh, she never did want to go back to her old self. No, never would she submit again to society's constraining ideas of a proper wife in a proper marriage.

But the loss of the child—all her logic could not make up for the emotional pain she suffered. Everything Cristobal had done—his deception, his philandering in their marriage, his blatant taking of her money to run the cotton—were nothing compared to his rape of her. His total disregard of her pleas, of her as a human being, of his destruction of his own seed.

For that she could never forgive Cristobal.

As if summoned by her condemning thoughts, he appeared before her, his black shirt and britches almost blending with the shadows cast by the arching palms that lined the shore. She looked up into his taut face. For one naked moment their eyes met; then she continued on along the beach. He fell into step with her, his hands jammed into his pockets.

"Jen, I—"

"I came out here because I wanted to be alone."

He grabbed her arm and jerked her around to face him. The moonlight showed the agony that twisted his features. The blood that soaked the sheets—the vision was still vivid in his mind. When he realized what was happening, that she was losing the baby she carried, he was like a man demented. What if he lost her, too? The only thing that had brightened his life. Her laughter, her thought-provoking statements, her warmth, her challenging smile . . . the way she touched his soul, as no other woman had, when the two of them met and blended in lovemaking. And those torturous twenty-four hours of waiting to see if she would survive—he was responsible for all the pain she endured. Even Solis, Alejandro, and the others had looked at him with the greatest reluctance.

"Jen, I didn't know," he said, his voice hoarse with his anguish. "You never told me you were carrying our child."

"Oh?" she said coolly. "Does rape exclude pregnant women?" He winced visibly at that barb, but she continued. "And what makes you think it was your child?" She knew she was behaving vilely, but she couldn't stop the malicious words from coming. "How do you know it wasn't Mark's or some other man's? You know I would do anything for the Cause."

There was a terrible silence with the lapping of the waves the only sound about the two stiff silhouettes. Then Cristobal's fingers dug painfully into Jeanette's upper arms. "You little bitch. You aren't half the woman I thought you were."

"Good. Then go to Rubia when you feel like rape."

"I don't have to rape her."

The fight went out of Jeanette. Her head drooped. Weakened by the miscarriage, she would probably have collapsed there on the sand were it not for Cristobal's biting grip at her shoulders. "Take me home . . . back to Texas."

He released her and stepped back. "I can't. Not until I've finished the run."

"I'm strong enough to finish the return run." But even speaking seemed to require an effort.

"I can't trust you, Jen. You'd have the French on me in no time. I'll send a ship back for you."

Her head jerked up. "What? You mean to leave me here? In Bermuda?"

"It'll be only a month to six weeks at the most."

He started back in the direction of the house. She jerked at his sleeve. "I won't stay here—with another of your mistresses. I'm going with you."

He sighed. "That's the trouble with you, Jen. You're hell-bent on having your own way. But this time you're going to do what someone tells you. You're going to be the gracious lady and guest of Barbara Williams."

Like hell she would. Jeanette knew that Cristobal would pick the first moonless night to make the run. Already the moon was waning. At most, another day or two remained for her to make preparations.

Since she was unconscious when Cristobal brought her to Bermuda, she was able to persuade Barbara to take her on a tour of St. George's. The tour offered her a chance to reconnoiter the harbor, to locate the *Revenge*, and lay her plans for hiding away.

The next day Barbara took her out in a carriage with a fringed surrey top to see the island. The Bermudas, comprising a British Crown Colony, were the most northerly coral islands, in the world. "But unlike most coral islands, which are flat," Barbara explained, "all the Bermuda islands are carved with hills and ridges like St. George's."

She instructed the black boy to halt the carriage on one of the bluffs, rising 250 feet above sea level, that overlooked St. George's and its harbor. Directly below the bluff madcaps dashed against the boulders. But toward the harbor the water was a peaceful blue and green. Farther out, schools of porpoises sported, and Jeanette thought she sighted a flying fish.

A winding road lined with verdant tropical foliage descended to the whitewashed town with its wide, palm-shaded streets. Like Bagdad, St. George's harbor was awash with ships of every nationality. "Where is the *Revenge* anchored?" Jeanette asked.

"Just beyond the bend of the cove. All four warehouses are on that side. St. George's only has one dock for each of the warehouses for loading and unloading cargo. So each ship must wait its turn."

So the run was to be soon. "I've heard so much about St. George's warehouses—that they're a lifeline to the Confederacy. May I visit your husband's?"

Barbara's pale-blue eyes skimmed over Jeanette's face. Was this the first time Cristobal had taken his wife on a run with him? It was not uncommon, especially during the first two years of the war when blockade running was not so risky, for Southern women and children to travel on the blockade runners, though the fares were exorbitant.

But most women, unaware of the profits to be made in trade, had little interest in dirty, musty warehouses. Yet Jeanette Cavazos did. At least Jeanette and she had that in common. And Cristobal.

Jeanette located the *Revenge*. In that British port it no longer flew the flag of France but rather Mexico's eagle and serpent. At the Williams warehouse Barbara showed her crates piled to the ceiling. They were marked MER-CHANDISE or NAILS or COMBUSTIBLES and in reality held greatcloth, shoes, blankets, and other Confederate Government commissary stores awaiting shipment.

Jeanette gave the warehouse only a cursory examination while she studied the *Revenge*'s crew of thirty-six men as they moved back and forth between the warehouse and the dock like ants. On their shoulders they toted boxes, barrels, and bags of boots, candles, tea, coffee, preserved meats, and even wire frames for hoop skirts. None of them took notice of the two women standing in the shadows of the warehouse, watching. But Jeanette marked everything. She knew that the pliant bags of green coffee would be her best hiding place.

That evening on the terrace she managed to behave civilly to Cristobal. She would be having her way soon enough. In turn, Cristobal was giving his attention to Barbara, who wanted to know how he'd managed to become one of the few blockade runners to successfully elude the men-of-war thus far.

"Rules," he replied simply, his gaze lingering on Barbara's full breasts perched high in her gown's décolletage. "The crew wears gray clothing at night. And as you may have noticed, the ship is painted a dull gray. Smoking on deck is strictly forbidden. Even our engine-room hatchways are screened with tarpaulins. The lookout posted in the crosstrees is rewarded a dollar for every sail sighted. But if the sail was seen first from the deck, his pay is docked five dollars."

From there the talk drifted to the many Southern refugees who were swarming Bermuda. "Not peaceful like it used to be," Owen declared. "Sailors, cotton brokers, rum sellers—Jews and Gentiles of high and low degree coining money and squandering it as if they owned the secret of the transmutation of metals!"

Cristobal's chuckle was low, so different from the assumed chortle Jeanette had known. Her hand gripped the glass of mint julep. She couldn't get to the French soon enough.

The house was dark, except for the light that peeked from beneath Cristobal's door, when Jeanette slipped out of her room. Was Cristobal preparing to join his crew—or was he at that moment joined with Barbara?

Black bile rose in Jeanette's throat, and she spun away, stealthily making her way down the darkened stairs. A good three miles stretched between Magnolia Hill and the harbor. Forty-five minutes at a fast walk. She swung out onto the pebbled lane, keeping to the shadows of the large oleanders. Even wearing her hat and the dungaree britches and buckskin shirt that Barbara had instructed her maid to wash, Jeanette knew her fair coloring would call attention, for three-quarters of the local population was black.

She circumvented the town and arrived at the dock to find it still bustling with last-minute loading. The tide would soon be running, and the ships wanted to be ready. Head kept low, she moved among the sailors, sidestepping the mounds of supplies waiting to be loaded. Lanterns suspended from posts lit the area, and the usual fishy smell pervaded the air.

She found the *Revenge*'s crew busy hefting cargo across the gangplank from the dock to the ship. She timed their comings and goings—three to five minutes—and waited for the point where one man departed the dock and the next had yet to arrive. Quickly she untied the stout cord around a huge bag of coffee and tugged at one end to dump out a portion of the contents. Coal. Black coal instead of green coffee!

Too late. The whistling of a sailor portended another arrival shortly. She pushed her way inside. Perhaps fifteen minutes went by, while she huddled among the jabbing chunks of coal. Then the bag was moved. "Top's open," a voice grumbled. It was Alejandro.

Dear God, don't let him look inside.

And he wouldn't have, had the coal dust not choked her, sending her into a paroxysm of coughing. Light shafted in her face. "Señora!"

She peeked up through the opening of the bag. Alejandro's grubby face peered down at her in shock. "Please, Alejandro," she wheezed. "Please don't tell. I've got to get back to Texas."

Indecision played on his face, then the light disappeared as the top was secured. A moment later, she heard
another voice, a gruffer one than Alejandro's, and she felt
herself hoisted and tossed over a shoulder. She had done
it. She had stolen away on the *Revenge*.

It seemed like she had crouched in the bag for hours
before she felt the slight swaying of the ship and heard the
creaking of its timbers. Unable to bear the enforced
rigidity a moment longer, she pushed toward the opening.
It did not give! Why hadn't she the foresight to bring
along a knife? She pushed and shoved at the bag's top.
Coals scratched her arms and face. Surely Alejandro
would remember she was down in the hold and come to
let her out of the bag.

Her struggles brought on another convulsion of coughing, and a voice sounding suspiciously like that of Cristobal said, "What the—?"

31

During July and August, when the Gulf's summer heat was at its maximum, heavy thunderstorms were a daily happening. Cristobal counted on this natural phenomenon to make good his run into Bagdad. He could even count on the hour—about four in the afternoon—that the thunderheads would begin their buildup.

Looking at the clear azure sky, a novice sailor would find no indication of an approaching thunderstorm. But one by one scattered masses of cirrocumulus clouds would join with marvelous rapidity and instantly darkness would prevail. Then came the mutterings of thunder. One telltale sign of this natural force was the almost unnoticeable way the breeze tugged at the wisps of Jen's unbound hair. She stood toward the prow, overlooking the bowsprit. Cristobal did not need to see her face to know she wore an expression as brooding as the black, gathering clouds. For just a moment his own brooding gaze lightened as he recalled the black face that had confronted him down in the hold the day before. He had tried to sound stern, berating Jen for using Alejandro's friendship to stow away, of being stubborn and willful—but he didn't remember everything else he had said. Only that he had ended up breaking out in laughter at the little black boy glaring up at him. Oh, Jen!

Would she give him away to the French? He'd have to take that chance now.

The hate still flamed in her eyes. Yet desire flickered there, too. But desire was a cheap commodity. He could find it—or easily arouse it—in a number of women. Love . . . that was something else. It was something that he, used to commanding, could not command of Jen.

As it was, he had surrendered his cabin to her, while he tossed restlessly on a slung hammock in a cabin with Solis and two others whose snores drowned out the noise of the ship's engine. He dragged his gaze from her lissome form and made his way up toward the wheelhouse. When it came time to make the dash for an inlet, or to run before weather such as was accumulating on the horizon, he preferred to be at the helm.

Solis was on duty and surrendered the wheel gladly enough. "Tell my wife to go to our—" Cristobal paused and grinned. "No, *inform* my wife of the approaching bad weather and *request* her to go to our cabin."

Already blue-black clouds boiled over the sea's edge and raced toward them. For the first time in days Cristobal relaxed. He enjoyed vying with the elements. In their unpredictability they were predictable. Not so Jen. *Dios*, if he could only chart that maze of her mind, perhaps he would find her of less interest—perhaps then he could rid himself of her.

As if his thoughts had summoned her, she was at his side. "Solis told me of the storm," she said stiffly. "I want to watch."

He looked down into her upturned face and read there, beyond her anger and contempt, the same excitement he felt when faced with a challenge. That afternoon it would

be the most difficult of all challenges, the powerful force
of nature. Understanding that need, he nodded and
turned back to the helm.

Before them the mass of clouds foamed, dragging its
braids of rain beneath it. The wind began to shriek like a
thousand harpies. It seemed no time before the rain fell in
torrents, accompanied by invariably peculiar discharges of
electricity. Single fireballs followed each other every second, darting straight from the sky to the sea with a hiss
like an enormous shell and exploding as they struck with a
sharp retort.

He heard Jen's soft gasp of awe and looked down to see
the excitement glittering in her incredible eyes. Then he
turned his attention to fighting the slam of the wind. On
the Gulf, the thunder came in quick, stacatto concussions,
distinctly separate, and of such volume as to stun the ear
and make the ship quiver in every timber.

Balls of fire perched upon the bulwarks, and Jen exclaimed, "What a magnificent electrical matinee!"

He smiled down at her. "Jen, Jen. You're incorrigible.
When will you ever learn to be afraid? And how sad if you
ever do."

Her blue eyes turned on him with a strange look, as if
she were trying to fathom his depths for the first time.
Before she could reply, another sharp retort vibrated along
the ship, rocking it. Jeanette staggered against him, and he
caught her and steadied her as he tried to correct the wildly
spinning wheel. "Lightning struck," she breathed, her
eyes wide.

"No! It's a broadside hit! A blockader!" His normally
lazy voice was sharp and commanding. "Get below!"

"No!" she echoed. "I'm staying!"

He hit her then, a sharp slap that caught her on the
temple more than the cheek. He saw the tears that
flooded her eyes. "I command this ship, and at least here
you will obey me. Now—"

But there was no time to argue. Shell after shell screamed across the decks of the fleeing *Revenge*. Now the real excitement was beginning. Nothing Cristobal had ever experienced could compare with it. Hunting, pig-sticking, big-game shooting, polo—he had done a little of each. All had their thrilling moments, but none approached running a blockade.

Suddenly the *Revenge*'s foremast exploded in a shower of splinters and fell drunkenly to port as one of the Federal cruiser's shots found its target. Cristobal's hand shot out to grab the back of Jen's neck and push her down on the floor.

His long legs braced against the jarring, he shouted, "I'm going to run her in ashore—before we're all blown to eternity."

"The *Revenge*?" Jen asked, her body stretched prone, her face raised to peer up at him. He knew what she really wanted to know—was he risking his ship for her? Was he?

She scrambled to her knees. Black smoke smudged one cheekbone, and her hair looked like a bird's nest. He thought she had never been lovelier. Where some natures were crushed by overwhelming difficulties, others, like hers, were stimulated by them. "What about you?" she demanded.

"I plan to run like a jackrabbit, my dear."

"A coward through and through! I was right about you all along!"

Alejandro appeared in the doorway. Even the grime could not conceal his pallor. The cigarette stub between his lips bobbed uncontrollably. "The port paddle box— Señor Solis says to tell you the *Yanquis* gave a hit."

Cristobal cursed in mixed French and Spanish. Then in a cold, cutting voice: "Alejandro—escort . . . Señora Cavazos to my cabin."

She tugged at Alejandro's grip. "And what am I to do,

Captain Cavazos?" she demanded sarcastically. "Sit and knit?"

"Your insolence is charming. When the hull scrapes bottom, you can come on deck. Tell the boarding officers the truth—you were abducted. At the worst you'll be detained as a witness at the prize court proceedings."

If he and the crew were caught, the vessel's French registry could only compromise them further. At the most he could hope that they would be taken to New Orleans instead of Key West for trial. Key West was little better than a sandbank penal colony. If they were found guilty, they faced at least five years hard labor in the Dry Tortugas.

Without another glance in her direction, he ordered, "Get my wife below, Alejandro."

He hooked his hand over one of the helm's spokes and spun it like it was a roulette wheel. The *Revenge* tacked sharply. Suddenly the steamer lurched, her hull grinding against a shoal. He was thrown against the wheel. At that same moment a torpedo plowed across the deck, and he heard Jen's strangled scream.

He took the bridge's steps two at a time. Below him he sighted Jen and Alejandro—both of them sprawled on the planks, Jen's body draped over the boy. *Dios, no!* He reached them just as Jen lifted her head. The rain plastered her hair to her forehead and cheeks. He grabbed her shoulders. "Are you hurt?"

She blinked, shook her head slowly. "No . . . Alejandro, I think he . . ."

He knelt over the boy. Blood splattered the back of Alejandro's shirt. The boy wasn't moving. He rolled him over, and one arm flopped against the planks. Cristobal looked up into Jeanette's ashen face. Rain streamed down his jaws like tears. "He's dead," he said tonelessly. "And it's your fault, Jen. Your determination to have your own way—at every bend in the road—has cost Alejandro his life."

Her hand flew to her mouth. "I didn't know this would happen, Cristobal. I couldn't have foreseen it. I didn't think—"

"You never do—except of what you want." He rose to his feet. His eyes were hard, his lips flat with anger that had been long building. "You're free of me now," he said in an empty breath and pivoted away.

He made his way below decks to destroy the cargo. The hole he planned to blast in the hull would flood the place and damage the silks, the sugar, the gunpowder—rendering them useless to the Yankees. In the dark of the hold he threaded his way through the kegs and crates and clambered over boxes stacked end over end. The storm raging outside still battered at the beached ship, and a keg was sent toppling from its perch to crash against Cristobal's temple.

Waves of colors washed over him. Then utter blackness. Next he realized he was on his knees in the dank hole. A sticky fluid coated his hands. No time to feel around for damage. He had to sabotage the cargo. He lurched to his feet, and the contents of the hold seemed to tilt precariously about him.

"Kitt?" Solis peered into the darkness.

"Here," Cristobal mumbled and groped for something to steady his wobbly legs.

Solis prowled through the jumble of boxes and barrels until he located his friend. "We've got to get out, Kitt," he said and slid a hefty shoulder under Cristobal's arm to support him. "The *Yanquis* will be boarding at any minute."

"The others?"

"Already on the beach. Scrambling for the cover of chaparral."

"Good," Cristobal grunted. Negotiating the stairway was no easy feat. The steps cagily shifted positions under his feet.

"Mrs. St. John—I mean your wife—is up there waiting for them."

"The minx will carry off her part magnificently." With the back of his sleeve Cristobal wiped at the blood that streamed in his left eye. "And I fear she'll have her revenge on me—and on you, too, Solis—if we don't get out soon."

The wind slammed against the two when they emerged from the hatch. Cristobal blinked against the sudden light of the lantern held up to his face. A semicircle of bayonets pointed at him.

32

"*Sacré tonnerre!* Aawwk. Rape!"

"Tia Juana, will you shut up that infernal bird!"

Jeanette tossed her pen down on the secretary and put her hands to her temples. Behind her the old negress shook her head and rolled her eyes. Her mistress had been riding a broom ever since her return from that sea voyage. If Tia Juana didn't know better, she'd say Halloween was today instead of next week.

"I'd think you'd be tickled pink that that ol' coot of a general done retreated." She picked up the cage. "No mo' of dem curfews for us free folks—eh, Washington?"

"Rape! Help!"

Jeanette waited, head in her hands, until Tia Juana had left the bedroom. Slowly she pushed back from the secretary and walked to the window. She didn't know what was wrong with her. The October day was bright and balmy. A perfect day for—for boating on the salt lake.

Oh, damnation. Why had not three months wiped her memory clear of Cristobal? The whole voyage seemed an odyssey. She tried to tell herself her restiveness was because Morgan had moved his army out of Brownsville.

Brownsville's citizens were rejoicing, but Jen had been deprived of her revenge on the general.

True, Morgan still maintained a few regiments of Federal troops out on Brazos Santiago; mostly the black Union Corps d'Afrique—a more even match now for Ford's troops who had moved back into Fort Brown, which especially delighted Annabel. The week following the triumphant return of the Confederate troops, she married her Major Hampton.

Perhaps, Jeanette thought, it was the thrill of running the cotton that was gone for her. Perhaps the removal of the Yankee soldiers had taken the challenge out of it. Yet she was just as determined as ever to drive the Yankees from Texas—and to have her revenge. That goal had never changed.

She had. Cristobal had changed her in some subtle, indefinable way.

Her fingers curled about the window curtain. Where was he? Oh, Heavenly Father! She never really wanted to see him swinging from some frigate's yardarm. But, damnit, after all the underhanded, vile things he had done to her, he deserved to rot out the rest of the war in some moldy Northern prison!

So why did her heart lighten when she told herself that, though all logic dictated against hope, he might have gotten away with the others? When he and Solis had shoved their way through the boarding soldiers and leapt overboard, she had held out little hope they could escape the rain of Northern bullets.

Rubia had disappeared from Columbia shortly before Jeanette's return. Yet Jeanette knew, with a woman's intuition, that Rubia was waiting for Cristobal somewhere— if not in Bagdad. Trinidad reported that the woman had not returned to her place of employment. Rubia, Jeanette sensed, was a *soldadera* now, a woman following her warrior.

Behind Jeanette, Tia Juana cleared her throat. Jeanette turned. "Yes?"

"Trinidad is a-waitin' downstairs."

She sighed. She supposed she should be grateful that it was time to make another run to Alleyton for cotton. Cotton trading was running more smoothly once more from Brownsville to Matamoros, where the Imperialist government now ruled and was friendly to the Confederate cause. The twin cities were once again thriving emporia. Commercial ventures flourished because of the backlog of business that had built up during the Federal occupation of Brownsville and the fear that the current conditions would not last.

The situation in Matamoros was more precarious. The French Imperialists held Matamoros, but in the countryside bands of Juarista liberals roamed undisturbed. Was Cristobal with them now? All Jeanette knew was that the *Revenge* no longer anchored in Bagdad's harbor.

She put on the broad-brimmed straw hat, though it was beyond her why she attempted to protect her complexion when she was already as brown as Trinidad. *Old leather. That's what my skin looks like. No wonder Cristobal preferred Rubia to me.*

Trinidad seemed as restless as Jeanette. He followed her into the chapel while she squeezed through the aisles of stacked cotton bales, counting them for the next run.

"Señora?"

Jeanette swung in the direction of the voice. A man— Solis—emerged from a crevice formed by the bales. That explained Trinidad's nervousness. He had known Solis was there, waiting. "I have brought you something, señora." Solis came forward, his hand outstretched.

Wordlessly she took the object. It was wrapped in crinkled paper. She unfolded the paper to find her wedding ring. She looked at Solis. "The paper is for you, also, señora."

The dimness of the chapel made it difficult to read the writing. "What is it?"

"A draft. Drawn on the Bank of England in Bermuda. Cristobal has been keeping your money for you—in British pounds instead of Confederate dollars. He meant for you to have this when we were in Bermuda."

She looked into the smooth-skinned face, trying to decipher how much he wasn't telling her. "Where is Cristobal?" She saw his hesitancy. "Please," she begged.

He saw in her eyes the same yearning mixed with relief that he had seen in Rubia's eyes when he and Cristobal had returned to Juárez's headquarters, now in Chihuahua. At first he had thought Rubia's sentiments directed solely toward Cristobal. But now, having spent time alone with her and listened to her speak of her life at her husband's rancho or later in the bordello, now he had hope. If for no other reason than the way he caught her covertly studying him across a campfire or in a cantina or late at night when he pored over maps with Cristobal.

"I will tell Cristobal you have asked of him," Solis said at last. He wheeled away before she could ask more.

Jeanette wanted to call him back, but what could she say? Could Cristobal ever forgive her for her stubbornness, her nasty words, the grief she had brought on him and his friends? Without meaning to, somewhere along the way she had forgiven him.

"*Sobrina*," Trinidad said.

Preoccupied with remorse for the first time in her life, she looked back to her overseer. "What is it, Trini?"

Trinidad fixed his eyes on the lint-strewn floor. "I theenk I knew all the time Cristobal was the Frenchman. I remember heem as a keed. A wild one—untamable as the mesteno. Like you, *sobrina*."

She closed her eyes and laid her head back against one of the stacks of bales. The ring—the banknote—in her hand, they were only objects. "I think you may be right."

"I respected Señor St. John—but, *sobrina,* never did you laugh—never were you the wild mesteno unteel after he died. Weeth Señor Cristobal—you were free to be yourself, no?"

What was Trinidad trying to tell her? That all those years of marriage she had conformed for Armand? But she had loved him. She still did. But that love . . . it seemed fuzzy, like a badly taken daguerrotype. Like her memory of him.

33

Jeanette jammed her hands in the pockets of her pants. Now that she lived alone, she wore the pants more often since there was no need for simulation. She had even taken to keeping Washington in her bedroom just to break the silence in the great house.

Outside her bedroom window the spring rain had been funneling down the glass panes. Now there was only the percussion of the dripping leaves. So much for the planned run to Monterrey. First the winter rains and now the spring rains. It was just as well. Reports had it that cotton trains above and below Brownsville were mudbound these days. Between the weather and the rumors that the South was contemplating surrender, goods were stacking up in Brownsville and the price of gold was suddenly declining on the world market.

It did not help that the Juarista forces, who had the support of the United States, had driven the Imperialists from northern Mexico two weeks earlier, cutting off the South's communications with the outside world through Mexico. And that was the worst of it—she did not know if Cristobal was alive or if his body had been dragged off and tossed on the mound of bodies formed by both the Imperialist and the Juarista dead.

Her friends believed that she and Cristobal had gone to visit her father and Aunt Hermione, but did they believe her story that Cristobal had stayed to cover the war's effect on New England for some European paper?

How she missed Cristobal! The months had not lessened the ache or the memories. Some instinct told her that he was still alive. Did he ever think of her? He had to. Though he had never actually declared his love in so many words, she knew he loved her. *Had* loved her. Did he still? Could he still . . . after all that had happened?

Alejandro's death—all the tears she had shed for the boy would not bring him back now or change Cristobal's feelings for her, whatever they were. She could do nothing but hope . . . and wait.

Waiting—it was a woman's lot in life. And she chafed against it. Other matters needed her wayward attention. Columbia faced financial chaos unless she divested herself of the cotton stored there. For once Jeanette knew hardship. No longer was Tia Juana able to serve roast mutton and boned turkey, plum pudding and oyster soup, Madeira and *pâté de foie gras* all in one meal.

Now Trinidad mixed the oil of cottonseed and ground peas as a substitute for coffee. Tia Juana was pulling the blue thread from bed ticking in order to patch worn clothes. Felix mixed soot and cottonseed oil to make shoeblack, and Jeanette and Pedro and the other *campesinos* were making their own bullet cartridges with one musket ball and three buckshot, dipping the paper cartridges in melted beeswax.

Yet all the scrimping did not seem really to help that much—not when a barrel of flour was going for $1,250 in Confederate currency. Jeanette was tired of waiting for a change in everything—Cristobal, the weather, the war, finances. She was determined at least to take control of the serious financial situation.

She swung away from the window and took the hall steps two at a time. Snatching her hat from the hall tree, she hurried outside and hailed Trinidad, dispatching her instructions. The cotton was to be hauled to Brownsville for sale.

However, by the time she and the *campesinos* arrived in Brownsville that afternoon, her idea did not seem like a good one.

All was gloom in the city. Activity centered around the auctioneers in almost every street crying, "Going, going, gone!"

Beside her in the wagon sat Trinidad, who shook his head sadly. "Eet ees hopeless. A cousin—he told me, *sobrina*, that store owners—they damage their goods now for the insurance."

From beneath the boardwalk's porticoes Jeanette glumly watched inventories sell for as little as twenty cents on the dollar. All of Brownsville seemed to crowd the streets watching, from infants-in-arms to infantry with arms. And even their uniforms were dismal—homespun cloth dyed from organic matter and called butternut made at the Huntsville penitentiary. Before Jeanette's cotton reached the auction block, a cavalryman galloped down the streets, waving his saber above his head. "The Yankees are attacking!"

A padre in the brown robe of the Oblate Brothers stepped out into the horse's path and grabbed the bridle. "Where?"

"Palmito Hill!" the soldier gasped. "General Ford needs all able-bodied men!"

It was like a stampede of buffalo. Women and children fleeing to the safety of their houses. Men—the infirm, the old, those on leave—yelled the Rebel war cries and ran or hobbled for their horses and wagons. The frantic hope that the Confederacy could still win surged through the crowd, sweeping over Jeanette as well. Without waiting for Trinidad, she whirled and ran back to the yard where her wagons waited. "Unload the cotton!" she called to Juan and Felix. "Pronto!"

It seemed an interminable length of time before the heavy bales had been dumped and the wagons were on the road leading to Palmito Hill, twelve miles northeast. All the men were far ahead of Jeanette's wagons. And because of the salt marshes, her wagons were forced to keep to the winding River Road rather than take the more direct route. While she cursed the oxen's creeping pace, she also belatedly realized she had only the revolver—and her *campesinos* were armed with their rifles and one round of ammunition. Not much to wage a battle with. Still her blood raced with the excitement of the conflict.

In the distance she could hear the intermittent whoomphing of cannon. The closer the wagon rolled the thicker grew the smoke that hazed the sky. A large strip of salt marsh that was little more than a mire hole forced her to abandon the wagons. "You wait here with the wagons, Trini."

He shook his shaggy head. "I go weeth you, *sobrina*."

She saw the determined look in the rheumy eyes. But she was just as determined. She wouldn't be responsible for the death of yet another beloved soul. He was finally dissuaded when she agreed to take Felix and the other *campesinos* with her. It seemed they loped through the chaparral for miles and hours. Rifle fire pinged the air the closer they crept through the palmito bush and mesquite thickets on the broad hill. Men stretched on their stomachs and crouched on their knees and signaled that she had reached the battlefront.

The Rebels fired at a nebulous enemy somewhere beyond and below. Her stomach knotted, as it had in that ultimate moment when the Frenchman—when Cristobal—had taken her beyond herself. Strange that the body's responses to generate opposing feelings—of love and war—should so closely resemble one another. But then hadn't Cristobal called that one mystical moment of lovemaking "the little death"?

The shouting, the roar of the cannons, the boom of the rifles was deafening. Jeanette, flanked on either side by her *campesinos*, edged to the top of the bluff. A dense fog of smoke hung in the air below, obscuring the thickets and the Federal troops who returned the fire. She called out to the nearest Reb, a young boy of no more than twenty, "How many Yanks down there?"

He turned, and she saw the gunpowder that blackened his face and rimmed his weary eyes. "Maybe three hundred."

Three hundred against a hundred ninety or so. The odds weren't in the Confederacy's favor. Yet her blood seemed to sing in her veins. At first she fired blindly into the thickets. Once a blue-coated soldier staggered out and crumpled to the ground. Ironically she hoped it wasn't her bullet that had killed him. Then when the young Reb just down the line from her buckled and rolled, exposing the shot that gaped open his jaw, she paused and with a chilling cold-bloodedness took more deliberate aim. Never did the fear occur to her that soon she could be lying contorted and mutilated like the Reb.

An hour later when Ford charged by on his horse shouting, "Attack!" Jeanette experienced an exhilaration that almost made her dizzy. She forgot all else but the battle. With the hundreds of other men she surged to her feet, shouting hoarsely and brandishing her rifle like it was a scimitar.

Felix grabbed at her arm to hold her back. "No, señora!"

She shook off his hold and charged down the hill between Pedro and Juan. Behind her Felix broke into a sprint to catch up with his mistress. Bullets creased the air all around her and hummed in her ears. The breeze ruffled against her face. Her hat blew off her head and her braid swung free. She continued to run, stumbling once. But Pedro was there to grab her up, and she took off again. Ahead the Federal soldiers sprang from the thickets like rabbits and fled in retreat.

Then General Morgan loomed before her eyes. The general's saber swiped furiously at the Rebel soldier who clung to the bridle of his horse. The saber embedded in the Reb's shoulder, and he went down beneath the prancing hooves. In midstep Jeanette halted and raised the rifle to her shoulder. All her anger—all her hatred—of Morgan poured forth into the minute movement of her forefinger that would be needed on the trigger. For some inexplicable reason, perhaps the instinct of the wary beast, his head spun in her direction. At that second their eyes locked, and she saw stark surprise in his. His thin lips mouthed her name.

She thought of Armand. Left to rot to death because of Morgan. No wonder soldiers became inured to killing. It would take so little to kill the monster now.

"Drop the saber!" she commanded. "And dismount. You're my prisoner."

His eyes glittered, and she knew *he* would not hesitate to kill her if she were careless enough to give him the chance. Like a wall, the other *campesinos* shielded her from fleeing Federal soldiers as she prodded Morgan ahead of her.

The makeshift camp was at the nearby Palmito Ranch. The captured soldiers, most of them black men from the Corps d'Afrique, were herded either into the dilapidated barn or the corrals. Already the Confederate soldiers were celebrating the battle they had won, passing around cheap *aguardiente*. One bearded soldier tilted to his mouth a bottle of Kentucky mash he had rescued. But everywhere activity stopped as Jeanette moved among them. A woman in man's clothing!

Unperturbed by their reactions, she marched General Morgan to the ranchhouse to report to Ford. He was as surprised as the others. From behind the kitchen table he eyed her suspiciously. "I'd think I was hallucinating if I didn't know better." Then he smiled. "My little Mexican gunrunner, a lady."

She looked down at her dirt-stained britches and broken, scuffed boots. "Hardly a lady, Colonel."

Laughing, he swept his hat from his head and ran his fingers through his mussed hair. "I'm sure there'll be some commendation from President Jefferson for your meritorious deeds, Miss—?"

"Lavender Blue," General Morgan smiled coldly. "Our government would delight in making her acquaintance." Jeanette shivered with the malice that laced his voice.

"So I see," Ford said slowly. Then he slapped the table and laughed again. "Oh, this is too good! Can you imagine, General Morgan, what effect this will have on your reputation?"

Before Morgan could reply, Trinidad appeared in the doorway. His guarded gaze went to Jeanette. "Yes?" Ford asked.

The old man beckoned to his mistress with a gnarled finger. "Excuse me, Colonel Ford," she said. "My overseer."

Ford nodded his head, and she followed Trinidad into the ranchhouse's shabby parlor. Wordlessly he handed her the newspaper. "A bunch of them were thrown from a passing steamer. The passengers—they were shouting and crying."

Puzzled, she looked from the old monkey face to the crumpled newspaper. The paper, dated five weeks earlier, rattled between her hands as she scanned the headlines: LEE SURRENDERS TO GRANT AT APPOMATTOX."

All her dreams—all the South's dreams—of victory were shattered. But a worse realization followed. The captors were now the captured. As soon as she turned this over to Ford, the Federal prisoners would be released. Morgan would be her jailer!

"We leave now?" Trinidad whispered, making it more of a statement than a question. Like her, he knew it would be sheer foolishness on her part to remain. Imprisonment, a hangman's noose, a firing squad—such fates awaited traitors. And Morgan would certainly label her a traitor.

"Eet's not too late to get away," Trinidad pleaded.

Lee had not run. There was such a thing as honor. Yet paralyzing fear twisted like a coiled serpent in her belly.

"*Sobrina*, let us go, now! You weel rot as deed Señor Armand!"

34

Brilliant sunshine warmed the old adobe walls of Fort Brown, and mockingbirds and kildees warbled notes of summer's balmy promise. The only occupant in the cell of Fort Brown's jail stared through the small cell window, her vision blurred from a succession of sleepless nights. Her fingers curled around the iron bars. Outside a wagon rolled onto the parade grounds. On its bed was a coffin. When Morgan read Jeanette her death warrant, holding her responsible for the death of 111 men at Palmito Hill alone, she had calmly requested a tight, metallic coffin and asked that it be placed near where she was to be shot. She sighed. Still possessing a woman's vanity, she wanted as few to view her corpse as possible.

She had counted on a fair trial. But the military proceedings had been more like a Spanish Inquisition: She had been kept in irons during the entire trial. General Morgan's testimony, along with that of other staunch Union sympathizers in Brownsville, had been damaging. As final proof Morgan had presented the Oath of Allegiance to the Federal Government that she had signed— "and violated," he finished, pointing an accusatory finger at her as the Holy Office must have pointed at the heretic.

Watching the soldiers unload the coffin, it seemed to her a dream—that it was not possible that within the day she would cease to breathe, cease to live. An appeal was put forth by a number of Brownsville's citizens who had been loyal to the Confederacy—among them, surprisingly, Annabel's father, Judge Goddard, and Elizabeth Crabbe. But as yet President Grant had not responded. And Jeanette knew that one female spy had already been hanged for aiding in the assassination of Lincoln. She had little hope.

Despite her resolve to face the ordeal bravely, she turned from the cell window and began to vomit all over her bunk's moldy mattress. In the past week she had eaten little, and her stomach at last contracted in dry heaves. One hand anchored in the mattress to hold her up. Weakly she wiped her mouth with the back of her other hand. Not now. She couldn't turn weak now. She could be no less valiant than the common soldier who had faced death day after hideous day.

But, dear God, she was scared. As usual, fear stirred in her that uncontrollable urge to wet her pants.

"Aawwk! *Sacré tonnerre!* Lavender Blue. Aawwk!"

Incredulous, Jeanette pushed herself erect. Slowly she turned. Next to her posted guard stood one of the most disreputable men she had ever glimpsed. A black eye patch hid one eye, and the other drooped with a leer. Tobacco spittle drooled from the corner of his mouth. A slovenly beard, also stained with tobacco juice, graced his slack jaw. Stringy hair slid over his forehead. Dirt begrimed his bare feet, and his trousers were held up by an even dirtier rope.

But, impossibly, Washington perched on his shoulder. Had the man ransacked Columbia? She knew it was happening all over the South without any kind of law yet established.

"This here greaser built yer coffin, ma'am," the guard

said in a most respectful manner. His boyish face, still shadowed with peach fuzz, wore an apologetic look, as if it were his fault she was to be shot at sunset. "The general okayed yer inspection of it and all."

She nodded dumbly. Such a macabre thing to do—inspect one's own coffin! She would much rather have had her last words with Trinidad and Tia Juana and Annabel and Claudia, who had come from Tampico, but they all had been turned away. Morgan had derisively offered the services of a priest. She had refused. There was nothing to repent for; she would not change her life—no, that was not quite right. She would not have scorned Cristobal's love.

Suddenly her gaze switched from the guard to the coffinmaker. The oaf had the nerve to wink lasciviously at her. A laugh started in her stomach and rumbled upward, and she had to fight it back. "Let me see the coffin," she said with the straightest face she could muster.

The guard bent to place the key in the lock, and at that moment the butt of the coffinmaker's pistol thunked against the soldier's head. Cristobal swooped up the soldier's hat and jammed it on Jeanette's head. "Let's go!" he said and grabbed her arm, yanking her over the sprawled soldier.

Excitement sang in her veins again. At any moment they both could be shot—her back felt terribly exposed. Yet she was no longer afraid. To die fighting—no, to die living, that was all she asked.

She clambered up on the wagon seat beside Cristobal. Washington called out from his precarious perch on Cristobal's shoulder, "Help!" Cristobal looked down at her and grinned. That was all the courage she needed.

Still, her heartbeat accelerated as the wagon approached the gate. Would the guards remember that only one man had come through on the wagon? When Cristobal reined in the team at the gate, she saw two men talking to the guards. In their hands were pads and pencils. Reporters! One reporter turned to Cristobal and asked, "You the coffinmaker? What did the woman look like? Pretty as they say?"

Cristobal spit over the side of the wagon. "Ugly as an old hag, señor."

Caught up in the prestige of being interviewed, the guard carelessly waved them past, and all of Jeanette's pent-up laughter burst out. Tears rolled from her eyes, and she knew she was close to hysteria. Cristobal's large hand closed comfortably over hers. "I'm all right," she hiccoughed. "I guess it's just the letdown—after all the years of pretense and fighting. And now the South is no more." The last was uttered on a sigh.

"You still don't understand, do you, Jen?" Cristobal said, but there was a tenderness in his voice. And there on Levee Street with people coming and going and despite the urgency to flee town, he turned to her and caught her chin with his hand, forcing her to look up into his warm brown eyes.

"It was never the South you were fighting for. You were fighting for pure pleasure, my dear girl. You've always enjoyed the challenge of conflict."

She searched his face—and searched her mind—and she knew in that instant that what he said was true. "But it's over now," she moaned.

"Oh, no," he chuckled. "We've still got a war to fight in Mexico. And after that, Jen, we'll find another war somewhere else. If nowhere else, I'm sure there'll always be just enough conflict between the two of us to make life challenging!"

"Why—how did you know to come?"

"Trinidad. He and Felix searched half of Mexico for me. The entire Cervantes family is at our camp now. Great Juaristas they'll make."

He took her face between his two hands and lowered

his lips over hers, kissing her as thoroughly as the Frenchman ever did. The thought dimly occurred to her that he
had not asked her if she loved him or wanted to come with
him. He was that sure of her—had always been that sure
of her. Then she forgot all else in the pure joy of the realization that she had found her complement in life. She
had found her mate. A man who tempted her spirit of
independence as it had never been tempted before.

And she let her kiss relay that knowledge, her arms
coming up around Cristobal's neck, her body pressed
close to his, seeking also her physical complement.

Washington chose that moment to tug at her hat's brim,
and her hat and braid tumbled free. Still Cristobal did not
release her. Both were oblivious to the passersby who
stopped to stare at the passionate couple.

"Aawwk!" cooed Washington. "Rape!"

or the soldiers coming
after them

Parris Afton Bonds

A favorite of romance readers everywhere, Parris Afton
Bonds is the author of ten books and mother of five sons,
in addition to teaching creative writing at a local commu-
nity college. She is co-founder and board member of Romance Writers of America and was the recipient of the
Best Novel of 1981 award given by the Texas Press
Women for *Dust Devil*. Her previous Fawcett trade pa-
perback, *Deep Purple,* was a best seller, and *Stardust*
recently received an enta best seller, and *Stardust*
recently received an enthusiastic response from her many
ardent fans.